About the cover

This deliciously beautiful art, is the work of world-famous artist Raina Hopkins. Raina lives in Cornwall, England where she designs and produces some of the finest art of this kind. We are delighted that she has agreed to provide this one, originally titled the 'Sun Goddess', and for 'Annie Abbott and the Druid Stones' represents the 'Keeper of the Light'. Thank you Raina!

You may find more of her work on the website, Deviant Art.

Copyright © 2022 by Isabelle & Michael Nelson
All rights reserved

First Edition Published May 2022
by Indies United Publishing House, LLC

978-1-64456- [Paperback]
978-1-64456- [Mobi]
978-1-64456- [ePub]
978-1-64456- [Audiobook]

Library of Congress Control Number: 2022936382

INDIES UNITED PUBLISHING HOUSE, LLC
P.O. BOX 3071
QUINCY, IL 62305-3071
www.indiesunites.net

Annie Abbott
and the Druid Stones

The Annie Abbott Adventures
Book One

Isabelle & Michael Nelson

INDIES UNITED PUBLISHING HOUSE, LLC

Forward

Every year since I was very young, as soon as the school year was out for the summer, (and sometimes before it was out), my father would plan an adventure for just the two of us. Sometimes to the Northwoods of Wisconsin or Minnesota, the Florida Keys, or Big Sur, California. My Dad believed that life was about broadening your horizons, and learning as much as you could in the time you were granted.

Our 'adventures' were exciting and most of the time, educational. I believe they helped me to see the intricacies of the environment and the life forms that inhabit it. This book mirrors some of the lessons these experiences taught me—and then goes deeper. To see the life in all things and feel the life that surrounds you is to know real magic.

We are all Annie Abbott in one way or another.

Isabelle Anne Nelson

There is one kind of magic that is easily available to everyone; learning. Learning is a magical experience. It is fuel that drives the meaning in our lives, and makes our journey interesting and exciting.

All the places mentioned in this book are real and can be visited if one would wish to. We never stop learning, we only stop being interested.

Michael D. Nelson

Annie Abbott and the Druid Stones

Mike Abbott climbed down the steep attic steps, a stack of small boxes in his arms. Staggering while balancing the heavy stack, he hurried to the kitchen, where he dropped the three boxes with a loud thump onto the table.

"What was that noise?" Annie, Mike's twelve-year-old daughter exclaimed, rushing into the room, the book she had been reading immediately forgotten. "You scared me."

Mike sat down on one of the wooden kitchen chairs to catch his breath. Sweat had beaded on his forehead, and his hair was festooned with dusty cobwebs from the attic.

"I was looking for something up in the attic," Mike regarded the boxes, "I didn't know what these were. They were tucked way back in under the eaves in a little alcove I'd never noticed before. I don't recall ever seeing them."

Annie looked at the three cartons. They appeared to be very old. The tape holding the seams and edges had yellowed, separating itself and rolling at the edges. Two of the boxes were fairly large, the last no bigger than a shoebox.

"They're all pretty heavy, but that smallest one, that one weighs a ton." Mike was finally catching his breath.

Annie picked up the littlest one. It was a lot heavier than she had expected. It took both hands to lift it and look at the bottom. There was nothing on it or anywhere else that gave a clue as to the contents. The other two boxes were the same. Anonymous in all regards. Annie's detective spirit immediately twitched.

"What do you think's in it Dad?" She asked as she tried to shake the heavy box. And before he could voice an answer, "Can we open 'em.", "Let's open 'em."

"Let's finish what I was going to do before I found these first."

"C'mon Dad! Let's just take a peek. C'mon Dad, it's a real mystery! Let's just open one then, then the other two later?"

"Ah, I give up." He'd dealt with Annie's curious spirit before. "As old as they look, I can't imagine that it's anything very important, but I'm a little curious too, which one?"

"Let's open the little one. It's *so* heavy. It's got to have a clue about what's in the other two."

"That makes sense, I guess." Mike took out his pocket knife and carefully cut the tape securing the top. Even before he had closed the knife and replaced it in his pocket, Annie was already folding back the flaps and diving in.

"Look at these old newspapers Dad; they're so old they're falling apart."

"Wow!" Mike peered at the old sheets. "Look at the dates on these! This one is from the year nineteen-eleven and…Oh my Gosh!"

"What! What Dad?"

"This is the wedding announcement for my grandfather, Conor Padraig Abbott to Margaret Siobhan McKillip!"

"Let me see please? Wow! Married on June 21st; that's the summer solstice! They were married at Stone Church on Washington Island. Where's that?"

"Washington Island is in northern Wisconsin. On the Door County Peninsula, to be exact. I don't think I ever heard about a stone church though. Washington Island is where my father was born," said Mike, wonder in his voice. "I didn't know anything like this still existed."

"It says the best man was somebody named Jean Luc LaBeaux. Did you ever know him?"

"Way before my time Annie, but Jean Luc LaBeaux is a name I've heard of. A legendary brawler. Something about him being a 'Keeper of the Peace' or a lawman in the wild days of the north woods. Hmm, wonder if it was the same guy. Oh well, what else is in there?"

Annie dove back into the little box. "Oh WOW!" With two hands she lifted out the huge and ancient Navy Colt revolver, almost dropping it on the table in her haste to be rid of it.

"What is that! I had no idea something like that was in this house." As he looked closely at it. "At least it's not loaded."

"The bullets are still in the box Dad. See?" Annie tipped up the box on its side.

"Oh great! Just don't you worry about that right now," he moved the lethal weapon to the other end of the table, "what else is in there."

"This." She lifted out a small metal strong box by the handle on its top. "I'm almost afraid to open it."

She wasn't fooling anyone; she couldn't wait to get it open. Her father felt the same way. They both fumbled to open the small latch, and holding their breath, tipped back the lid.

"I don't believe it!" Mike Abbott rocked back in his seat, completely flabbergasted. Annie's eyes were as big as saucers as she looked at her father's face.

The rest of the box contained only three things. Two of these were exactly alike. The third was a small envelope addressed simply to 'The Finder'. The other two things, ingots of solid gold.

With fingers that trembled, Mike opened the ancient envelope carefully. Inside was a fine piece of stationary, addressed in a fine hand:

The Finder

Greetings, I Conor Padraig Abbott leave this earthly coil a frustrated man having not finished the task that the Lord has set before me. The great treasure of my house still eludes me and alas my body can no longer support the search. I am in hopes that you are a true searcher, and gifted intellectually in ways that I did not possess. In this box you will find the means to afford to continue my search, and the means to defend it should the treasure be found. These contents are reward enough if your steadfastness be wanting, but I exhort you to continue in my endeavor and make it your own.

The other two containers, should they have remained together, contain all the many clues and maps such that I have been able to gather in my lifetime, along with my diary.

May your search be fruitful. Follow the signs, and trust your instincts. And good luck to you.

C. P. Abbott

Annie looked at her father and his eyes met hers. They both smiled. Finally, an adventure for both of them.

The diary of Conor Abbott
Thursday June 22nd, 1911, Mid-summer's eve

We gathered, myself and my clansmen, at the stone church at evening time. The moon was in the final crescent and so had set earlier than the sun. Then came the elder and the thirteen. The great elder of our clan and the crones gathered in a circle around us, and the elder spoke of knowledge and wisdom, our divine task. The crones each individually came forward and presented both a promise and a curse to my bride. Foolishly or wisely, she accepted their gifts, forever to be one of the wise and a part of their circle. We pledged our troth and danced in the moonless night. In the morning we were husband and wife and the elder and the thirteen had gone.

And from that moment we are set with a task. She to pursue the great truths hidden within the Book of Spells, and I to seek the treasure of the ages with only my wits and her gifts. We begin this life together, she with beauty and confidence that I can only hope to measure up to.

The final words of the Druid were, "Seek the stones and feel their life. First before all things, feel the life in all that you see and touch. Only then will the steps to the great mystery become clear to you. Seek the stones that bear the mark."

"What does that mean Dad?" Annie looked up, confused. "What kind of 'mark'?"

"Well Annie, I think it means that we need to go to Door County, Wisconsin, and Washington Island at the end of it. I think we need to seek the stones."

"Oh boy! When?"

"It's summer break at the school, so *soon.*"

The Big Water

For the third time in the last fifteen minutes, Annie opened one eye and peeked at the luminous face of the clock on her bedside table. The time didn't seem to be moving fast enough for her. There was no light coming in through the bedroom window; it was still dark outside. With a big sigh, she flounced the blankets and closed her eyes again. She knew she wouldn't be able to go back to sleep. She was too excited.

Her father had told her that they were going to be leaving early in the morning, and as far as she was concerned this was nice and early. She had packed her knapsack the night before, making sure she had plenty of snacks. Her father, usually never told her where they were going to go, it was always a surprise for Annie, and Annie loved his surprises. She had never been disappointed and with every adventure he had planned, she learned so much more about life and the world that surrounded her.

Today they were going on a new adventure. She and her father had read the long-lost diary of her great-grandfather, Conor Abbott. He spoke of a lost treasure that he had searched for until his death. He had left clues maps and in the diary urged the finder of the book to continue his search. It had been his dying wish. Today, Annie and her father were going to start where Great-grandfather Conor Abbott had marked the map as the place to begin.

Then she smelled it! Coffee! The smell of coffee meant that her father was up and had started the coffee pot. At last! She threw back the bed covers, gave one more glance at the darkened windows and started pulling on her clothes. It was time, and the adventure awaited. What would it be this time? She could hardly wait.

Taking the stairs two at a time, she slid into the kitchen slightly off balance and was greeted by the sight of her father leaning against the counter and taking his first sip of hot coffee. He was dressed in his old blue jeans, flannel shirt and laced boots. It was late June and the weather had been hot, but judging by the way he was dressed, today was going to be somewhere cool, and maybe even chilly.

"Did you pack a sweatshirt? Maybe even a jacket. Might get a little chilly before the sun comes up."

"Where are we going Dad? Rock Island right?"

"Ah, well that's part of our adventure today, but there is also a surprise, but I'll tell you a little. First, we're taking a long drive, a few hours really, then we're meeting an old friend of mine. He's in charge of this part of the adventure, and I'm kind of excited myself."

"Is it really a long drive?"

"Yep, we've got to get all the way up into northern

Wisconsin today, and we've got to get there before the sun rises. So, grab some grub to go, and we'll saddle up. Don't forget your sweatshirt though, and grab a baseball hat out of the front closet too."

"Dad, you know I hate wearing a hat."

"You'll be glad you did before the day is over; I promise."

Annie filled a bowl with granola and added yogurt. Slicing a banana over it, she asked again, "Can't you give me a little more information than that Dad?"

"Okay. We're also going to learn a lot, and I'm going to show you the church where my grandparents were married too."

"A church? That doesn't sound very interesting. Where is it?"

"This church you'll find interesting I bet. But maybe not, we'll see."

"That's it, that's all your going to tell me?"

"That's all."

Once, out in the front yard, Annie peeked into the back of Mike's old pickup truck. The truck bed was usually empty, but today there were two bicycles, one was hers. The other one was her father's that he rode back and forth to the college campus, where he was a professor of history. There were no other clues there. Where could we be going that we need bikes, she thought. She asked him again, but he just smiled.

"Honey, you've got to be patient. If I start telling you about it, you'll start expecting something that might not happen. Let's just see how the day rolls out."

"Huh, okay Dad."

"Why don't you hop in the back seat and try to

catch a little sleep. There won't be anything to look at in the dark, and I'm going to try and make up some time. Besides, if you stay awake, you're just going to pester me with more questions."

"I can't sleep. You always try that but you know I'm not going to be able to fall asleep. It's too *'interesting'*."

"Suit yourself, but I'm telling you right now, I'm not looking for conversation."

With that he turned the key in the truck's ignition and backed out of their driveway, heading up the street toward this newest adventure.

Hours later, Annie was awakened when the truck engine shut off.

"Wake up Annie. We're here sleepy head."

"I wasn't sleeping; I was just resting. You said you didn't want to talk."

"Okay, I guess we must have had a swarm of bees buzzing in the back seat. I'll have to do something about them as soon as we get back to port."

"Get back to where?"

The sky was still dark, but a line of light had started to form on the horizon directly in front of the truck. There was nothing but darkness all around them except for right in front of them. A wooden dock stretched off into the darkness, and along its side, a large boat. Its lights blazing brightly in the inky blackness of the water behind it was bustling with activity. A crew of two men climbed in and out, loading packages and other gear. Nothing else was moving on the dock or in the rest of the harbor.

Mike Abbott stepped out of the truck and one of the crewmen hailed him.

"Hey Mike, I was beginning to think you weren't going to make it before we shoved off. C'mon aboard we're almost ready to go."

"Comin' right up Rafer. Kind of a chilly one."

"Gonna' be downright cold once we get out on the big water. Water temperature is still around fifty-five or fifty-six. Comes right up through the hull. Got some extra socks?"

"I do, can't speak for Annie though."

"I thought you were kidding." Annie spoke softly so that only her father could hear. "But I did pack extra."

"Well bring them with. Rafer's got plenty of food, but we better get aboard Annie. We mustn't keep him waiting."

"Where are we Dad? What is this place?"

"Surprise! We're way up in Door County, Wisconsin. At Bailey's Harbor actually. This boat is the 'Nirvana II' and its captain is my friend Rafer Tate. He's a commercial fisherman and he's taking us out this morning to try our luck with him."

"So, we're going fishing?"

"Not just fishing, hopefully catching too, but that's not all. We're going to see how healthy the lake is, and we're going to learn something, I hope. No one is more in tune with this big water than Rafer Tate. And that's really the point I think."

"What do you mean when you keep saying 'the big water'?"

"These are the Great Lakes, Annie. This one is Lake Michigan, but there are four others. Lake Michigan is not the largest, but it's plenty big enough. It lives and breathes just like any other thing on this planet. It has its own ecosystem, its own climate, and its health is tied to the health of all of us and how we treat it."

Reaching back into the truck, Annie grabbed her knapsack and hurried to catch up to her father as he strode down to the dock.

"How big?"

"Well Lake Michigan is almost five hundred kilometers long and about one-hundred-twenty kilometers wide. I think it's almost a kilometer deep, but my math isn't always dependable. It's got a lot of water in it."

Annie was quiet for a full minute while she puzzled out the math.

"Three hundred miles! That's more than three hundred miles long! And almost seventy-five miles wide. That's really big. That's almost as long as Illinois is, isn't it?"

"Almost. Rafer will be able to tell you more about it, if you're interested. He likes to talk about his lake."

"His lake? It's not his, is it?"

"Nope, not really. The native Americans consider themselves the stewards of the land and waters, the caretakers. They were here long before we were, and they consider all living things sacred. That includes the lake itself because it is a living thing. Not surprisingly, that is also the belief of the Druids that Grandfather Conor spoke of in his diary. Around here the local native Americans are Winnebago, Fox, Sauk and Sioux. Their people don't believe that we can own the land and that it is our job to care for it and everything that lives on it."

Rafer Tate

In the bright Klieg lights of the boat and surrounding dock area, Annie regarded Rafer Tate. He was big man, with long shiny black hair tied back in a pony tail. His big arms bulged with muscle below the sleeves of his short-sleeved shirt as he lifted buckets and boxes in both hands. He smiled at her from under his hat with bright white teeth, made brighter by his sun-darkened skin.

"Hi Annie! Looks like a pretty calm morning on the lake. We should have pretty smooth sailing. This is my mate, Rob. Rob is one of my tribal brothers, so I'm kind of stuck with him."

Rob smiled and winked at Annie, showing perfect teeth. "Are you ready to have some fun?"

"Yes sir. I think so."

Rafer laughed a smooth, easy laugh and stuck out his hand for Annie to shake.

"You call me Rafer. Okay? I'm not a sir to any man."

"How you doin' Rafer?" Mike Abbott shook his

hand too.

Rafer put his hand on Mike's shoulder.

"It's been a long time, old friend. You should come around more often."

"I'm still working for a living. Not everybody can go fishing every day you know."

"And don't you forget it buddy. Do what you like, never work a day in your life. Isn't that right 'zuva wichashaought'?"

"I've always thought so." Mike smiled and added, "I am no zuva wichashaought anymore old friend."

"For me you will always be. Climb aboard, trains pulling out and the sunrise will not wait."

Annie and Mike climbed over the side of the big boat and in under the cabin roof. Mike had been right, the morning was chilly, and the damp air made it seem cooler still. Finding seats next to the pilot's chair, Mike dug out his big coffee thermos and poured a cup into the cap.

"Here you go sweetheart. This will warm you right up."

She wasn't sure that she wanted any coffee, but then she smelled the rich aroma of hot chocolate. Hot chocolate was a different thing altogether and she took the cup eagerly. She burned her lip on the first sip but it tasted very good.

"It might be a little hot just yet. This is a really good thermos."

"What does that mean? What he called you 'zuva whatchamacallit'?

"Rafer knows about my time as a soldier. He also knows that I don't like to talk about it so it's his idea of a little joke. It means 'going to war man', or something like that in the native dialect. He's just poking fun at me."

The men finished their preparation and jumped into the boat pulling in the ropes behind them. Rafer made his way up to the pilot's chair and started throwing switches. The big boat hummed into life. Then with a wink to Annie, he pushed a button and the mighty engine growled to life, vibrating the deck under their feet.

Slowly, the big boat backed out of its slip and began its careful journey out of the harbor and onto the 'big water' beyond. The sky ahead of them was beautifully lit with bright yellows, oranges and a hint of blue. The clouds were aglow with the promise of a magnificent sunrise. Once out beyond the harbor buoys, Rafer Tate pushed up the throttles. Higher and higher he pushed and faster and faster the Nirvana II leaped out to meet the sunrise. The speed breathtakingly exhilarating, as the harbor faded and the boat raced from wave to wave. Soon, the harbor lights and the sight of land disappeared over the horizon behind them.

"This is a fishing boat Annie." Her dad spoke in her ear. "Rafer is an old friend of mine, and this is his livelihood. When I spoke to him about the diary, he was intrigued and offered to help. We could take the ferry from the mainland to Washington Island and then go across the Island and take the ferry on to Rock Island but the ferries are always full, and it's a long wait at times. Having Rafer ferry us around will give us the opportunity to get a lot more done in one day than we normally would. That's why we brought the bikes too.

We can ride them once we get on the islands.

"But first we need to help Rafer make up for some of his lost fishing time. So first, we're going fishing on the big water and that's an adventure in itself."

"We're going to go out about five miles this morning," Rafer shouted over the roar of the engine. "We'll be fishing in about three or four hundred feet of water for a while and see what happens. The water hasn't had a chance to warm up yet, so the fish can't decide what level they want to settle into."

Annie looked puzzled. Rafer explained.

"*Michi-Gami* never gets really warm. It's a cold lake, like *Gichi-gami*. The sun warms the surface during the summer but the water stays very cold down deep. When the water starts to warm, the little fish come up to feed on the little critters that grow in the sunlight and warmer water. The big fish follow them, but until the change settles in, they can be anywhere."

"What's a *Gichi-gami*?" Annie shouted back.

"Lake Superior is *Gichi-gami*. It is a native American name. Just like 'zuva wichashaought' is. I have a lot of friends who speak this language and I respect the sacredness that these names hold for them. I speak some of it myself, and I have learned other phrases and names." Rafer yelled so he could be heard above the roar of the big engine. "*Gichi-gami* means 'Big Sea' in your language. Michi-gami is Lake Michigan where we are today."

"Lake Superior is the biggest lake. We learned that in school."

"Very good. Did they tell you that there is enough water in Lake Superior, Gichi-gami, to cover the entire continental United States in about a foot of water? I bet they didn't."

"That can't be true." Annie was skeptical, "Can it?"

"You can look it up. It's true. It has its own weather system. It is also a very fickle mistress. No one goes out on Lake Superior lightly; she is very unforgiving to people who do not respect her."

"We don't have to worry about that today, do we?"

"Nope, just look at that sunrise. This is a blessing of a day. It is going to be beautiful. Let's catch some fish today and go in early. How does that sound, little one?"

"What do I have to do?"

"We fish for the salmon and trout. They get fairly large and the restaurants in town pay pretty well for them, which is good for me. We have a limit on how many we can take on any given day. They count the limit individually, which means five Coho salmon for each man, or girl, or twenty all together. That' a lot of salmon, so that would be good for us."

"I thought salmon and trout lived in fast rivers and stuff."

"Not these guys. Brook trout, or other river fish don't get too big. We've caught Cohos that weigh up to twenty-five pounds. That's a really big one, but they're out here."

"That's a lot bigger than the sunfish and bluegills that I catch."

"That's for sure Annie. After we do our best catching fish, we're taking you guys up to Washington Island so you and your dad can explore. You could take the ferry across but there can be a lot of traffic."

"Yeah, and this is more fun!"

"Also—if I know your dad, he's going to wanna' look in more than one place. The Island is nice but getting around on it without a car would be really tough. This way we can go all the way around to the back side and go in from there if we want to."

"So what do I have to do now?"

"We'll rig up and then when we get something, you reel it in. That'll be your job—if you're up to it."

"How do we know where the fish are? This is a pretty big lake." She asked looking out over the water stretching all the way to the horizon.

"Do you see this monitor up above the console? That is a GPS unit. When we were out here yesterday, we marked a school of fish right where we are going. The GPS will show us how to get back to that exact spot. With any luck they will still be in the area. Then Rob and I will get our tackle rigged and set it out. With a little luck, we'll be on the fish and they'll start striking the bait. Then we're going to get busy bringing them in. Think you can reel them in?"

"I'm ready Captain."

"That's the spirit! Well, the lake trout have been a little spotty so far this season. They like the cold water, but they seem to be up a little higher, around fifty or sixty feet. There are also Coho salmon in here and they are fun too."

"That sounds pretty easy. I caught a couple of trout last summer in the Brule River over near Cable; the biggest one weighed almost a pound. So sure, I can do that." She shouted back.

"We'll see." Rafer smiled a knowing smile. "We're almost there now."

With a signal to Rob, the first mate, Rafer throttled the engine back and the two men got busy.

"We never shut the engine completely off Annie. By keeping the boat idling along we won't get turned sideways in the wind. Getting turned in the wind like that, the waves hit the side of the boat and it rocks and tips. Pretty easy to get seasick when that happens so we keep going just a little to prevent that."

The boat had about a dozen big fishing poles stuck out from the sides and the roof of the pilot house in all directions. Each one had different shiny bright lures rigged on the end of their heavy line. One by one, the men attached large weights to the lines. Each weight looked like a small cannon ball, weighed as much as eight pounds, and had its own separate line and reel.

Once the weights were attached, they were lowered into the water. A motor attached to the line counted how far the weight sank. When it reached the depth that they thought there would be fish, they stopped it. The bright fishing lure then trailed out behind the weight at the depth they wanted to fish. When, and if, a fish would strike the bait, the weight would detach from the line when the fisherman set the hook. Then a motor attached to the reel for the weight would reel it back up to the boat. That way the weight didn't hinder reeling in the fish, and it was ready for the next fishing pole.

Soon there were six lines in the water and the fishing began while the men prepared a few more poles. The boat continued to plow slowly through the calm morning water as the light grew and the sky brightened.

"FISH ON!!!"

Rafer's yell was preceded by a sharp jerk in one of the large poles. Rob jumped to the pole and unhooked its heavy weight. A small motor reeled the weight up while Rob wrestled the pole that was bent into the shape of a large question mark.

"Mike, you take the first one. Show Annie how *easy* it is!"

Mike took the pole Rob offered him and began reeling. The fish suddenly realized it was hooked and decided he didn't like it and was going to run away, and run he did. The reel screamed as the line peeled off, and the fish made its run for freedom. Mike continued to reel against the pressure. With his feet braced and the rod bent at a sharp angle, he slowly won back some of the line the fish had taken. Far out behind the boat a big fish jumped, breaking out of the water, and dislodging the shiny lure. The pole went slack and the fish was gone.

"Well darn it. Did I do something wrong Rafer?"

"Nope, those lake trout just seem to know if they

can get any slack in the line, they can spit the bait."

"FISH ON!"

"This one's yours Annie, get ready!"

Annie was ready and eagerly took the pole from the first mate Rob. It was a lot bigger pole than any she'd ever handled before. The fish pulled with a mighty force and Annie had to brace her feet and knees against the transom at the rear of the boat as the fish made its first run.

"Just reel steady Annie. Looks like a good one." Rob stood next to Annie to be ready to help if she needed it.

Annie didn't know how she was supposed to reel steady when the fish was peeling line off so fast that the reel was a blur of spinning motion and buzzing like a swarm of bees. Holding onto the pole and trying to steadily reel, the fish fought and jerked the pole, yanking it this way and that way. Whatever was on the other end of the line, it was very strong. Annie almost thought it might pull her over the side and into the water. At last, the fish ran straight toward the boat. Annie turned the reel as fast as she could to keep as much slack as she could out of the line. When it got close to the boat, the fish decided to run again. The line screamed out of the reel and the thick rod bent into a C shape, losing all the progress that she had made.

The fish fought hard for its freedom and Annie bravely fought back. Her arms were starting to tire, and she found herself thinking about how cold her feet were.

"I'm going to put the boat in reverse Annie, so that we can gain a little ground on this one. It's a big one for sure and we don't want to lose him." Rafer yelled from the pilot's seat as he started slowly backing the big boat toward the fighting fish. "Do you need to rest, or any help?"

"No, I've got this."

She wanted to be the first one to catch a fish this morning, so she stubbornly reeled as fast as she could. Annie didn't want to admit that her arms were getting so tired that her shoulders were starting to ache. Her feet, braced against the transom, felt numb from the cold and her thighs started to weaken from her efforts.

"Are you sure you don't need some help Annie?"

"No dad, I've got this. This is a big fish."

"That it is. Get him girl. You've got this."

"You're doing great Annie." Rafer Tate slowed the boat and Rob brought in some of the other poles. "Just keep reeling and hold her steady."

Five minutes had become ten and the fight continued. Each time the fish came close, it would see the boat and run again and the line would scream out off of the reel. Annie raised the pole high and kept reeling but it was getting difficult and she was starting to worry that she might need to admit defeat and hand the pole to someone else.

Suddenly, a thought leaped into her head!

A voice, soft and tender, a thought of great depth whispering in her ear. A voice so powerful, it took Annie by such surprise that her knees buckled a little.

"Find your power; use your strength! Take our strength with your own and use it. WE are here for you."

With the voice a feeling of great energy blossomed

from inside her chest. The ache in her shoulders and arms melted away, and her thighs felt strong again. She felt determination and resolve as she straightened the thick rod and turned the reel again. She felt the fish at the end of the line and suddenly felt its tremendous strength and vitality. She willed the great fish to stop fighting against her. She felt a strange strong connection to it. She suddenly knew that she would win in the end.

The fish fought on, and Annie worked the reel and held the pole tight. Her forearms no longer tired and aching; it seemed she had been trying to reel the fish for a very long time. But the fish was now only heavy, and its fight had suddenly relented.

But even with her newfound strength, the fight was not over. As the boat slowly backed up, waves sloshed up over the broad rear end of the big vessel. In no time, Annie was soaked with icy cold water from the knees down, but still the fish dragged back against her, its weight and reluctance heavy. It was hard work and very exciting.

At last, the fish came close and everyone on the boat could see it.

"Wow! Nice healthy fish. Get him in here Rob!"

Rob grabbed the gaff, a long pole with a sharp hook on the end of it. He reached out with it and in one swift movement, brought the huge Coho salmon in over the side of the boat. It lay in the bright morning sun displaying all the colors of the rainbow down its flanks.

Taking the pole from Annie, he placed it in one of the holders and relieved her. Annie dropped into one of the seats and stared at the big colorful fish. It was beautiful, with bright hues of blue and a stripe of orange down its side. It didn't matter that her arms were exhausted or her feet were very cold. She had never seen such a big beautiful fish and she had caught it all by herself.

The experience had been exciting and confusing. She couldn't explain the powerful voice that had suddenly arrived, nor the strength and endurance that it had brought with it. And that the strength was now slowing ebbing away. Nor could she understand it. She looked up at her father, confused. Her eyes met his. For a moment he just looked deeply into her eyes, his face asking a question, then with a small smile he nodded his approval.

"Wow! I bet it's at least fifteen pounds." Mike's voice was filled with awe as he looked down on the fish.

"Closer to twenty I'd say. Really early in the season to see such a big one. Looks like you're good luck Miss Annie." Rafer voiced his pleasure. "I guess we'll need to take you with us all the time from now on. Let's get a picture of your big fish. Pick it up for me."

"Maybe Rob could pick it up? My arms are a little tired."

"I bet they are," said Rob, with a grin, "that was a lot of hard work. Here you go, stand next to me so that everyone knows it was you who caught it."

Rob hoisted the fish up and held it next to Annie. It was such a big fish that it reached all the way up to her shoulders. No wonder it had been so hard to catch she thought as Rafer snapped a picture with his cell phone.

They fished the rest of the morning. Everyone

caught fish as they slowly worked their way north in the direction of Washington and Rock Island. Soon they were in sight of the islands and had caught their limit. But no fish even came close to the big fish that Annie had managed.

Little did she know that that was just the beginning of today's adventure. The day was still young.

The Hunt for Clues

They skirted the side of Washington Island and crossed the channel toward Rock Island. The boat was big and powerful, and they raced across the water. As they approached the small harbor where the ferry docked, Rafer turned to Mike Abbott.

"Do you want me to pull into the dock here Mike?"

"Yes, please Rafer. I think we can take the bikes off and ride to the couple of places marked on the map here. A couple of them are pretty far."

"The island is not as big as Washington, but it's big enough, and it's getting kinda' hot. Wouldn't it be better if we cruised the shoreline and went into the island on a shorter angle?"

"Ideally yes. You're already doing me a huge favor Rafer. I don't want to impose."

"Annie's already made my day, old friend. And I will never be able to repay the debt I owe you."

"Well, that's good, the Annie thing, but you don't owe me anything Rafer."

"What? I owe you my life. How can you say that?"

"That's enough Rafer; it was a long time ago. Memory is a funny thing; it makes things seem bigger than they might have really been."

"Suit yourself Mike, but I'll still keep it the way I remember it."

"Thanks Rafer. Let me out at the dock for a few minutes, will you? I want to see if there's anybody around here that knows the inside of the island."

"Okie dokie, I've got to change my shoes and get into some long pants if I'm going to hike in the woods, so take your time."

"I'll be just a minute."

With that Mike climbed out to the front of the big boat and as it approached the dock he jumped across to the deck, waved and on foot headed toward the visitor center.

"What did you mean...Mr. Tate?" asked Annie.

"It's Rafer, call me Rafer. What did I mean about what?"

"About owing my Dad."

"Oh that, I don't think your father likes to talk about it."

"About what?"

"Nothing Annie. It's just that your father wasn't always a Professor of History. Before that he was something else entirely, and that's when I became his friend." Rafer looked out over the water wistfully, thoughtfully rubbing a sun-whitened scar over his left eyebrow. "Way back then; a very long time ago it seems nowadays."

Shortly Mike came down the hill from the small

visitor's area. With him came two others. One seemed to be ancient, bent like trees that have endured years of strong winds and weather, the other a young boy of seven or eight years old. As they approached the boat the old man spoke in a strong voice that seemed out of place within his ruined body.

"This boy knows the Island as well as anyone else on this island. He will show you the way to what you are looking for, but he cannot find it for you. That will be up to you."

Mike and the young boy jumped back onto the boat, and the old man continued; this time he spoke to Annie.

"It is a long time, a very long time since the last came seeking. Well met young one, welcome midsummer's eve." He called as the boat slowly backed away. "Follow the boy, but trust your own feelings."

"Dad what does he mean?"

"Today is the summer solstice Annie; it's June 21st."

"I'd forgotten that, so today's the longest day of the year?"

"All days are the same length sweetie, but yes today the sunlight lasts longer than any other day of the year."

"And it's one of the hottest!" Rafer chimed in. "Glad we're out on the cool lake water."

"No Dad, I meant the other things he said. What did he mean?"

Reaching into his backpack Mike pulled out Conor Abbott's diary. Opening it he read aloud.

"Beneath the ground, food for worms forever gazing toward heaven and the stone above."

"Boy, I've puzzled over that sentence for quite a while, but I think I've got it figured out. It sounds like he's talking about someone's grave, and maybe their headstone, or something like that."

"But where?"

"Well, that's the mystery Annie. There are three cemeteries on Rock Island. I've marked them on this map of the island. Only one is used these days, this one." He pointed at the mark on the southern end of the island. "The others are very old. I think we should start with the old ones. There is a real chance that there are many buried here that were never marked as well. People have lived here for a long time, and written records are relatively new here. What do you think?"

"Sure, I think that's a pretty good plan Dad. Which one first?"

"I think the one that's hardest to get to, for some reason that sounds right to me."

"Okay, which one is that?"

"This one on the eastern side, there's a trail to it, maybe a couple miles. Do you think you can get us close to it Rafer?"

Rafer had been looking over his shoulder.

"I can get you close, but I can't get the boat all the way to the shoreline. You'd probably have to swim the last fifty or so yards."

"Those graves are haunted. Everyone knows that."

The boy had climbed onto the boat and taken a seat at the back. Up until now he had not spoken.

"No one goes there at night—ever."

"That's the one then. That's where we should start

Dad."

"Say no more," Rafer consulted the map one more time, shoved the throttle and the boat leaped forward.

In minutes they approached the densely wooded shoreline. The rocky beach was deserted, but they spied a narrow path that led away and up the hill into the woods. Rafer, Mike and Annie got ready to jump out and swim. All three hesitated, knowing the water would be freezing cold. The young boy dove in headfirst, and with strong strokes, struck out for the shore. Mike looked at Annie, shrugged and jumped in himself. Rafer was not far behind him. Annie took a deep breath, waved at Rob who was staying with the boat, and jumped herself.

The icy water took her breath away for a moment. The two men had already reached a spot where they could stand in the water and they waded the rest of the way. Annie swam as best as she could hoping to not hold them up. The boy was already waiting for them and half up the trail. Once on the beach, Annie hurried to catch up, her shoes squishing water with each step.

They climbed to the higher ground on the overgrown path, but once at the top of the hill it disappeared. The young boy did not hesitate but moved ahead into the thick undergrowth, bearing to the left. The air was still and hot. In no time, their wet clothes were no longer cool, and now made them break out in a sweat. Annie stayed close behind the men who pushed through the brambles and brush with effort.

At last, they broke out of the trees into a small clearing. A faded wooden fence surrounded a small space and inside the space, several gravestones were scattered about. The boy stepped back, his posture indicating reluctance to go any closer, but he pointed without speaking. The men climbed through the slats of the fence and Annie scooted underneath it.

Inside, the grass was deep, the gray stones barely visible. Any names that had been carved into the stones had faded, eroded away by rain and time. Mike reached into his knapsack and studied some of his notes while Rafer walked from one to the next.

As soon as Annie stood up inside the fenced enclosure, the voice spoke again. Cool and soothing, quiet but speaking with great strength.

"The sign is here; it is for you to find. Look within yourself before you seek."

Annie was dizzied by the feeling that the voice conjured. She glanced from one adventurer to the next, hoping that one of them had heard the voice too. Hoping that she wasn't actually losing her mind.

What did it mean, 'look within myself'? She was confused and felt very strange. Suddenly in the corner of her eye a shadow moved, turning quickly there was nothing there. She put a hand on one of the fence posts to steady herself. At the edge of the fenced space a huge oak had been uprooted in a recent storm. It lay on its great side, its leaves still green and shiny, close enough to touch from inside the fence. Looking at it she felt the sorrow of the tree and the trees that surrounded it. She felt its age and wisdom deep in her chest. She looked at the tree, suddenly studying it carefully. A huge network of roots had been exposed, the dirt and sod still clinging to them. A large crater had been created when they had been pulled from the ground. Directly in the center she spied a square white stone that pushed upward from the middle.

"Dad...."

Something in her voice got both men's attention.

"There's something under that tree." She pointed.

Both men climbed the fence and approached the tree studying the white stone as they approached it. It was certainly a grave stone and very old to be buried among the roots of the great tree.

"Should we pull it out I wonder?" Rafer's voice held a hint of awe in it.

"NO! Don't touch it!" The boys panicked voice sounded from the edge of the clearing. "It'll be bad luck for us all!"

"He's right of course. This is an antiquity and shouldn't be disturbed. But we can examine it where it is I think." While Annie's father spoke he was busily pulling the dirt and grass away from the bottom of the stone. The carving at the bottom was clear, unexposed to the weather all these many years.

"Well what is this then?" His voice filled with wonder. "This is the one!" Mike was excited. "Look!"

On the face of the stone was a clearly carved sigil.

The name on the stone was faded, but clear—L'Abbee.

"L'Abbee! That is French for 'Of the Abbey'. Of the Abbey—Abbott! This is one of our ancestors I believe. One of our ancestors was buried here!"

"What does that little picture mean? Is it just decoration Dad?"

"That is known as a sigil Annie. A sigil is a carving or picture that represents something important, something 'magical'."

"Is it? Is it magical?"

"This one is special in a different way Annie; this is the sign of the druids."

"Seek the stones, they bear the sign! Dad that's what the diary said, Seek the stones they bear the sign! This is one of the stones, isn't it?"

"It certainly appears to be. Let's get some more of this dirt off the lower part and see if there's anything else on it."

They carefully removed most of the remaining dirt from the stone and below the name of L'Abbee was a bible verse, the carving much clearer than the rest of the stone.

And the apostles said unto the Lord, Increase our faith.

"The stone was obviously buried long before Conor Abbott began looking for it. 'Seek the stones, they bear the mark,' those were the words of the elder. But he would have never found it here; it was already underneath the tree by the time he began looking. He was doomed to not complete his task, but now we have the answer."

"That's right Dad, but it also said, 'Seek the stones and feel their life.' What does that mean?"

"How do you feel the life of a stone, it's just a stone." Rafer was confused. "It has no life, it's a rock."

"It's sad that it has been under the ground so long. Kind of lonesome, 'forever gazing at heaven and the stone above." Annie felt the sadness of the tree and the loneliness of the stone. As Annie reached out to touch the headstone, a bright blue spark flashed and leapt from the stone to her hand—and the world went black around her.

"Annie! Annie, are you alright? Here take a drink of this water. Oh my God, Annie are you alright?"

Annie opened her eyes. She was lying in the grass looking up at a moon in its last crescent and the blue sky above, the two men leaning over her with concerned expressions.

"Seek the Apostles, seek the fisherman."

"What? What are you saying Annie? Oh God, I've let you get dehydrated. What kind of father am I?"

Annie pulled herself up into a sitting position.

"What? I'm fine. What do you mean Dad?"

"What you just said, 'Seek the Apostles, seek the fisherman." Where did that come from?"

"I don't know what you mean Dad; I never said anything like that."

Rafer and Mike looked down at her with concern.

Rafer said, "Maybe we should get her back to the boat Mike."

"I agree, let's go."

"Wait a minute Dad, did you see the spark? Didn't you feel it?"

"Feel what?"

"The spark."

"Honey I think you've been out in this heat too long."

"No, you don't understand, I touched the stone like this and….

"Seek the Apostles, seek the fisherman."

Annie's voice didn't sound like Annie. It was strong, loud and with a foreign accent. Again, she dropped to her knees.

"It's a message from the stone. It's message for the true seeker." The boy had approached without them taking notice. He looked at her with huge eyes and pointed. "She is the seeker."

The two men looked from one to the other, eyebrows raised.

"What does that mean?" Said Annie, recovering and rising to her feet.

"It must mean that the next stone will have something to do with Apostles. But what I can't imagine." He looked at Annie, "Well, this isn't going to be an easy answer for sure." He smiled, "but it appears that we now have our ***seeker.***"

Again, Mike met her gaze, and again she saw something in his eyes that she didn't recognize. He gave her a slight smile and a wink.

"It looks like we've got some homework to tackle Annie. We're going to have another look at the clues that Conor left us again."

Seek the Apostles

The sound of birds calling and woodpeckers hammering was too loud in the trees and woods surrounding the little tent where Annie was trying to sleep. Squirrels and chipmunks made their own racket as they scolded each other, searching the leaves and pine needles for seeds and fresh pinecones. With a loud, "Harumph," Annie pulled her pillow over her ears and rolled over in her sleeping bag, trying to go back to sleep.

"Wake up sleepy-head," Annie's father called from outside of her tent, "it's going to be a beautiful day. Adventure awaits!"

It was no use. Going back to sleep was out of the question once her father was up. Annie again felt the excitement that she'd fallen asleep with the night before. When Annie's father said 'Adventure awaits', it meant that he had something special planned for the day, and up until now he had not let her in on the secret. If last night was going to be any indication of what was to come, she was sure she didn't want to miss a minute of it. With a deep sigh, she threw open the sleeping bag and started pulling on her shoes.

The heat of summer had finally begun to fade, and the evenings had become pleasant. Although it was too early for the autumn leaves to begin to color the campus of the college farther south, they had arrived in earnest in the north woods. Late August was giving a last deep sigh as it faded into September.

They had driven from their home many hours until they reached the very top of the United States and the pebbly shores of Lake Superior. By the time they had arrived in the little fishing village of Bayfield, Wisconsin, the sun had set and the light was fading from the sky. They needed to hurry to catch the last ferry from the mainland across the bay to Madeline Island. They had kept their truck windows rolled all the way down as they drove through the town. It was a cool summer evening and they heard the ship's horn sounding just as they approached the harbor. They had made it with only minutes to spare and was the last vehicle allowed on board.

Once the ferry, named the 'Madeline', had cast off, the journey across open water had been exciting. In the twilight of the evening, the twinkling lights of the little fishing village became smaller and smaller. The calm water and cool air were refreshing and tiny fish leaped and flashed their silvery sides in the boat's wake as it plowed its way across the wide bay. Their destination - the harbor at LaPointe, the only town or settlement on Madeline Island in the Chequamegon Bay of the vast Lake Superior.

Full darkness had fallen by the time the big ferry

docked and tied up. One by one the cars and trucks had driven off, taking their sleepy passengers to their homes and beds. Because they were the last vehicle to board, they were also the last vehicle to exit. Mike Abbott had not hesitated but drove straight out of town, and into the forest and bright starlit night. In almost no time, they arrived at the campground where they would be camping for the weekend. Annie was an old hand at setting up camp, even in the dark. Once they had their lanterns lit and their gear unloaded, her father started a small campfire and they finished setting up their two small tents and fixing a late meal.

"So Dad?" Annie couldn't contain herself any longer. She looked around the darkened campsite, "We're on an island right? Madeline Island."

"Yep, named after the Native American wife of the fur trapper, Michael Cadotte. She apparently was quite a lady. Her father was Chief White Crane of the Ojibwe Nation. She and her children are buried here on this island. Not far from here actually."

"So, this is a history adventure Professor?" She smiled at him.

"Well, I am a Professor of History, but not really, but I always enjoy learning about new places and things. The history of the Apostle Islands is centuries old, and Madeline Cadott is only a small but very important piece of that."

"Islands, you said islands. The Apostle Islands?"

"There are twenty-two islands in all. Twelve of them are fairly large, which the early Jesuits named for the twelve apostles, I think."

"So, that's the big secret?" Annie's eyes sparkled in

the firelight. "Seek the Apostles, Seek the Fisherman." You figured it out!"

"Well maybe, I thought about all the possibilities, churches and churchyards with names of the Apostles, but none of them had all of them, and back in the days of Conor Abbott, it was still pretty wild around here. The same people who lived on Washington and Rock Island were the same ones that lived here in large part. So I thought it was worth a shot. What do you think?"

"That's a really good idea Dad, but what about the second part? 'Seek the fisherman.'?"

"Well Annie, I didn't want to 'spill the beans' too soon, just in case the weather turned against us. We are out in Lake Superior now and the weather can turn in a few hours, and then almost any kind of travel is not safe. So, I wanted to wait and see, but it looks like smooth sailing for tomorrow now."

"Sailing! We're going sailing? Tomorrow? Really?"

"Well not sailboat sailing, but we're adventuring out into the Lake and it promises to be almost perfect weather."

"Did you say it was dangerous?"

"I said it can be dangerous. One time, a storm came up in September out here. It came so fast that it caught everyone by surprise and over half-a-dozen big ships sank in about twelve hours. Many lives were lost. But tomorrow's forecast is for another day like today, but this is September, and strange things happen on Superior in September."

"But we'll be careful, right?"

"We're always careful Annie, but we are always adventurous too, so we are extra careful. Always. I'm not forgetting how much the last trip took out of you honey."

"Six ships sank in one day; is that really true?" Annie was perplexed.

"Yes, but actually it was more than that, those ships were the really big ones. Huge iron ore freighters from hills near Duluth, Minnesota and the copper ore freighters from the mines in Upper Michigan. One of them was the Edmund Fitzgerald, you know? Like the song? There was a train-car ferry out of Ste. Sault Marie on the Canadian border. There was no way of knowing how many smaller ships and boats were also lost. It must have been quite a storm.

"How do you know all this stuff? But, Geez Dad, that must have been awful."

"The College has unlimited library resources; it's half the reason I like my job. But that day must have been really awful, as you say. Lake Superior is not to be trifled with. Now crawl in there and try and get some sleep. We got here a lot later than I wanted to and now it's even later. So good night, sleep tight."

"Sleep? Now? You've got my brain going a million miles an hour. How am I going to go to sleep?"

"You might be surprised. This fresh air is magical."

"I'll try. Is there anything else you want to tell me?"

"There are black bears on some of the Apostle Islands, but as far as I know there aren't any here on Madeline Island." He paused and scratched his chin. "As far as I know."

"Thanks Dad, sometimes I really hate you. Now I've got that to think about too."

"Good night Annie, it's almost tomorrow, so I'll see

you soon."

Captain Gabe

That had been last night, and now an adventure awaited! Ready to face the new day and their adventure, Annie crawled out of her little tent into a mystic world. Tall pines grew thick, the air sharp with their scent. The ground was soft, thickly padded with their pungent needles. A morning fog hung low in the trees, limiting how far she could see in any direction. The air was damp and cool on her face.

Mike Abbott, his hair neatly brushed and flannel shirt tucked into his jeans, was busying himself over their small camp stove on the nearby picnic table, and a cheerful fire was burning in the firepit. The smell of bacon frying was mixed with the aroma of fresh bread.

"I'm trying out the new Dutch oven for some biscuits and the bacon and eggs are almost done."

"I think I might be starving!" She yawned and stretched while she peeked over her father's shoulder.

"It's the air, makes you extra hungry."

After she had eaten a big breakfast of two eggs, four pieces of bacon and a couple of dinner rolls, Annie put her elbows on the table and looked across at him. He was watching her with a twinkle in his eye.

"That's a healthy appetite you've got there. Take after your father I see."

"Don't try and dodge the question Dad, what are we really doing today?"

Mike reached into his knapsack lying next to him on the table and took out the diary of Conor Abbott. Opening it, he said, "There are no dates on the clues that Great-grandad put in here. It's anyone's guess what order we should look for them in. I think this one seems the most likely for now. Especially because we are supposed to be looking for a fisherman.

"With the fish he eats, with the fish he sleeps, above the waves beneath the ground.

"That doesn't make any sense. Does it?"

"I've been puzzling over it for a while now. The statement contradicts itself. For sure it's a riddle of some sort. The second line is even more confusing.

"Above the waves, beneath the ground he waits in vain, his peace is found."

"How do we figure it out?"

"Well today, I've got a secret weapon."

"What kind of secret weapon?" She smiled.

"Today?" He smiled at her and winked, "well today you are going to be introduced to none other than Captain Gabe."

"Captain Gabe? What's a Captain Gabe?"

"We're in the Apostle Islands, but now we need to 'seek the fisherman.'" Gabe MacDonald is a person who knows these islands almost better than anyone else around here. He's also quite a character—to say the least. If anyone would know how to find a mythical fisherman, it'll be Captain Gabe and he is taking us out on an island tour and adventure."

"How do you know all these interesting people Dad?"

"Well Annie," he winked at her, "once upon a time, I used to be interesting too."

"That does sound pretty cool. When?"

"We will have to wait until this fog burns off, but once we've straightened up the campsite, we'll head back to the harbor."

The little harbor in the village of LaPointe was bustling with the many fishermen who had been waiting for the fog to clear off of the lake. Now engines were starting, and ropes were being cast off, as they made ready to start their day of hard work. Mike walked through the activity, talking to some of the men and waving to others. Near the end of the dock stood a big man, drinking coffee out of an equally big mug and looking out over the water. He was tall and broad in the shoulders, wearing Bermuda shorts and sandals in spite of the chill in the air.

"Hey there Gabe!" yelled Mike as he approached.

The big man turned around with a smile that matched his size, bright teeth flashing in a burly beard covering most of his face, and eyebrows that seemed to be trying to climb up into his shoulder length hair. A good crop of chest hair showed through the unbuttoned portion of his floral print Hawaiian shirt. It occurred to Annie that Captain Gabe looked more like a bear than a man.

Well, she thought, there's one bear on Madeline Island after all.

Mike shook Gabe's hand, and then they embraced.

"Long time no see Big Mike."

"It's been a while, that's for sure. So, this is what you're doing now?"

"Yep, you know me," Captain Gabe swept his huge arm in a broad arc taking in the harbor and the lake beyond it, "I've got to be on water and this is a place where my heart has always wanted to be. I love this place."

"Now who's this beautiful creature? Annie, right?"

"Yes sir," Annie stepped forward to shake his hand. The closer she got to Captain Gabe, the bigger he got.

"It is a pleasure to meet you, Annie. Welcome to Lake Superior. Are you ready to learn about her?" He said with a wink. "If you are, let's get aboard and shove off."

Annie scanned all the big boats in the harbor getting ready to leave. There were some with one or two masts gently swaying in the waves and big fishing boats with trawler winches and gear hanging over their sides, "Which one is yours?"

"Why this one. This little beauty right here." Gabe pointed at a small open boat tied to the dock near them. "She's small so that she can go places that the bigger boats can't, and she's fast and plenty safe. Just hop in and we're on our way Annie."

Annie wasn't too sure about the boat. It looked so small next to the others along the dock, and only a fraction of the size of Rafer Tate's boat in Bailey's Harbor, but she climbed in anyway.

Captain Gabe stood at the wheel of the boat and guided it almost casually out of the harbor, steering with one hand while he drank his coffee with the other. Once out on the lake he turned the boat to the left and began following the shoreline of Madeline Island.

"What are we going to see?" asked Annie, speaking above the thrum of the engine.

"Well first, we're going to go around Madeline, which is the largest of the islands. Long Island, which you can see on the horizon over on the right, is longer but very narrow. Once we go around the end of the island, we'll cross the channel between Madeline and Stockton Island. There we'll see a sunken shipwreck and maybe a few black bears. How does that sound?"

"A real shipwreck? Really? And bears?"

"Yep, there are actually more black bears per square mile on Stockton Island than any other place in the world. I see them on the beach all the time. They eat shellfish, clams and mussels, and anything else that washes up on the shoreline. If the day doesn't get too hot, we should see one or two."

"That would be cool!" Annie had forgotten about any worries she had about the size of the boat and now was looking forward to Stockton Island.

"Right now, we're on the leeward side of the island. That means we're out of the wind. The wind always blows a little on the lake, and sometimes a lot. When we round the end of the island it is almost five miles across to Stockton. The wind will be blowing and the waves will be considerably bigger than they are here. I'll be throttling the boat up to make the run, so make sure you hang on Annie. Okay?"

Annie thought that sounded pretty scary, but she nodded. She settled in next to her dad on the seat.

As soon as the end of the island came into view, Big Captain Gabe pushed the throttle up and the little boat shot out into the open water. His prediction had been correct. The waves were three or four feet high and the breeze blew directly into their faces. Ahead of them, Stockton Island looked far away as the boat leaped from wave top to wave top, giving them a wild and bouncy ride while big Captain Gabe steered with one hand and sipped coffee from his huge mug. Annie had to admit to herself that it was very exciting, especially when she remembered that the nearest land was almost a hundred feet underneath her feet.

Once they got to the island, they were again out of the wind. Captain Gabe slowed the boat as they made their way along the lakeshore as quietly as they could. Rounding a point of land, they saw something in the water.

"What's that? It looks like an old dock or a pier or something."

"That is the wreck of the Noquebay Annie. It lies in the sand in about fifteen feet of water."

He drifted the boat directly over the wreck and they looked down into the crystal-clear water of Lake Superior. The hull and windlass were visible clearly and the ship's wheel could also be seen in the golden light of the sunshine.

"The Noquebay was over two hundred feet long and carrying a full load of lumber. She had taken shelter from a storm in Bayfield back more than a hundred years ago. After she left the harbor, she only made it this far before a fire broke out on board. The captain grounded her here on the beach to save his crew and the ship. The cargo was recovered and the crew survived, but what was left of the ship never moved again."

"You can see everything so clearly. That is really something." Mike was impressed.

"There's another thing you can see clearly," said Captain Gabe pointing at the beach only a few dozen yards away. A large black bear and two cubs had just emerged from the edge of the forest and were strolling along the beach, unaware that they were being watched. Gabe shut off the engine and let the boat silently bob in the water while they watched the bear cubs frolic in the water, investigating everything they encountered. Suddenly, the sow sniffed the air and rose up on her hind legs looking directly at the little boat.

"Whoa! Don't even think about it Mama, we mean no harm." Gabe's voice didn't sound too confident as he spoke to the large and protective mama bear only separated by a narrow strip of shallow water.

The two cub's feet in the water also stood and regarded the boat, frozen in time.

"Greetings Mother! We are the seekers. Go in Peace!" Mike stood in the front of the boat, legs spread, voice steady and strong as he held his hand up, palm outward.

The three bears dropped down onto their front feet, and the two cubs turned and followed their mother back into the dense undergrowth of the forest without a sound.

"Holy Cow! That was one of the most amazing things I've ever seen!" Annie was really excited. She looked at her father, "What was that?"

They had already seen two amazing things and it was not even lunchtime yet!

"Just a trick my own Dad taught me. Glad it worked though. It mighta' gotten a little crowded in the boat there for a minute."

"Wow! Where are we going next?"

Gabe looked up at the sky. "It's getting hot. I think from here we'll go across to Oak Island, a very pretty place, and we'll walk the beach and hunt for agates. What'dya say?"

"Agates?"

"Agates are a kind of quartz stone that is made in a volcano. They have a glassy kind of rock in them called chalcedony. They are reddish or brown in color because of all the iron around here. They are really quite beautiful, and some are valuable." Annie's dad explained. "They're easy to spot if you know what to look for."

"But first, Annie, I think you might like to take a little '*Nantucket sleighride*'. What d'ya think Mike?"

"I don't know; she's kind of a fraidy cat," he said with a crooked smile.

"I'm not a fraidy cat! What's a *Nantucket sleighride*?"

A Sleighride, the Seiche and Some Stones

"Well, in olden days whale hunters, called whalers, sailed out of Nantucket, Rhode Island. This was before we learned it was wrong to hunt whales, so it wasn't considered a bad thing back then." Her father explained.

"They used harpoons that they threw by hand from longboats rowed by a crew of six or eight men. The harpooner stood in the front of the boat as they tried to get as close to the whale as they could. The harpoon had a long rope fastened to it," continued Captain Gabe, "when they successfully 'hooked' a whale, it would dive or run as fast as it could trying to get away. But it was attached to the boat by the rope, and the mariners were pulled on a very fast, very wild ride. They called it a Nantucket sleighride. It was probably terrifying, but it sounds very exciting from this distance. Are you up for it Annie? How about you Mike, you rode the sleigh better than anyone I've ever seen once upon a time."

"No thanks Gabe, my days on the rope are behind me, I hope," smiled Mike as they shared an old memory.

"I don't know, I think so" Annie was interested but not sure. "It sounds exciting, but there's no whales around here."

"Nope, that's why we have a boat with a really big motor on it," he gave Mike a wink. "Let's go then."

Captain Gabe tied a rope to the front of his boat and handed the end to Annie.

"Stand way up in the front of the boat and hang on to the rope, just like the old mariners this is your harpoon rope. Once we get out into the channel again, where the wind is blowing and the waves are up, we'll see if you like being a whale hunter, okay Annie?"

"Sure," she said, leaning back to pull the rope tight, trying to grip the deck with her toes, "I can do this," she said to herself.

Gabe turned the boat away from the beach and the sunken wreck of the Noquebay, and turned up the shoreline to the end of the island. As soon as he cleared the point the breeze picked up and the waves got higher. Gabe pushed the throttle forward and the boat started jumping from wave to wave. With each bounce the water splashed from the bow and sprayed Annie. She had to keep her knees bent to absorb the shock as the boat slammed into the next wave as she kept the rope tight. A big grin spread across her face as the ride got wilder by the second.

Captain Gabe pushed the throttle farther up and the little boat leaped forward. Jumping from the crest of a wave it would vault into the air, crashing down in a rainbow of water and race ahead only to climb the next wave and leap ahead again.

Annie threw one arm in the air and whooped, "This is fantastic!"

And then the voice within spoke again,

"First before all things, feel the life in all that you see and touch."

"Faster!" She yelled over her shoulder.

The engine roared like a wild animal, and the boat flew out across the water. Annie felt a strange compulsion as the boat leaped from wave to wave in an impossible sunlight dazzling spray. She let go of the rope. She spread her arms and tipped her head back, an incredible sense of total freedom washed over her. The boat raced on, one with Annie and the water.

In no time they arrived at their next stop, Oak Island. Annie was soaking wet from the spray and out of breath, but the ride was over far too soon for her. She had never felt so alive. Captain Gabe shut off the boat's motor and smiled down at her.

"Well, no mistake about it. You're your father's daughter, that's for sure."

Taking the rope out of Annie's hands he jumped overboard into the waist deep water. Wading toward the shore the big man pulled the boat closer and then tied the boat to a large tree root that lay half submerged at the edge of the lake.

"You'll have to walk from there. If the seiche goes out, it will ground the boat and we'll be stuck here until it comes back. Don't worry, the water's pretty cold but not very deep."

Annie couldn't get any wetter, so she jumped out

and waded onto the stony shore.

"There's lots of agates along here. There's not much sand on this side of the island, so any of these little stones might be agates."

Annie looked down at the millions of stones, excited to find a gemstone.

"What's a seiche?"

"Think of it like the lake is breathing Annie," Mike Abbott answered, "A seiche is like a huge wave that moves in and out from the land. There are usually a few every day. The water can go out in a matter of minutes."

"Yep, and it would leave our boat high and dry while we wait for the lake to return the water to us. Just like it's taking a breath and letting it out."

"That's amazing!"

"That's nature, a truly amazing design to all things. All the islands here are affected by the seiche, but because of how they are oriented, it affects them all differently. For some the water just rises and falls, for others it can even make the streams and creeks run backward, and for still others it helped make the huge sea caves on the outer islands. Right Mike?"

"Right! Well, let's go find some stones."

Annie was surprised how tired her legs were after the Nantucket Sleighride. She remembered when she had heard the voice on Washington Island and touched the stone she had been exhausted. Her father and Rafer Tate had had to carry her to the boat afterward. As in the first time, she felt a wave of fatigue wash through all her muscles.

In the shallow water she could see the stones on the bottom clearly, but there were so many she couldn't pick out just one that was more beautiful than any other one. Finally, she just sat down in the bright sunshine on the beach and watched the waves lap the shore.

The next thing she knew, her dad was touching her shoulder.

"Hey sleepy-head, I think we better get going. It's starting to get late."

"I guess I dozed off for a few minutes."

"More than a few, I think."

"I didn't find any agates though, Dad," she said looking around quickly.

Mike reached out his open hand, in it, five fire-bright stones shone in the bright sunlight.

"Yes, we did, and here they are. Just for you."

"Geez, they're really beautiful!"

"Yep, forged in fire and polished by nature, but it's time to go. The seiche is turning."

"What's next?"

"Next? Well next we're gonna jump across to Manitou Island. It's a bit of a jaunt, so hang on. Probably going to take us about thirty minutes and we'll be out in the channel again, so hang on."

"What's on Manitou Island?"

"It's just an old fishing camp." Captain Gabe explained, "But it's haunted."

"Seriously?"

"That's what the locals say, and I'm a local."

"Excellent!"

"There are lots of stories about Manitou. Lots of people talk about the watchers they get a glimpse of in the trees."

"The watchers?"

"Yes, they claimed that they saw someone watching them from the woods, but when they approached, there was nobody there. For a while, it was kind of a tourist attraction. People looking for someone hiding in the woods. It was almost like they believed that Bigfoot was living on the island. But no one was ever found and nothing ever came of it that I know of."

Gabe started the boat back up and as soon as they were away from the shallow shoreline he pushed the throttle and they picked up speed. Once again, they were flying across the open water, not too fast as to be dangerous but fast enough to make it exciting. As soon as they approached the island they could see the old fishing camp, with its weathered grey shacks and a wooden dock that extended out into the water.

"For the last hundred years, someone has lived here almost constantly, fishing through the ice in the winter, and out of boats in the summer. They would salt the herring and smoke the bigger fish, selling it on the mainland. They hauled their fish to Bayfield by dog sleds over the ice. There was never more than one or two men here at any time and some were considered to be 'interesting characters', Black Pete lived here for a few seasons, and Captain Bark. It was a place of hard work, and people that wanted, or needed, to be away from society. Some of them were crazy, and some of them were dangerous but all of them were interesting characters."

"They're all gone now. The National Park Service owns the islands now. They conduct tours, and there's usually someone here most of the time these days. But the legends live on. No one knows for sure what became of them all, but it's clear that some never left the island."

Captain Gabe pulled the boat neatly up to the dock. Mike and Annie jumped out eager to explore.

"Take your time. It's almost lunchtime, so we'll have ourselves a little lunch. I'll get a fire started and we'll have shore lunch. I'll catch it while you're looking around."

"That quick?" Mike was skeptical.

"I've got a secret weapon Captain." He winked back.

"Not anymore Gabe, not anymore."

Fish Camp

They took their time and hiked up the hill to the camp. The cabins and shacks had been restored for tourists, and there was a picnic area above the camp. They explored the shacks and other buildings and refilled their water bottles at the old pump. Annie kept a sharp eye out for ghosts even though it was broad daylight.

At the top of the clearing, Mike stopped to examine a small plaque mounted on one of the shacks marked 'Smokehouse'. Suddenly, Annie felt something buzzing in her pants pocket. At first she thought that an insect had somehow gotten into it. She pushed her hand down in to pull it out but there was no bug, however her pocket continued to vibrate. Reaching down she felt the agates that her father had collected. They were the source of the vibration. They were alive in her hand. She looked in her hand as the stones danced about in her palm, each vibrating against one another.

"Feel the life in all things that you see and touch."
Annie felt the sunlight around her dim and her

vision narrow. She was no longer aware of her father, or the small 'Smokehouse' with its plaque behind her. In front of her she saw a small opening in the edge of the woods. Without hesitating she stepped into the shade of the trees and followed the path as it climbed up toward the top of the island. The stones, back in her pocket, continued to vibrate more and more as she climbed.

The path led to a stand of cypress trees. Their fragrance heady in the bright sunlight. Beneath them the shade deepened to twilight. Once inside Annie looked around, not sure why or how she had found herself to be there; the stones in her pocket suddenly quiet as her vision returned to normal.

The light was a mixture of shadow, deep and verdant green. She found herself staring at the varied shades of contrasting shadow. Then, unconsciously she fixed on one spot, not entirely sure what she was seeing. She knew something was there, but could not make it out. A sureness came over her and she found her voice. She spoke in a loud voice.

"Who are you? Come out."

In front of her the leaves of the nearby tree stirred and a shadowy figure appeared. A man, dressed in careworn clothes and boots materialized before her. He was not much taller than Annie, but he was much older, ancient in comparison. His grey beard covered most of his chest, and his hair hung to his shoulders from under an old stocking cap. His weather-creased face regarded her with curiosity.

"You were watching me."

"Been watchin' ya'"

"Why, who are you?"

"I am Rolf."

Annie did not sense any danger from Rolf. As he smiled at her, he seemed friendly and benevolent.

"Rolf? Just Rolf?"

He looked puzzled for a minute, then scratched his beard and said, "Yes, Rolf, just Rolf., only Rolf, always Rolf."

"My name's Annie Abbott. Hello Rolf. Why were you watching me?"

"You are the seeker."

Annie took a step back.

"What do you mean? How do you know that?"

The voice spoke in her ear again, ***"Seek the Apostles, seek the fisherman."***

Annie looked at the old man in front of her with sudden certainty, "You are the fisherman."

He nodded. "I am the fisherman."

The Fisherman

Annie's eyes grew wide. When she and her father had discussed their search, they had assumed that they would find another gravestone, or another marker of some kind. It had not occurred to them that the next clue to their mystery would be alive and she had found him all by herself. It didn't really matter to her that he had found her instead. The fisherman they had come to look for was standing right in front of her.

Rolf smiled at her and turning stepped back into the dense undergrowth at the edge of the little clearing, instantly lost from sight.

"Wait! Where are you going?"

"To the cliffs." He called, "There's something fer ya ta see there."

"The cliffs?"

"Yes, You must hurry, before the seiche comes back in."

"Wait, stop! I can't go anywhere with you. I don't know who you are. Wait until my Dad catches up so we can all go together please."

Rolf stopped in his tracks. Turning slightly, he cocked his head to the side and listened.

"The Mariner remains, but the Soldier is coming." With that statement, Rolf backed quickly into the underbrush behind him and immediately disappeared from sight.

"Wait! The Mariner? Who's the Mariner?"

"Annie, where are you?" Her father's voice carried through the quiet of the woods from down the hill. *"Annie!"*

"I'm up here Dad!" She called while her eyes desperately searched for any sign of the old man.

"There you are!" Mike arrived slightly winded. He squatted down to look at Annie at eye level, "You shouldn't wander off like that without telling someone Annie. I don't know what kind of stuff you might run into alone. There are probably bears on this island just like all the rest of them."

"Dad!" Annie cut her father off, touching his shoulder. "Dad, I found the fisherman!"

"What? What do you mean?"

"He was right here a second ago. He said he had something to show me, but then he got scared and ran away."

"Slow down for a second Annie. You met someone up here, and he was trying to lure you away?"

"No Dad, it wasn't like that. He knew I was the Seeker."

"What? How would he know that?"

"I don't know Dad, he just said he had to show me something, then he disappeared into the woods right before you got here."

"Why would he do that?"

"He said something about a '*Mariner*'(?), and a '*Soldier*'. He said the Mariner was waiting, but that the Soldier was coming, then he disappeared."

Mike Abbott rocked back on his heels, his eyes narrowing. "What did this 'fisherman' look like? Can you describe him?"

"I think I could, but he's standing right behind you."

Without a sound, the old man had somehow appeared again. This time, on the opposite side of the small space. He stood behind Mike Abbott with a large wooden fishing cudgel in his hand.

"I warn you; I won't be taken." His voice was strong and he held the heavy weapon at the ready.

"Rolf! This is my dad. He's not going to take you anywhere." Annie stepped between the two men. "Please? He's my dad."

"He is the soldier. He has come for me."

"No! No, I haven't. I didn't even know you were here. I'm not here for anybody."

"I don't believe you." Rolf raised the club, ready to strike.

"Soothe the wounded, end the war."

As the voice sounded in her head, Annie's vision again darkened, narrowing down into a tunneled vision, strangely dark. He looked at the old man, but saw someone different standing there. In his place, shimmering in the sunlight, stood a young man, almost a boy. She felt the pain of his loneliness; and his secret shame. She regarded her father; instead of the graying college professor she knew, a young man stood at the ready to defend them, with countless shadows of others standing behind him, tall and straight, with eyes as cold as steel, the layers of his strength laid bare.

In a strong voice, that spoke of age and power she spoke; *"I am the seeker, the sister of many sisters. Crimes of the past, are not wounds of the present. Speak of our quest and nothing more."*

As before, as soon as she spoke the words, her strength abandoned her and Annie fell to her knees breathing hard.

"I…I don't know where that comes from Dad. I…I can't…explain it."

"The seiche is coming, we must go." Rolf spoke with urgency, the club in his hand seemingly forgotten.

"Where? Where do you want us to go?"

"To the cliff, we must to hurry. The Mariner is coming."

Rolf turned and hurried into the undergrowth. Mike helped Annie to her feet.

"I'm okay now Dad. Should we follow him?"

"He is the fisherman; I think we have to."

They hurried to catch up to the old man, who moved with surprising speed and agility through the dense brush. As they approached the northern edge of the island, they could hear the waves crashing onto the shoreline. Before they broke through the trees however, Rolf stopped. Pushing back the branches of a large bush, he pointed to an opening in the ground.

"We must hurry. The chamber will flood when the seiche returns."

"What chamber? You don't seriously want us to go in there, do you?"

"Yes, there are things you must see."

"Dad! *Above the waves, beneath the ground he waits in vain, his peace is found.'* I think that's what the fisherman is supposed to show us."

With that Rolf turned, dropped to his hands and knees and entered the darkness of the tunnel. "We must hurry."

"Looks like a pretty tight fit for me." Mike was skeptical.

"I'll go Dad. You can stay out here."

"Not a chance Annie, 'In for a penny, in for a pound' as the saying goes. I'll go first, stay close; it looks pretty dark in there."

The Cave and the Grave

Mike dropped on his stomach and crawled into the narrow opening; Annie was right behind him. Once they were inside the darkness was total. Annie could hear her father breathing and the shuffle of his clothes as they scraped against the sides of the passageway.

"Whew, pretty tight in here." Mike whispered, "I don't enjoy tight places."

"Hurry! It opens up in just a little way further. We must not get caught in it when the chamber floods." Rolf's voice sounded from the distance, panicked.

Annie crawled forward and suddenly a larger space opened in front of her. A flickering glow from a small candle in Rolf's hand offered meager light. As she and her father got to their feet, Annie looked around. They were standing in a small grotto, the sides of layered sandstone were damp, dripping water, and the ceiling festooned with tangled tree roots that had made the journey down to this depth. Two or three inches of water had collected on the floor. In the half-light, Rolf pointed to a high corner raising the candle over his head.

"He has been waiting for you. He is the pirate, Black Pete."

"Oh my goodness! Annie, you shouldn't look!"

Seated on a high shelf above the high-water line marked on the room's walls, a desiccated skeleton, still dressed in rags and worn boots perched. A ghastly skull showed a hideous toothy grin as it gazed back at them. The flickering light and darkness gave the room a macabre feeling.

"Well, he used to be Black Pete anyway." Taking the candle from Rolf, Mike stretched up to look more closely. "How did you find him here Rolf?"

"He is my father." He said without emotion. "The water's rising. The seiche is coming."

"What have you got to tell us Black Pete? Do you have a message?" Mike scaled as much of the wall as he could and held the candle into the small hollowed out space. "Well now what's this, something is carved on the wall here. John 1:5, hmm that's cryptic."

"Is that all you've got for us Pete?"

The water was rising rapidly. It was now over Annie's shoe tops. The small opening they had crawled through was almost halfway closed behind them.

Annie felt a strong urge to touch what was left of Black Pete. Reaching past her father she stretched out her hand toward Black Pete. This time they all witnessed the blue spark that jumped to her outstretched fingers in the darkened room.

In a voice that was dimmed by distance and time, she spoke; *"Trust me not for I am betrayed by madness, still I guard the stone and await the seeker."*

Again, Annie's knees buckled and she would have fallen into the almost knee-deep water if Mike hadn't caught her.

"Rolf? Do you know what those words might mean?"

"For a long time, he kept the lighthouse at Raspberry Island, but my mother died. After that, he left the island and brought me here. We have remained here hidden away from the outside world since. He often talked about a stone, and that someone would come for it. He prayed that someone would come. He lost his mind waiting."

"He is guarding the stone Dad, where could it be?"

"Let's have a look, but we're running out of time." He looked carefully around Black Pete. "Well I'll be! It's underneath him. He's sitting on it, I think. Rolf can you help me lift him."

"I cannot. The seiche continues to rise; it will take your bodies out when it goes. Just as it did mine."

"What? What do you mean?" But when they turned to question him, he had vanished. The small candle rested on a rock shelf alone.

Mike Abbott struggled to roll the skeleton away and underneath him a small carved headstone barely fit in the small space of the skeleton of Black Pete. Next to the stone lay another gold bar. With difficulty he pulled both down. The stone was too heavy for one man to hold. Dropping it into the pooled water he leaned it against the wall. As Annie held the candle near it, Mike read the carving.

"Here is the sign of the druid again, see! Below that it says Lucille, that must have been his wife. My gosh, it says 1892! Taking the candle and holding it closer he read:

The light shines in the darkness, and yet the darkness did not overcome it. John 1:5

"Dad!" The water was past her knees and rising rapidly.

"The tunnel is full to the top now, we are caught." Annie's father said matter-of-factly.

There must be another way out, otherwise the water couldn't get in."

"Wait Dad, he said it washed his body out of the cave. There must be a way down below where the water's coming in?"

"The water comes in from over there." Mike pointed toward the far corner, lost in the darkness. "But it must come in under the rocks."

Mike waded across the small room looking for the source of the water flowing in.

"Here it is, but the tunnel might be pretty long and probably pretty tight. I don't think we can hold our breath for long. Can we get out the other way?"

"I can't see the tunnel anymore Dad."

"Well then we swim, leave the stone and the gold. We've got to go before we are really caught."

Annie was terrified, this was a part of their adventures that she didn't like at all. She trusted her father, but she was not a good swimmer.

"Annie, it will be very dark. I'll feel my way out; you hang onto one of my feet. Don't let go. Hold your breath as long as you can."

The water was now well over her waist and cold.

"On the count of three take as big a breath as you can, then follow me. I love you Annie, hang on, we'll get through it if we keep our heads."

He took a few deep breaths, "One, two, three!" He dropped out of sight beneath the water. Annie followed his example and after three deep breaths, she dropped into the icy water. She felt her way forward toward the opening in the floor of the small cave. She could sense her father right in front of her. Reaching out she gripped his heavy boot and entered the narrow opening.

Annie tried to think about anything but breathing. The rocks scraped against her bare arms, and the corners of the passage pulled at her feet. The darkness of the tunnel was total, and made the experience even more terrifying. In only moments her lungs began to burn. It was taking too long. The tunnel seemed to go on and on. She felt herself beginning to weaken.

"Courage sister, he is almost free. You must trust the guardian."

Ahead of her light began to grow and she could see the opening of the tunnel ahead. She felt her father's efforts speed up, and she pushed harder against the rocks. The light grew brighter. She could see the surface of the water above her now.

But she couldn't hold her breath any longer and the air burst from her lungs in a shower of bubbles that raced upward toward the surface. She was spent; it was too far. She tried to struggle upward but she was suddenly exhausted. Her grip on her father's boot weakened and she let go. Without air, she began to drown. The world darkened around her. Her arms and legs began to drift, useless as she began to sink into the darkness below.

Against the darkness an impossibly bright light flashed. She opened her eyes.

Before her an apparition appeared, floating in front of her. A woman, dressed all in white, the impossibly bright light emanating from within her. Her glowing diaphanous clothing floating; drifting with the current as she spoke:

"Courage and strength little sister. Trust them. Follow the guardian. Trust the Mariner. Listen to the wind. Share our strength little sister, we will help."

Rough hands encircled her, lifting her and rising toward the surface. Grabbing her shirt, she was lifted up and out of the water. She found herself coughing and gasping for breath, staring up at the blue sky above, lying on the deck of a boat next to her father. Captain Gabe stood over them, his long hair plastered down and his clothes making a puddle of water where he stood.

"I came as soon as you called Mike," he said with a worried expression on his face. "Are you gonna be okay Annie?"

"We are now Gabe, thank you yet again. Holy mackerel! That was a close one."

"Dad, where's Rolf?" Annie was recovering, and in a panic, she pulled herself up and scanned the water's surface around them.

"I don't think he followed us, Annie. I don't think he actually could have even if he had wanted to. He didn't make it out this way." Annie's father put a hand on her shoulder, "He's been watching a long time, and I think his work is done. He's completed his task. Maybe now, at last, he will be at peace."

Gabe pulled out some warm blankets and wrapped the two in them. He handed them cups of hot coffee. "It's all I've got, sorry Annie. I didn't have time to make sandwiches before I got called away."

Annie was saddened, "But dad, do you mean that he probably drowned? I don't want him to be dead. That's horrible."

"No Annie, I don't think he drowned—today, but that's not to say that he didn't once." He gave Annie a knowing look.

"What do you mean?" She continued to look across the water; then realization slowly spread to her reviving brain. She turned to look at him, "You mean?"

"Yes, I think you've met your first visitor from the other side Annie, from the spirit world."

"Oh…", she felt she was on the verge of tears, "oh that's so sad. He was waiting alone all this time."

"Yes Annie, but no longer. You've given him peace, I think."

Gabe quickly piloted the boat back to the dock at the fishing camp. In short order he had a good fire burning. Even in the warm afternoon sunlight, all three of them were shivering from the cold of the lake water and the terrifying events of the afternoon. Annie sipped the hot drink and felt the heat start to revive her. Now that she felt herself returning to normal, questions rapidly started crowding into her thoughts.

Almost too much had happened today. She was very sad about the fate of poor Rolf, an orphan alone his whole life and she was perplexed by the clues they had found in the cave, and their near-death escape. She slowly pieced all the events together in her head and realized that there were big pieces missing from the whole story.

Looking up at Captain Gabe, she asked, "You got called? I don't understand, who called you? Do cell phones even work around here? Do you even have a cell phone?"

The two men, seated on the picnic table next to each other exchanged glances.

"Dad?" Suddenly remembering, "the voice; I saw her! She was right in front of me. She told me to trust the 'guardian'. Who is the guardian? What is a guardian? Why would it say that?"

Gabe looked at Mike and raised one eyebrow. "Well Mike?"

Mike stood up and paced back and forth in front of them agitated, then with a long deep breath he sat down again. Finally, he nodded to himself, having come to some internal decision, he slapped his hands on his knees and fixing his most serious face, looked at Annie. Both men were tense, their gaze on Annie as she shivered under the blanket.

"I guess you would need to know sooner or later anyway Annie." He took a deep breath, "especially now that you are starting to show your powers."

He stood again and squared his shoulders. Captain Gabe, almost twice the size of her father stood just behind him, one hand on his shoulder. He met her questioning gaze with a serious face.

"I am the *Guardian.*"

The Guardian Appears

Annie was confused. She looked at her father again. In spite of the fact that he was dripping wet and making a puddle where he stood, he looked just the same as he always did. There didn't seem to be anything guardian-like about him. He just looked like a dad to her.

She looked past him at Gabe. Her father was pretty tall but Captain Gabe was at least another three or four inches taller and huge across the shoulders. He stood there smiling down at her, his hand still on her father's shoulder.

"And you're the Mariner."

"Yes Annie. I am the Mariner." There was no bright grin with his statement like before. He regarded her with a small solemn smile.

"Is this some kind of joke? You guys are setting me up for a laugh right?"

"Look closer, see with our eyes little sister. Behold the Three."

As the voice in her head spoke Annie's vision narrowed and the edges darkened. Directly in front of her stood a man she recognized, but barely. He was clad in a kilt, a sword at his belt and a longbow in his hand. He wore his chest and face painted in streaks of red and black. As he held her gaze, undeniable power radiated from the figure before her.

Behind him on his right stood a giant of a man with long hair and beard. On his head, he wore the head of a bear, the skin draped down his back. His face fearsome; he held a long trident in his right hand and his left was firmly on the shoulder of the warrior in front of him

Over the left shoulder of the warrior a shadow wavered, not quite visible but present none-the-less. It shimmered in the sunlight, transparent. The face slowly taking shape, only to melt again in the sun. With a gasp, she recognized the face. It was the face of Rafer Tate. As he too smiled down at her a feeling of peace and relaxation settled over her.

Her vision remained as she struggled to understand.

"Who…? Who are you?"

Mike Abbot continued, but spoke from within her vision. His voice speaking differently, impossibly old, wise and powerful.

"We are the Three. It is the curse and the blessing of our houses, handed down from father to son from origins lost in time. I am the Guardian; I serve only the One. I am Michael, guardian of the seeker. I am the fire that burns and the guardian of you, the true seeker."

Then the voice of Gabe spoke from the vision, strong and equally powerful,

"I am the Mariner. It is the curse and the blessing of my house. I am the protector of the Guardian and the Seeker. I am Gabriel. I am the water that brings truth

and understanding against the powers of doubt."

"Who is Mr. Tate? Is he one of you?"

"He is Raphael. He will soon join us. We are the three, the powers of the Great Ones of old—We are Fire, Water and Air."

Annie's vision cleared. Once again she was sitting on the ground next to the fire. Her father and Gabe looked the same as they always did. Her head was spinning. It was too much to take in all at once.

Her dad sat down on the corner of the old picnic table and smiled at her. "I knew it was about time for us to have this discussion, but I didn't know when the right time was. Ever since your twelfth birthday, you have started to show the signs."

"Signs? What signs?"

"You have come of age, so this explanation is a little late I'm afraid, and in truth, you're a little early."

"What are you talking about Dad? Are you trying to scare me?"

"Not on purpose, but you'll have to decide if you should be."

Annie didn't know what to think. The beautiful afternoon, the waves lapping the shore, even the sandwich in her hand were all forgotten as she concentrated on her father.

"A very, very long time ago. Centuries upon centuries ago actually, the druids were the keepers of the secrets of the earth. They traveled the world, offering their advice and understanding to all that asked for it. They were schooled in science and art, and practitioners of medicine and magic."

"What's that got to do with us?"

"You'll see Annie, patience. There were many famous druids, some you've probably heard about. Merlin the Magician for instance. And perhaps the most powerful woman of her time, and for a long time after, Morgan Le Fey, the Fairy Queen."

He paused and took a long drink of hot coffee, gathering his thoughts.

"Then came the bad times when the druids were suddenly persecuted. There were many that coveted the power that the druids wielded over other cultures. Many of the druids were executed, the women burned at the stake. As a result, much of their wisdom and lore were lost to the world. The druids went into hiding and disappeared from the face of the world. But they retained their internal gifts—their magic. It passed down the line from then until now, always a well-kept secret. It is passed from mother to daughter and with each new incarnation, there is a guardian. For this generation, I am that guardian." He took a breath and met her gaze. "And my charge is to defend the 28th generation descendent of the Fairy Queen, Morgan le Fey. That descendent is you, Annie Abbott."

"What! That's crazy. Magic isn't real. It's just pretend."

But somehow, she knew it wasn't crazy. Somewhere deep inside she felt that it was true.

"The voice and the woman that appeared to me?"

"I cannot tell you any more Annie. I am the Guardian, and although I have a few gifts, the power is in your hands. Only you can accept it, and only you can use it."

"I know someone that might help," Gabe spoke up, "Let's go over to Raspberry Island. There's someone there that might shed some light on the subject."

Annie suddenly remembered something. "Dad, Rolf said that Black Pete was the keeper at Raspberry Island. And the stone said, "The light shines in the darkness, and yet the darkness did not overcome it. Right?"

"Yes, that's right! There's a lighthouse at Raspberry Island. Do you think he was talking about that?"

"Yes," Annie felt sure. "Yes Dad, I'm sure that there is something there."

"Well then let's go, the day isn't getting any younger." Gabe began packing up the remains of the lunch as Annie struggled up from the ground wrapped in the heavy blanket.

Raspberry Island

Once they were back in the boat Captain Gabe skirted the long shoreline of Manitou Island keeping out of the wind as long as he could until they reached the westernmost point. Throttling up they raced across the channel toward Raspberry Island in the distance. Above the deep thrum of the motor Gabe shouted, "Lake Superior, or Giche-Gumi as the natives called it, is considered the most dangerous body of water on the planet. The storms are legend, and there is usually only one thing that stands between mariners and the bottom —the lighthouses. The Apostle Islands have the largest and most important ones in the world.

"The water in Superior is plenty deep, but around the islands it gets shallow and rocky really fast. That makes it especially treacherous. The lighthouses and their keepers have stood watch for over a century.

"Some of them, like Devil's Island are almost a hundred feet tall. Raspberry is nowhere near that, but it and Sand Island stand watch over the most important and dangerous stretch from Superior and Duluth going toward the sea channels. Their history is legendary and heroic. They are a huge part of the history of the inland sea."

Annie looked forward to the island, "I don't see it."

"It's on the other side, facing west where the big freighters are coming from and going to. You'll see it once we round the corner."

As they came around the bend, the red brick lighthouse stood high above the trees, its red roof bright in the late afternoon sun.

"My goodness it's beautiful."

"That she is, and like everything else—haunted by the mariners who've lost their lives along this channel. When the Pretoria sank off shore, five men were pulled to safety by the lighthouse keeper, five others drowned before he could save them. The lighthouses have saved many a ship and many a man."

It had been a very long and taxing day already, but as they approached the landing Annie felt a surge of energy. She knew that there was something waiting for her, and she wanted to seek it.

Docking the little boat, Annie jumped out and climbed the steps that rose up the long hill to the lighthouse. The lighthouse was indeed not just a big lamp in the sky, but a complete house and other buildings. The paint was fresh and sparkling, and the lawn and flower beds neatly trimmed.

"It looks brand new!"

"It is now managed by the National Park Service, but in the old days it was a solitary job, and demanded a solitary person." Said Captain Gabe as he puffed his way up the hill toward Annie. "When Raspberry was built, they tried to make a house and sight that could attract a lighthouse keeper with a family. Raspberry is one of the jewels of the islands."

"Do people live here now?"

"The Parks Department keeps full time people here now, but the light is automated."

"Can we see it?"

"I asked permission and she said she would arrange for it. She's living out here this summer. C'mon let's go meet Allegra and see what a big light bulb looks like, shall we?"

Standing outside the building, shading her eyes from the afternoon sun, a young woman waved as they approached.

"I saw your boat round the point Gabe. You're a little later than I expected."

"We stopped for agates, and Annie insisted on a 'sleighride'. Annie this is my daughter Allegra, Allegra meet Miss Annie Abbott."

The woman named Allegra touched her forehead and bowing slightly toward Annie said, "Well met sister." Straightening back up she smiled and added, "I bet you liked the ride, didn't you Annie. He's been doing that to me since I was about five years old, but it's still fun!" She smiled a big smile at her. "I see you got all dressed up for the day Dad."

"This is business casual; I'm being casual."

"Okay Dad." She gave him a wink.

Turning toward Mike Abbott, "Greetings Michael, and a gracious welcome to the Guardian." Again she touched her forehead and gave a slight bow. "So, the three are assembling at last."

Mike returned the gesture, touching his forehead, "Yes, things are beginning to move. Rafer said he could feel it in the wind."

Allegra nodded solemnly. Turning back to Annie, "Well Annie, want to go see the light and foghorn?"

"Sure! You have a foghorn too?"

"We have to. Sometimes, when the fog is really thick, ships can't see the light. So, then we have a foghorn that sounds so that the ships can hear that they are getting too close to the rocks."

"Do you use it all the time?"

"No, it's automated nowadays. It works on a laser beam. The beam shines out into the lake and can sense when the air is getting too thick. Then it activates automatically. The sound can carry a long way across the water."

"That's pretty cool, lasers and stuff, pretty amazing."

"The light's really amazing. "There are over ninety stairs from the dock up to the lighthouse itself. Once you're in the lighthouse it's another sixty to the top of the tower; c'mon let's climb some stairs, so you can see the view."

At the top of the staircase, they caught their breath and came into the light chamber.

"The tower itself is only forty-seven feet tall, so it's pretty short by most standards. But it stands at the top of the hill which is another fifty or sixty feet, so all-in-all it ends up being one of the highest lights. The original light was made from cut glass in France. It was about three feet tall and eighteen inches wide and powered by a kerosene lamp. The keepers had to clean all the windows and the light every day to keep the soot from the lamp darkening the glass. The original is in the maritime museum back in Bayfield. This one is a modern marvel, but the light itself is pretty small. It's how the light is magnified and focused through various lenses that makes it spectacularly bright and the beam amazingly narrow. It's pretty impressive at night; you should see it."

"I wish I could, but I think we need to get back pretty soon." Annie looked out the windows at the water that stretched to the horizon and the sun that was beginning to set.

"It is a lot to take in all at once, isn't it?"

"You can't imagine Allegra. It has been an amazing, terrifying day. I've never been so scared in my entire life. I can't explain it; it's all too much."

"Is it? Does it seem unreal?"

Annie looked at Allegra; their eyes met.

"You have something in your pocket, a talisman. Will you show me?"

Annie was surprised. She drew out the five agate stones from her pocket and held them out in the palm of her hand. Still puzzled at how Allegra knew they were there.

"Now don't be afraid Annie, concentrate on the stones and watch."

Annie looked at the stones. They were beautiful in the late afternoon sunlight. The bands of amber and gold seemed impossibly deep and beautiful. She looked at them more deeply, concentrating on the patterns of each one. Suddenly, one moved slightly, then another. Soon they were all vibrating together. They began to glow. Brighter and brighter, until their brilliance was blinding, filling the small room as they vibrated in her palm. So terrifyingly bright that Annie closed her hand to block out their fiery light. When she opened her hand the stones lay quietly again, cool to the touch showing no signs of what they had just been.

"You see Annie? Magic exists. The light shines in the darkness and the darkness does not overcome it."

"You? You are one of them!"

"Yes Annie, I am one of *them* as you say. I am one of the sisters." Again, she touched her forehead and gave a slight bow, "Well met sister."

"I don't know what any of that means. I'm just a kid. What does all this mean?"

"I have a message for you from the sisters." She reached forward and placed her fingertips on Annie's forehead. Immediately, the voice spoke from within,

"Wisdom belongs to the aged, and understanding to the old. The three can help you, but you must learn for yourself. Seek the eldest, learn your strength."

Allegra removed her hand.

"I wouldn't advise going back to LaPointe in the dark. My father, Captain Gabe's one of the best, but you just never know on Lake Superior, and it is quite a way back. As it is, you're not going to be back before dark. Once it gets dark though you'll see the light at Chequamegon Point, as you come past the point at Bayfield. When the beacons are lit, it is awe inspiring."

"I'm sorry I'll miss it."

"Oh, you won't. The sun is setting right now and it's more than twenty miles back to LaPointe. Even with Dad's wild driving you won't be back before full dark.

You'll be able to see Chequamegon Point and the LaPointe lights if that happens.

It was much easier going down all the stairs than it had been going up. Annie's legs were already tired from her adventure of the 'Nantucket sleighride' and the stairs. Once back in the boat, Captain Gabe pulled a couple of big blankets out of one of the storage compartments, handing them out to Mike and Annie he said, "The water is always icy cold, once the sun goes down the heat of the day will be gone pretty fast and the cold will come up from the bottom of the boat. Annie's already wet, so we don't want anyone getting a chill."

He looked at Annie fondly, "You've had a long day young lady; let's get you home."

Casting off, Gabe stood at the wheel and turned toward home. Annie snuggled up against her father wrapped in the warm blanket, as the sun set behind them.

Even with Captain Gabe running the boat fast across the now evening calmed water, it was well over an hour before they came in sight of Madeline Island and the sky had darkened. As they passed the small village of Red Cliff on the mainland, the beacon at LaPointe lighthouse blazed alight and stabbed its amazing light out into the darkness of the lake rousing Annie from a dreamy sleep. Almost immediately, Chequamegon Point flashed its brilliance out across the water as well.

"Look they're lighting the way home for us Annie." Whispered Mike as he put his arm around her shoulders.

Annie smiled as she closed her eyes again.

The Three

The large bed was soft and warm, as sunshine streamed in the windows. The air in the room was fresh and cool. Somewhere voices softly conversed and she smelled fresh coffee.

The room, bright in the morning sunlight, was decorated all in white. Lacy curtains and walls of white. The bedframe, dresser and nightstands were all white as well. Even the soft sheets and blankets were pristine and white. The ceiling was slanted under the eaves of the roof and the gabled windows looked out onto a street below where busy conversations and foot traffic drifted up to her. For a moment she was confused, she didn't recognize this strange bedroom under the eaves.

Slowly memory returned. She recalled Gabe's small boat bobbing and bumping the dock as she was lifted out and handed to another set of strong arms. Then the thump of feet on a wooden dock as she was carried from the harbor and up a street while she dozed in the strong arms. And finally, she recalled being gently laid in this bed and covered with the wonderfully soft and warm blankets and drifting into a deep and dreamless sleep.

Sitting up in the bed, Annie stretched and rubbed her sleepy eyes. The events of yesterday began to run through her mind. She was not sure that she wanted any more days like that one. It seemed so completely unreal. She found it hard to believe that it had actually all happened. But the scratches and bruises on her arms and the stiffness in her muscles as she stretched were more than enough evidence; they were a testament to the rigorous activities of the previous day.

The face in the mirror from across the room regarded her with curiosity and horror. The girl in the mirror had dark circles under her eyes. With the bright light of the window behind her, her red hair was even redder; a wild haystack spread out in every direction. She was still wearing the now wrinkled clothes she had worn yesterday. Next to the mirrored dresser was a chair with her heavy boots and socks underneath; on the chair rested her knapsack and a white bath towel.

She found herself wondering how it got there. She had left it in the campground that she and her father had left yesterday morning before meeting Gabe. Was it Gabe, or was it the Mariner? She wasn't sure which was correct. As her confused and overwhelmed brain struggled with the puzzle her stomach growled. She was suddenly starving.

Throwing back the covers, she swung her feet onto the floor. She crossed to the dresser and picked up the knapsack. Swinging the towel over her shoulder she set out in search of a shower.

Twenty minutes later with her wet hair still wrapped

in a towel, she descended a narrow staircase near the back of the house and into a spacious and brightly lit kitchen also decorated in spotless white. Sunlight streamed in through windows that lined the room on all sides. Seated at the table in the center of the room were her father and the handsome Rafer Tate. Both looked up with a smile.

"Good morning, Annie. I hope you slept well."

"I think I slept like the dead Dad. I don't think I remember how I got here. And for that matter, where is here?"

"Welcome to 'Rose Hall' Annie." Rafer Tate spoke, "You are in the town of Bayfield today. We brought you from the harbor last night while you were asleep. It sounds like you had a pretty wild day yesterday. I'm sorry I missed it."

"I'm almost thinking that I must have dreamt it all."

"It all happened Annie. And after yesterday, things will never be the same for you I'm afraid, or any of us again." Her father's voice was serious and so was the stern look on his face.

Annie suddenly realized that besides the aroma of fresh brewed coffee, she could also smell fresh bread baking. She remembered again that she was hungry.

"I'm starving Dad. Is there anything to eat?"

"Oh my goodness! I almost forgot to take the bread out of the oven!"

From another room toward the front of the house, an impossibly beautiful woman breezed into the room. She was tall and pale skinned, adorned in a white sheath dress with three-quarter length sleeves, and stylish flat slippers. Her long, ebony hair fell over her shoulders and down her back. Her make-up, perfect as bright ice-blue eyes flashed a smile at Annie.

Grabbing a potholder from above the stove she reached into the oven and took two wonderfully fragrant pans of golden-brown loaves of bread out. Sitting them in the center of the table she bustled around the kitchen. Setting out jars of jam, a small butter churn and a pitcher of sweet-smelling syrup. A bowl of fresh fruit and an impossibly tall stack of hot pancakes. With each addition, Annie's eyes got bigger and bigger.

"Wow! That's a lot of food!"

"You should probably eat quickly; Gabriel will be here any minute. Once he arrives, nothing on the table will be safe." The woman's accented voice was deep and rich and vaguely familiar.

"Annie, this is Elspeth. Elspeth is keeper of Rose Hall."

"Greetings little sister. Well met."

"Oh?— *Oh!*" sudden recognition dawned on Annie, "It was you! You're the voice! You're the voice that spoke to me in the tunnel, when…when I was drowning."

"My voice was used, yes."

"Used?"

"Yes, Annie." She smiled down at her, "When I became aware of your danger. I summoned the sisters. But in the end, you saved yourself Annie."

"I'm confused—again." Looking around she added. "Where **is** Mr. MacDonald?"

Elspeth spoke again, "Gabriel took the boat back to LaPointe late last night. This morning he will take down your tent and your camping site. Then he will bring your father's truck back on the first ferry across from the island this morning."

"How did my knapsack get here?"

"I retrieved it after I knew that you would come to Rose Hall last night."

"When did you know that I was coming here."

"Why after Allegra told me, of course."

"She called you then?"

"In a manner of speaking, yes." Elspeth began cutting the bread into slices. The smell of sweet cinnamon joined the other delicious smells in the room.

"Now I'm really confused."

"Have something to eat. After breakfast we will have much to talk about." Her father smiled at her.

As Annie reached for the stack of pancakes, a door slammed somewhere toward the front of the house. It was accompanied by the loud stomp of approaching heavy boots.

"Well, something smells mighty good in here."

"We're in the kitchen Gabe!" Rafer shouted. "Quick Annie get everything you want before he sits down. There might not be much left once he starts in."

Gabe MacDonald stood, very nearly filling the kitchen doorway, almost needing to turn sideways to get his shoulders through.

"That's rude Rafe. Totally rude." Gabe looked down at Rafer, "I'll arm wrestle you for your share of breakfast." He added with a smile.

"You'd lose my friend. I would cheat," he added.

"There is plenty and then some. Eat hearty. It is a

long time since the Three were gathered in one place. It is fitting that it is in Rose Hall." Elspeth spoke warmly as she touched the arm of the giant.

Gabe looked fondly at her. "Allegra looked good yesterday; she would like to come home soon, if you will allow it."

"I've been considering it. It is hard to have two strong women under one roof though. But it is a good thing she was there when Annie arrived. Much was accomplished thanks to her."

Annie looked a question from one to the other. Elspeth gave a musical laugh.

"Oh Annie, forgive me, Allegra is my daughter." She smiled again at the giant standing next to her, "And for a very long time now, Gabriel has been my husband."

"And yet, the beast remains untamed by your genteel touch Elspeth." Mike smiled and joined the fun.

"You better believe it," Gabe laughed. "But she loves me anyway."

"Gentlemen, sit, eat. There is work to be done. A journey is beginning and you must prepare. We will join hands and give our thanks for our food and each other first. Gabriel sit at the end of the table, away from Michael and Raphael. I have too much fine glassware in the house if you please. The Three must not touch one another at the same moment."

Gabriel took his seat and reached for Annie's hand on one side taking Mike Abbott's on the other. The circle joined hands and bowed their heads. Immediately, Annie felt as if she had been plugged into an electrical outlet. As if all of the molecules in her body began to vibrate vigorously. She opened her eyes in shock. In place of those that had been seated around the table, she once again looked upon the three as she had on Stockton Island.

Gabe MacDonald, huge and menacing, his face painted in a warrior's pattern, his huge hand gently holding hers. To his right, a much younger version of her father, tall and straight, with flowing red hair and beard, heavily muscled arms, and eyes that seemed to glow from within. To her left Rafer Tate, also aglow, bright in the morning light. His long black hair was tied back from his handsome face. A long cruel scar ran from his hairline, across his left eye and down his left cheek. At the far end of the table, Elspeth, her pale skin aglow shone with an unholy light, her ruby lips parted and she spoke.

"Greetings and well met guests. I am Elspeth, White Witch of Rose Hall. I thank you for this breakfast with friends. We celebrate this gathering of the Three, and the appearance of the Seeker. We offer our thanks and we bless this food and lift it up in service."

Releasing her grip on the two hands she brought her palms together.

"Dig in everyone."

You didn't have to tell Annie twice as she dug in.

Wind River

After breakfast, the three men began to clear the table and wash the dishes, laughing and joking with each other. The clink and clash of dishes and silverware almost as loud as their boisterous teasing. Elspeth, cringing at the clash of every plate, knife and fork, prepared a cup of hot mulled cider for Annie. Dropping two sticks of cinnamon bark into the steaming cup, she handed it to her.

"Shall we go out to the garden Annie? Perhaps we could have a chat while the boys do their best to destroy my china."

Annie took the cup and in spite of having just eaten a huge breakfast, found the delicious aroma of the cider alluring. She followed Elspeth as she flowed to the back door and out into the sheltered English garden at the back of the house. A narrow path meandered through countless rose bushes, in all colors of the rainbow, their fragrance heady in the warm autumn air. The back of the house and fences that guarded the perimeter were covered with climbing varieties, and they shaded the small gazebo that Elspeth took a seat in at the very back of the space.

As she arranged herself in the comfortable chair, Elspeth began; "Annie, all of this is very new to you, and I'm sure it is quite a shock. Until you reached a certain point in your growth it was important that you did not see the things that now surround you. It could have retarded your journey to maturity. The very fact that you can see them is evidence that you are—that you have reached that point. I can tell you some things that might help, but many others you will discover for yourself."

Annie sipped the hot cider and thought about what she had said. The last few months had been a complete shock to her. First the adventure of Rock Island, and the revelation of the seeker. Then all that had taken place yesterday. Which included a near-death experience that she didn't wish to repeat.

Elspeth continued, "As I said, I am the eighth in a line that leads back to the original White Witch of Rose Hall. That woman was Annie Palmer, and the original Rose Hall was in Jamaica. When it became clear that she was about to be murdered by ill-wishers jealous of her power, she escaped to the United States. The presence of Rose Hall, and all that it is, is a deeply protected secret. As the descendant I keep the secrets of the Hall and all the power that dwells therein.

The White Witch is a benevolent force, but not to be trifled with. Her anger can be fierce at times, deadly when necessary. However, the power of the White Witch, and indeed most of the sisters, is but a shadow in comparison to the descendent of Morgan Le Fey, the

Faery Queen. All of the Fey people have waited for the arrival of the next descendent. It has been many hundreds of years since the last Seeker appeared, but when the *'Three'* arose, we knew that the time had finally arrived. Michael was the first, and by him you were born. Your mother was a good woman, a master of potions and spells but did not understand in the deeper ways or who we were underneath. It is a great sadness that she did not survive to see what you have become.

"Michael, Gabriel and Raphael have fought many battles in their past and they are a fearsome force to be reckoned with. Michael is the leader and the eldest, but they are all very old. In fact, they make me feel quite young in their presence. You must put your trust in them and their judgment completely. They each harbor a special gift and each shield their power, but it is there nonetheless. It is a mistake to underestimate them, as many have discovered to their great misfortune. In a moment, perhaps they will demonstrate for you what accompanies you on your quest which you are only now discovering as your fate."

"I don't know anything about this quest that everyone is talking about. I don't understand why I'm the one, as you say, and what that even means."

"I bet you don't. It is a lot to take in and I can only give you a little, but it will be a start. The keepers of the stones cannot be fooled, for you cannot deceive a spirit. They have identified you as the one. In addition, you have beheld the power of the sisters and the true identity of the 'Three'. That also proves our hope. It is therefore true that you are the 'Seeker', the true and only direct descendent of the Morgan of legend and lore. High priestess of the Druids, bewitcher of Merlin the Magnificent. You, Annie, are the next Faery Queen, Morgan Le Fey."

"What! That can't be true. Merlin was a myth; no one knows if he even existed."

"He was a powerful Druid and a practitioner of the arts at a very high level indeed. Much of what he learned was lost when he passed. He loved one woman completely however, and she learned all that she could of his craft."

"I read that the English and even the French hunted her. Didn't they try to capture her over and over? Even St. Patrick was supposed to hunt her. That seems a little fantastic if you ask me."

Elspeth continued, "The legend says that she was a changeling, a shape-shifter. That she could shift into a raven and escape. Morgan Le Fey was a changeling it is true, as many of the sisters are. She was also powerful beyond anything approaching what we are today and that you might become. The seeker is the one that searches for the lost secrets and the treasure that accompanies them. It will take someone of unusual courage and cunning to elude the darker powers who also seek."

"That is true Annie," Mike and the two men, having finished their kitchen duties, had joined them in the garden. "There are those that want the treasure out of greed and the acquisition of power. They would wield the power for evil and to control others. We cannot let that happen."

Turning to Elspeth, "The fall term has already started at school, so I will have to take a sabbatical from the University. Rafe has left orders for Rob to take his boat out of the water and store it in the shipyard. Gabe will finally have something to do besides cultivating the rose garden."

"Hey! I'm good at tending the roses. Don't belittle it."

"I think the roses are amazing Mr. MacDonald. Simply amazing!"

"At least someone here appreciates culture." Gabe smiled at Annie, "but you need to call me Gabe, or Gabriel if you like."

"Ok,—Gabe."

"I think we should decide what your next step from here is gentlemen."

"Right." Mike sat down on the grass, "what do we know so far? The clues are cryptic, and the diary is of no use anymore. The water from yesterday destroyed the inked entries. We are flying blind right now."

"Annie, I need you to concentrate for a moment." Elspeth reached out her hand. "Take my hand and concentrate only on what the keepers of the stones told you. What did it mean to you?"

Annie held Elspeth's cool hand. She thought about what had happened when she touched the stones and when she had spoken with Rolf on Stockton Island. Suddenly, there was a presence in her mind. A picture became clear, a woman old and bent, her head covered with a shawl and her face in shadow. In a voice that was deep and strong, Annie spoke out loud, *"Wisdom belongs to the aged, and understanding to the old. It is time—come to me."*

The vision cleared and once again she was seated in

the gazebo. The three men, their eyes wide stared back.

"She speaks of the eldest. The eldest calls for her." Rafer said in awe.

"Yes, it appears so." Closing her eyes in concentration, Elspeth spoke as if from far away. *"She is hidden, and far away. You must travel to her as she can no longer come to us."*

"But where?" Mike was already rising to his feet.

"She is at Wind River. Near the cut in the mountain where the river flows out." Elspeth frowned again closing her eyes in concentration. *"Others are seeking her, and she is in danger."* Eyes still closed she suddenly rose to her feet, head back. Again, in a voice as if from far away, impossibly powerful, ***"The Three are called."***

"Wait, what does that mean?" Annie appealed to them.

"Show her," Elspeth ordered

The three men rose to their feet. Michael stood in front and Gabe stood to his right and Rafer to the left. On a signal from Mike, they placed their hands on his shoulder.

A reverberating sonic wave blasted Annie with a deafening 'thrum' almost knocking her from her seat; her vision closed down so that only the Three were visible. Their visage a terrible thing to behold, their ferocity undeniable they pulsed with power as they held their weapons drawn and ready.

Elspeth spoke, "Behold the Three! Ancient warriors, fearsome in battle, gentle in life. Guardians of the Seeker."

Michael raised his right-hand palm outward and a

blast as bright as the sun exploded from it. Racing across the garden it struck the fence in a shower of sparks, setting it on fire.

"Enough." Elspeth spoke. The men removed their hands and returned to the peaceful friends that they had been only moments before. Elspeth waved her hand at the fence and the fire was extinguished. The rose vines quickly moved to cover the charred portion. In a matter of moments, it was as if nothing had happened.

"I have to go to Wind River," Annie said in wonderment. "I think I need to go now."

"First you must rest. Tomorrow will be soon enough." Her dad said with concern.

The Others

The next morning, the small company gathered at the front door of Rose Hall. Elspeth touched each one in turn but stopped in front of Annie.

"From here on out you will be hunted. The Others can sense the power that has arisen. But they also know of the Three, so they will be cautious. Safe travels sister."

As they all climbed into Mike's truck, Annie turned for one last look at Rose Hall. But it was not there. A small run-down shack, its shutters hanging askew and badly needing paint had taken its place on the street. The front yard was overgrown with weeds, and a faded 'KEEP OUT' sign stood near the sidewalk. She turned to her father in wonder. Mike smiled and shrugged, "The White Witch is very careful. She knows how to take care of herself."

"But, where did Rose Hall go? How does she do that?"

"Go back and ask her."

Annie skirted the 'KEEP OUT' sign and briskly

strode down the sidewalk. She tried to peak through the filthy opaque windows but failed. Trying the front door the knob turned easily and the door swung open. Stepping into the front room, she was once again in a white ornate foyer bathed in sunlight.

"What is it sister?" Elspeth, arms folded on her chest stood at the foot of the winding staircase as if waiting for her. She gave her a knowing smile. "Have you forgotten something?"

"What? Oh—it's just that…um…I guess I better start getting used to a whole lot of stuff pretty soon."

"Oh honey, it's just an illusion, like hypnosis. The Hall is still here always, but out there you couldn't convince anyone of that even if you had a million dollars."

The front door swung open and Annie's father hurried in, shut the door, then leaned against it.

"They are here."

"Oh, that was quick."

"Rafer and Gabe are scouting, we can feel that they are near, but so far, they're being elusive."

"You will have to find another way Michael, surely they'll be watching the truck."

"We'll need a disguise. Rafer and Gabe can create a diversion. What've you got Elspeth."

"It is her power that we need to hide not her appearance. They don't know what she looks like, but they can feel her power. It is like a magnet for them."

"What do you suggest then."

"I have a thought, but first you Michael. They do know what you look like, but there's only so much I can accomplish."

She steered Mike Abbott across the foyer so that he stood in front of a full-length mirror at the end of the room. "Here, try this."

In the mirror Mike's reflection blurred. Amid swirling colors, it slowly reformed, but in place of Professor Michael Abbott, an overweight middle-aged women stood wearing bib overalls and reading glasses on a pearl neck chain.

"NO! Seriously Elspeth? This isn't funny."

Annie blinked her eyes. Looking at her father he looked exactly the same as he always did, but the mirror did not reflect it. It was an amazing illusion and she blinked her eyes several times.

"Oh Michael, you are going to breeze right past any opposition." She chuckled. "Actually, I think this is some of my best work."

Her chuckle turned into a full-out laugh and for a moment she could not stop; she was still shaking when she turned to Annie. "Alright now, your turn."

"Oh please! I want to be a grownup. Can you make me a grownup?"

"If I did, it would not hide the power you hold. No, I have something very special in mind. Here you go," she moved Annie to the mirror. "Just relax."

Nothing changed as far as she could tell. She felt exactly the same, but things in the mirror had taken a decidedly unexpected turn. Standing at the edge of the mirror stood Elspeth the White Witch of Rose Hall. On her extended left arm sat a coal black raven gazing back at her.

"Behold the Changeling; the Faery Queen.

"Now you must fly, go with speed but safely, the time is short. Michael, protect her until the three are together again."

Escape Into the Wild

To Annie the ninety miles from Bayfield to Duluth, Minnesota seemed to take forever. Wherever possible Mike pushed the speed limit while he watched for pursuit in the rear-view mirror. They had no news from either Gabriel or Raphael before they left and Mike had his phone turned off in case the 'Others' were able to trace it.

The hour-and-a-half that the trip took proved to be nothing in comparison to how long the ride from Duluth to Fargo, North Dakota would be. There had been almost no break in the monotony of endless forests that bordered the shoulders of the road on both sides. Crossing the northern end of Minnesota had taken far longer than either of them wanted, the presence of danger and the possibility of traffic police an ever-present complication.

Annie couldn't relax. The scenery was beautiful but unchanging. She fidgeted, restless in the comfortable bucket seat, but unable to get comfortable. She tried to be patient and had tried a few conversation starters with her father, but Mike Abbot was too busy to carry on a conversation. Although she recognized that Elspeth had probably been correct when she had said that the 'Others' would know her father's pickup truck and be watching for it, her idea of something less conspicuous had been a little questionable.

The low, sleek bright red Maserati was neither anonymous nor inconspicuous. Annie felt that it looked like a louder, longer and faster version of any James Bond car she had seen in the movies. In actuality the car turned heads whenever they passed by. People would stop what they were doing to see the classic super car and its high-powered engine whine by. That there wasn't much of a chance that the two of them would be suspected of driving such a machine that was certainly true, but they were also not very forgettable. Just their passing through a small town in northern Minnesota would be remembered for more than a few minutes. The car was beautiful, powerful and unbelievably fast. It was also more than a handful for Mike. The slightest touch on the gas pedal resulted in the car exploding away from a stoplight. Minor touches on the brake pedal caused it to almost stand on its nose. The steering was tight and over-responsive, with any minor correction resulting in the car swerving sharply and the six-speed manual transmission had proved challenging for Mike to master as well.

At first Mike had joked about the challenge, but as the drive lengthened the constant need to remain intensely alert had started to wear on him.

"Leave it to Elspeth to think that this was better than my truck. It figures that she would have something like this just sitting around. I'll bet she's maxed out the speedometer more than once."

"What do you think this thing will do Dad?"

"The speedometer shows a top end around one hundred-sixty. I'd be surprised if it wouldn't go a bit more. It's like having a tiger on a leash. This thing wants to go, go, go and by that I mean really go. If I so much as blink, it will jump up ten miles per hour it seems. Once we get out in North Dakota, we'll see just what it will do though."

As they approached Fargo, the dense forests thinned and then disappeared altogether. It was replaced by seemingly endless prairie stretching to the horizon in every direction. From forty miles away they could already begin to see the city.

"Boy, it's really flat out here."

"Yes, it is. Someone once told me that in North Dakota the land was so flat that you could watch your dog run away for three days."

"Is that a dad joke?"

"Yep, I got a million of 'em."

"Trust me. I know."

As she turned the events of the last few days over in her head, she was increasingly confused.

"Dad? Who are the 'Others'?"

Mike rubbed his forehead for a moment, leaned back in the seat and sighed. "Ah, that's a tough nut to crack Sweetie. It's more a question of which one is it this time."

"Dad!"

"Right, right. If anyone deserves a complete answer to that question it's probably you. The answer is simple and short, or long and complicated."

"Simple and short first."

"The 'Others' are the bad guys."

"Geez Dad, a little bit longer than that please. C'mon, I don't want you to joke about it, I need to know—I think."

"Yes, you do. I can fill in the details mostly but learning about them, and us, is really a process. There are multiple parts to it, and each part leads somewhere else."

"How much farther is it to this Wind River place and what is it?"

"I don't really know the answer to the first part of that question, another fourteen or fifteen hours maybe."

"Well then we've got plenty of time Dad. What about the other half of the question?"

"Okay; touché'. Wind River is deep in the mountains of northwestern Wyoming and it's on the Shoshone Reservation. Where we want to go is a small settlement where the Eldest is living right now. Rafer is Native American too, but he is Sioux. I really don't have any idea what race the Eldest is; she's tricky that way."

"Okay, good enough for now I guess, but now what about the 'Others'."

"The first answer is pretty easy. After that it's part history, part mystery and part epic adventure."

"I know you're a history teacher Dad, but can you, just for once, skip the history before you give me the answer?"

"Why? Do I do that a lot?"

"All the time."

"Hmm…I see. I'll have to try and watch that from now on."

"The story Dad…please."

"Okay, but you need a little history just to get the gist of the problem, okay?"

"Sounds like you're stalling."

"Okay, okay, let's see. Over the millennia of time that people have walked the earth…"

"Dad stop! I just want to know who's chasing us— and maybe why they're chasing us. For right now that's all."

"Sheesh! Okay. The short answer is that I don't know who it is that is chasing us. At times it can be one faction, and then the next time, it is someone else entirely. They are not interchangeable though. Some of them are new and lust for power, some of them are very old and lust for power, still others are just plain evil and lust for power. They see those that hold power that they want as tools, weapons if you will, to be subjugated and used to their advantage."

"Wait! What's subjugated?"

"It means conquered and enslaved."

"Oh? That sounds kinda medieval."

"In every sense of the word actually. They see the 'Seeker' as the keys to the kingdom. Quite literally actually. If they can make use of the power of the Seeker, it can unlock secrets to limitless power."

"So? Who's chasing us Dad?"

"It's hard to say. Think of you, the world, and the universe. Each one in motion, each one with an internal clock with its own timetable. The pendulum of each clock swings back and forth. For some of those things the clock, and its pendulum are very big. For others it's small—tiny even. The longer the pendulum, the longer it takes for it to swing back and forth, right to left, left to right."

"Okay, I'm with you so far."

"Some clocks, like those for men, are relatively small. Only a few swings of their pendulum can be an entire person's individual life. For other things, the solar system, for example, the clock and the pendulum are immense, taking centuries even light years to complete one swing. But for either one, that swing is only one tick of their clock. The pendulums bring change with each swing. Right to left, left to right. So that things that are important today, let's say personal values for instance, can change to a complete opposite when the pendulum swings the other direction. Does that make sense?"

"Sorta."

"There's an old saying, 'Rags to riches to rags in three generations. What that means is a man, or woman sees what they want to achieve in their lives. They chart a path to achieve their goals and do, to whatever extent they can. The pendulum swings back the other way, now the person, or persons, that were benefitting from the achievement, the next generation, of those goals are looking at life from a different perspective, from the other end of the pendulum's swing. The things that were motivation at first don't exist at this end. Now there's food on the table, money in the bank. Rather than strive for a new goal, they simply enjoy the fruits of someone else's labor. So, the gains that the first generation made are squandered and eventually lost. Rags to riches to rags."

"So it's about money?"

"No my love, it's about power. But in this day and age, money is power and power is more money."

"So what's that got to do with us?"

"We have both."

Race to Wind River

As they entered the Red River Valley, Mike finally opened it up and pushed the accelerator down. The flame red Maserati Bora blasted forward like it had been fired out of a gun.

"Holy Cow! Dad! Slow down, please!" Annie was pressed back into the bucket seat. "How fast are we going?"

"The speed limit is posted at eighty miles-per-hour Annie. I'm trying to make up a little time."

"No offense Dad, but that didn't feel like eighty to me."

"No, sweetie. That was one-hundred-twenty. This car didn't even work up a sweat."

"Dad? Seriously? A hundred and twenty? I was thinking like ninety, it was so smooth, but scary all at the same time."

"Leave it to Elspeth to own the only vintage Maserati in about five states. Inconspicuous my left foot."

"Still Dad, this is a really awesome ride. Don't you

think?"

"Yes, and as far as I know, we may be the first people that she has ever let drive it other than herself. Gabe can't even get in the darn thing. He just doesn't fit."

"I'm not complaining or whining Dad. Mostly I'm a little scared, and I don't even know what I should be scared of. But how much farther is it really? We've been on the road for about five hours now haven't we?"

"Closer to six pumpkin. I don't actually know how much farther, or how much longer. My guess is about another eight- nine-hundred miles though. So, we're going to see if this beautiful beast underneath us wants to stretch its legs."

"What exactly does that mean Dad? I've never seen you drive anything but your old truck."

"Trust me Annie, you only know about half of who I am. Now, I need a little favor if you please."

"Sure Dad, anything."

"First, eat some of the food that Elspeth sent along. It will perk you up and give you a little more energy. Then when you're ready, I want you to concentrate very hard, and I want you to have only one thought as much as you can. I know you've not had any practice, but our need is great right now, and I will need the Seeker."

"What do you mean Dad?"

"Okay, you know that someone or thing is chasing us. We don't want to have them catch us right?"

"Too right."

"Okay, now I want you to not think about who's behind us. Anybody back there, we can outrun with this car. Unless they have rocket handy."

"Okay…"

"We can outrun them, but we can't outrun a telephone. I need you to just concentrate on how you don't want the people behind us to call the people waiting in front of us. I need you to think about not letting them see us."

"Now I am scared."

"Good, in a way, it will be additional motivation. Okay?"

"Okay Dad, I'll try."

Twelve hours later, Mike Abbott wheeled the bright red Maserati into a parking spot outside of truck stop on the outskirts of Casper, Wyoming. The light was just beginning to grow in the east. Reaching across, he roused a sleeping Annie. "Wake up Annie."

Annie sat up, rubbing her sleep heavy eyes, and peered around.

"We're in Casper, Wyoming. We have about another couple hundred miles or so to go, but I need a little break. It's pretty early in the morning here; we've driven all night. I think it might be a good idea to get cleaned up before we see what the rest of the day brings. Stay in the car and out of sight. Remember if anyone sees you, you look like a big black bird. You don't have to talk to anyone. Okay?"

"Sure Dad," said Annie as she dropped back in the seat and closed her eyes again.

Minutes later voices roused her again. Sitting up and clearing her eyes she saw three tall rough looking men admiring the sports car in the early morning light. She sunk down in the seat trying not to be noticed.

Behind the men, Mike Abbott rounded the corner of the convenience store, his arms filled with bags of snacks and cradling a coffee cup in his left hand.

"Hey little lady, is this your ride?"

"Yes, yes, it is young man."

"Well, we'd like to take it for a spin around the lot. Why don't you give us your keys? We'll have it back in just a minute or two." The men exchanged sly smiles.

"I don't think so. I'm running a little late boys."

"No way you can ever run late with a ride like this," one of them said while he ran his hand over the silky-smooth fender of the car.

"Sorry fellas, maybe some other time." Mike Abbott disguised as a middle-aged woman tried to walk past the three.

"Well maybe we're not asking lady." One of them drew a large pistol from a hidden holster. Another followed suit, pointing both at Mike Abbott.

"I think you are making a mistake, gentlemen."

"There's no mistake Michael. We know who you are, disguise or not; your stink tells us all we need to know. Where is the seeker?"

"I said, I think you are making a mistake, gentlemen."

"You can tell us now, or when we are finished with you Guardian. Where is the One?"

In a blur of motion that Annie almost could not follow, Mike Abbott turned in a half circle. Taking the man on his right, he propelled him into the man in the middle. Both pistols fired but by that time, all three were falling to the ground unconscious. Mike Abbott plopped into the driver's seat panting and started the car. Spinning the tires in reverse he backed out onto the road and squealing the tires soon had the Maserati approaching one-hundred miles an hour while he watched the rear-view mirror.

"Were those some of the others?"

"Not very adept ones thank goodness. No, they were just minions, watchers. But now they know our route, and direction. Time is getting short."

"I guess it's good that we have such a great car to get away in though, right Dad?"

"Elspeth is going to kill me," Mike held up his left hand. It was covered in blood.

"Dad! You're bleeding! Oh Dad, we've got to get you to a hospital. Oh geez, what is it."

"One of the pistols caught me. Guess I'm not as fast as I used to be. Hospitals are out of the question Annie; under no circumstances can we risk something like that. Besides, it's not the first time. I'm pretty sure I've been shot before. I just need to find a place to pull off the road so I can get a look at it."

"Oh Dad. I'm scared."

"I understand, me too honey, but it's gonna be fine. Don't you fret."

A small dirt track appeared in the growing daylight that led away from the road. Mike steered the Maserati into it and carefully drove for more than a mile into the low hills and out of sight from the road. Shutting off the engine he pushed open the door but didn't get out at first.

"I'm just gonna see if I can stop some of the mess. I'm ruining the upholstery in Elspeth's car. You stay here Annie; you don't want to look. Okay?"

Annie gulped and nodded.

Mike put one foot on the ground and turned away from her but before he could rise to his feet, he collapsed, falling face first into the dust.

"Dad!" Annie jumped out of the car and raced around to the driver's side. She struggled to turn her father on his side. "Dad!"

"You must call them. Let Rafer and Gabe know where to find you. Let them know where you are Seeker." Mike's voice was weak and far away. "Let them know." l

"No Dad! It's going to be alright. We're gonna be okay. Right Dad? Dad? Don't leave me Dad. Please!"

"You must reach out; you must tell the sisters." He whispered.

Annie jumped to her feet, frantically looking around the desolate landscape; there would be no help. Frantically pacing, not sure what to do in her helplessness. She stopped and closed her eyes. Suddenly, she knew what she had to do clearly. She knew something that she hadn't known before. She reached out with her thought; *"Sisters, I am in need. One of the Three— has fallen."*

Instantly, she felt power flow into her. She felt as if she grew taller, stronger, her hands and legs flexed. She looked at her father. With newfound strength she turned him on his back. The left side of his shirt a mess of dark blood and dirt. She placed a hand over the source and felt great force flow from her hand into him.

"Awaken Guardian, your time has not come. The two are coming."

Mike Abbott opened his eyes and drew a deep breath. His breathing deepened and he rested. His hand reached out and clasped Annie's.

"You must go." He closed his eyes and coughed.

"Raphael and Gabriel are coming. They will be here soon."

Mike opened his eyes, and smiled. "You summoned them, I'm so proud Annie."

"You should rest Dad. I'll be okay for now. I don't know what I did, or how. I don't even know if it will last. We can wait."

"Okay."

The sun burned down brutally hot for the rest of the day. As evening approached the air began to cool as the sun dipped behind the mountains to the west. Annie dozed, leaning against one of the car's tires. She had fashioned a crude canopy using a blanket and the car door to shade her father, and given him the rest of their water throughout the day. For his part he had lapsed in and out of consciousness. When he was conscious, he expressed his support for her. He spoke of his pride and confidence in her before lapsing out of consciousness again. As evening approached, he became feverish and did not wake again. His breathing became shallow and distant.

A huge pickup truck roared up the track, sliding to a stop at her feet, its massive lugged tires only inches away from running over her legs. Annie, caught by surprise, leaped to her feet, ready to run.

"Howdy pardner! Looks like you got yourself in a bit of a pickle here." Rafer Tate dropped down out of the truck. He swept Annie up in a hug. "We came as soon as we could. It was hard to convince the owner of this truck that we needed to borrow it. Can you imagine? So rude right? Gabe got him to listen to reason though."

Gabe came around the front of the truck and dropped to his knees next to Mike. After a brief examination, he laid both of his hands on his chest. "Michael, it's me, Gabriel. You gonna sleep all day?"

Mike Abbott took a deep breath and opened his eyes staring straight up.

"Gabriel, good to hear your voice." His voice was only a whisper, "I stand at the veil, it beckons to me. Annie's been great, really brave. Get her to Wind River; they're right behind you."

"Not without you, old friend. Not without you."

Gabe rose and speaking to Rafer, "He's fevered and he's lost a lot of blood. His need is the greatest. You take the car, get him to the healer at Wind River. I'll follow with Annie. Don't spare the horses Rafe, he's fading."

They carried Mike to the passenger side and gently lifted him into the seat.

"Wow, Elspeth's gonna kill you Mike."

"I know, with any luck I'll die before that." Mike's smiled weakly.

"We're right behind you Rafe, don't wait for us."

The Maserati fishtailed and straightened out going down the narrow track. From a mile away, they heard it hit the road and squeal the tires. The high horsepower engine roaring even from this distance.

Gabe lifted Annie up into the tall truck and then

climbed into the driver's side.

"Don't worry Annie, he's in good hands. You did an amazing job."

Three and a half hours later, they entered a small gathering of houses and trailers near a wooded hill. There had seemed to be endless curves and slow spots as they wound their way into the mountains. Both of them wanted the hurry, but the road had made it impossible. It was late enough so that many of the windows shone light and shadows moved within. As the truck pulled up several men hurried to it.

"Alasita paytah (fire warrior) has been taken up the hill Taté-iyòhiwin (Wind warrior) is with him. The healer is helping him, but his danger is great."

Gabe turned to Annie. "You're as safe here as anywhere else these days. I've got to see to Mike; he will need both Rafer and I. I'll be back in a few minutes, okay?"

"I don't want to be left alone Gabe."

"You are not alone sister. You are home." +

A bent woman in a dark shawl stood at the edge of the light. "Come with me, for your time has come."

Annie looked at Gabe. He gave a slow nod, "Go with her." He whispered. "She is the eldest."

The Eldest

"You will be safe with her," Gabe continued. "She is who we came to see. Go with her,. We'll find you after I see to Michael."

Without another word, Gabe turned and hurried away. The other men following. Annie regarded the crone.

"Come with me Seeker, the time is short." With that she turned and shuffled away into the darkness leaving Annie to catch up.

The old woman walked in silence and in spite of her appearance, moved with surprising speed. Annie, exhausted by the events of the day, stumbled in the dark after her, having difficulty keeping up. They walked with speed for a long time before at last coming to a small cabin dug into the side of a steep hill. A dim light burned in the window, and the smell of wood smoke hung in the air. There was no door on the entrance, instead a rough canvas was draped over the opening.

The old one lifted the drape and holding it up indicated to Annie to proceed ahead of her and entered behind.

"I very much like the disguise; the raven is a symbol of the Seeker. Is it comfortable for you?"

"I don't feel any different than usual ma'am. Do I still look like a raven?"

She smiled, the rest of her face remaining in deep in shadow, "No, you do not appear as a raven, not to me little sister." She lifted the hood of the shawl off of her head. "Then you are the true seeker. Anyone else could not tolerate the form. "You may call me Circe, youngest. Just as I am eldest, you now are youngest." Her voice, despite her aged appearance, was strong and assertive. "It a blessing and a curse that we must endure to preserve and protect the secrets of the ages."

The old woman stood using a small cane to support herself in front of Annie.

"It is with the utmost pleasure and much anticipation that I welcome you little sister. I have waited a long time for you. Welcome to my home."

Annie looked around the small room. The only thing remotely appealing was the cheery fire that burned in the hearth. The peeled log walls appeared pale white in the firelight of the hearth. The beamed ceiling disappearing into shadow above was festooned with drying herbs and vegetables hung within arms-reach. In the corner a small cot waited patiently. The floor was hard-packed dirt. A small table in the corner was set with two plates, a covered pot sat in the center, smelling delicious. Immediately, her stomach growled.

"Forgive my poor manners Seeker. You have not eaten for almost twenty-four hours; you are in need. Come, sit. Afterward we will talk."

ANNIE ABBOTT AND THE DRUID STONES

Annie sat down carefully, not entirely convinced the ramshackle chair would support her. The old woman dished a rich stew from the pot into bowls for each of them. With it she served a crusty bread that tasted of cinnamon and honey. Annie was famished and the food was delicious. Annie ate with relish while Circe' watched with a wry smile.

Her hunger satisfied after she had finished eating, Annie looked up feeling suddenly strangely sleepy. She looked across at the ancient woman. Her vision suddenly blurred. She blinked. What was different? She was confused, had the old woman changed? She blinked her eyes again. She wasn't sure. Did she look different? Younger? Much younger. The room slowly tipped on its side, she was too tired to think about it. Her head rested on the table beside her plate, and she closed her eyes. The old woman smiled a satisfied smile.

Bright sunshine splashed into Annie's face. She squinted and turned away. Then she snapped her eyes open in shock. Where was she? What had happened at the dinner table? Had she passed out? She looked around. She was still in the woman's hut. The tarp covering the door had been tied back and the window coverings had been removed. She had woken lying on the small cot in the corner of the room. Looking down, she saw that she was still dressed in her 'two-days of wearing' clothes. The woman Circe' was nowhere to be seen.

In a panic, she swung her legs out onto the dirt floor and sat up. The floor was warm and dry under her bare

121

feet. *'Where were her shoes?'*

From outside of the cabin, the old woman's voice called, "It is a beautiful morning Seeker. Come out and welcome the 'Morning Star'."

Walking to the doorway, Annie stepped out into the twilight morning and chilly air. It smelled of sage and freshness, damp with the dew of the night before. Across the valley, the sun, only half of its blinding shape visible was rising slowly above the peaks. In front of her, the ground sloped away for miles still in the shadow of a line of mountains at the far side of the valley.

Seated on a wooden bench at the front of the small house, Circe' sat cross-legged, her head leaning back against the logs of the building, her eyes closed. In her hands she held a small pipe, a tendril of smoke still rising from the bowl. The aroma of the sweet-scented pipe tobacco added its heady fragrance to the odors of sage and sweet grass. In the morning light of the sun, every wrinkle and crease of her ancient face was highlighted and intensified.

"To greet each day is a privilege not afforded to everyone Annie. We should always appreciate it for the gift that it is. Without that appreciation, the deeds that we do have little meaning because we are doing them for the wrong reasons." Circe' spoke without opening her eyes. "Always remember, 'Above all else, thankfulness in all things.' Come and sit here beside me. Enjoy the moment."

Annie was still unsure. The sun had not yet brought any heat to the new day and she began to shiver slightly in the cool mountain air. After falling asleep immediately after her dinner last night, she was not convinced that she should trust this enigmatic woman.

"There is a serape inside the doorway Annie. I believe it is just your size. Why don't you try it on?"

Annie had been dressed for a long car ride. As such, she was wearing a lightweight cotton short sleeved shirt and jeggings. The ground under her bare feet was cold as she curled her toes trying to warm them. Looking inside the doorway she spied a beautiful woven jacket with incredible colors of the rainbow hanging just inside. Taking it down and pulling it over her head it was impossibly soft, warm, and a perfect fit.

"This is really beautiful!"

"Do you like it? Then you must have it; I insist." She opened her eyes and regarded Annie with satisfaction. "I made it last winter during the idle months. At the time, I didn't know why I wanted to. As usual, if one can be patient, the answer will eventually reveal itself. And here you are. Does it fit?"

"It's perfect! So many colors, really beautiful."

"Thank you. It will protect you from weather and storm, but I have also woven other protections into it. It alone has some power of defense. Wear it in time of need."

Annie joined Circe' on the bench and leaned back against the wall. The sun was now above the mountain range to the east and beginning to make itself felt.

Annie gave a deep sigh. A feeling of safety and calm washed over her.

"The Wind Warrior approaches. Can you feel him?"

"Good morning the house!" Rafer Tate called from down the hill. "Anybody home?"

"That's so weird. I could actually feel him as he was getting closer."

Circe' looked down at her with a smile, "That's very good Youngest. You are starting to get in touch with the many messages that are carried on the wind."

Rafer finished his climb to the house and greeted the two women.

"Good morning, Eldest! Hello Annie, what a beautiful day."

"How did you…how do you do that Rafe? Why is it that every time you are near me, I get all calm and relaxed? I hadn't really thought about it before, but it happens every time you're around."

Rafer just smiled at her.

"Would you rather feel sad and lonely?" Circe' holding her gaze, "He can do that too, if you like."

"NO! No thank you, I mean. Is that really true? You can control my emotions?"

"No, not really. It's just a parlor trick, but it can be pretty handy at times. Like right now." He gave her a meaningful look.

"Oh…oh, how's my dad?"

Rafer's expression changed; his smile vanished. He turned to look at Annie, "The news is not good Annie. I'm sorry. He will pass through the veil soon I'm afraid."

"No!" Tears sprang from her eyes, "No!...SHUT UP…you can't say that, he's going to be okay. Please tell me he's going to be okay?" She wiped her tears and sniffed, "he has to be okay," and then a little more meekly, "he has to be," sniff, "he's my…he's my Dad."

"I can't promise you something that I don't know if

124

I can deliver sweetheart. Your father has been shot in the chest. I honestly don't know how he managed to get you away, an amazing display of determination, but I would expect nothing less of the Alasita paytah. The bullet punctured his lung and is pressing on his heart. Without removing it, he cannot survive. We don't have the skill it would require to perform such a delicate operation. He would not survive it."

He looked a long look at the old woman. "He passed the night with difficulty Eldest. He is delirious with fever and he is calling for the daughter of Helios. He calls for you Eldest'," he repeated.

"Ah me, and so it begins. I must come then, I feared it was so. As in everything these days, the time is short."

"What? Can you help my Dad Circe'?"

"I do not know child, but I cannot deny the call, nor would I refuse it."

"Who is the daughter of Helios? Is it some kind of a medicine?"

"A good and proper question," Rafer said without breaking his eye contact with Circe'.

The old woman rose painfully to her feet and stepped away from the bench. Walking a few paces down the hill she turned to face the two as she removed the black shawl that she had been wrapped in. Rising to her full height she raised her arms and stamped her cane down on the ground.

"Behold! I am Circe', daughter of Helios, god of the sun, older than ages upon ages of man. Bring forth what once was and still is!"

With a blinding flash the old woman disappeared. In

her place stood an impossibly tall, young woman. Her long black hair blowing in the sudden breeze, her eyes flashing like emeralds. The woman before them was radiant in dazzling colors of green and gold that caught the sunlight and reflected it back, creating a halo of brightest light around her. On her head she wore a crown of gold. In her hand she held a long ornate staff.

"I am Circe', daughter of Perse, nymph of the seas. I Circe', Warrior Queen of Aeaea, sister to Medea, enchantress of Odysseus. Descended from mother to daughter through the ages, of time. Master of potions and poisons, changeling and traveler. I am revealed at last."

Before Annie stood the most radiant and beautiful young woman she had ever seen. Dressed as she was in multilayers of hues of deep colors, tall as an Amazon with full black hair that framed a face so lovely that Annie felt faint. Awestricken and dazzled she gaped at the vision as it faded, slowly returning to the ancient crone swathed in a black hooded shawl.

She smiled at Annie's look of surprise, "Yes, back in the day, I could break a few hearts."

"And a lot of other things as well, not just hearts." Rafer added to Annie out the side of his mouth.

"Hush Raphael, shall we go. Time is of the essence it would seem."

The Faery Queen Rises

Hurrying down the hill and back into the settlement the three approached the home of the healer. Several men stood at the door but parted when they saw them approaching. Once inside there was no mistaking that someone inside was very ill.

Circe' sniffed the air. "He has festered; there is death in this room. The bullet must have been poisoned. He is in grave peril." Addressing the healer whose house it was, "Take me to your potions and herbs I must mix an antidote before the infection spreads any further. I can only hope there is time."

On a raised table in the center of the room Mike Abbott lay. His eyes were open as he stared up at the ceiling. Gabe, his huge frame taking up most of the available space held his hand. His breathing labored as he struggled against the blood that had collected in his lungs, drowning him. His shirt had been removed and the left side of his chest was covered in a gauze bandage colored dark from the wound. Annie cowered against the wall, terrified by the scene in front of her.

Rafer approached the table. "Mike, old buddy, I've brought her. She's going to help. Hang in there pal."

Mike reached out his other hand and clasped Rafer's. He spoke no words but gave a small smile.

In the corner, Circe' feverishly mixed a concoction, speaking a strange language, the noxious smell of the potion added itself to the others in the room.

> *"Ta vótana edó símera, proséxte aftá ta lógia pou léo, deíxte ti dýnamí sas aftí tin óra. Therapéfste ton ánthropo, ópos móno eseís boreíte".*
>
> *(Herbs here today, heed these words that I say, show your power at this hour. Heal the man, as only you can.)*

With a steaming cup in her hand, she shuffled to the makeshift gurney. "Michael, Guardian of the Seeker, Leader of the Three, gather your strength. I offer this antidote; it has the power to stop the poison. Drink this first; then I will do what I can with your wound."

She raised the cup to his lips and slowly poured a small portion into his parted lips. Mike tried to swallow, triggering a cough. Blood seeped from the corner of his mouth as Rafer dabbed it away exchanging a worried glance with Gabe. Circe' continued to administer the rest of the antidote.

Circe' then removed the bandage from his chest. The wound was red and angry. Frowning she spoke again.

> *"Chéria tou therapeftí, chéria tou dolofónou. Fotiá, aéras kai neró, oi dynámeis tis prosefchís. Férte zoí kai dýnami, se aftón aftín tin óra"*

(Hands of the healer, heart of the slayer. Fire, Air and Water, and powers of prayer. Bring life and power, to him at this hour.)

She laid her hands over the wound and closed her eyes. Mike Abbott contorted, his face suddenly a twisted mask of pain, a cry escaped his lips as his body arched up from the makeshift bed, only his feet and shoulders touching. He drew a shuddering breath and collapsed back onto the table—and breathed no more.

Rafer and Gabe looked at each other in stunned disbelief. Circe's eyes opened wide in amazement as she drew back from the table.

§§§§

"TOUCH NOT THE GUARDIAN!"

The voice was forceful, imperious, freezing everyone in the room. Turning they beheld Annie standing in the center of the room. Her small frame surrounded by an unearthly light, her legs and arms spread wide. Her eyes aglow, flaming red hair waving in the still air. She moved forward as they drew back from her advance. Reaching the table where her father lay still and unmoving, she laid one hand on his forehead, and the other over his heart, she spoke again: *"Step not through the veil of death Guardian. Your task is yet unfinished. I so command it. Return to me and our quest. You are called to our need. May the strength of the Three be once again. As I speak, so mote it be."*

Beneath her hands, the Guardian drew a shuddering breath.

Annie moved her hand over the angry wound, again she commanded: ***"Let the weapon of our enemy be no more, I draw forth your assassin. Be at peace Guardian. You are returned to my side."***

She removed her hand and opened it. In her open palm a lump of bloodied lead nestled there. Turning she dropped the bullet into a small bowl next to the bed. Mike Abbott opened his eyes and turned to her.

"You called to me, Mistress. I return to serve again, my Queen."

Annie eyes rolled up and became vacant. She collapsed to floor, unconscious.

Behind her Circe' smiled as Gabriel lifted the small girl into his arms. "Return her to my cabin Warrior. The circle that was broken is complete at last. Once again, as in ages long past, the full force of the old ones has gathered. Water, Air, and Fire are joined at last by Earth. The Faery Queen has risen.

Smoke and Magic

"It doesn't seem real. All of this doesn't seem real, like it's some long dream. Even things that I see and touch. Somehow, I feel like I'm watching a 3-D movie with characters that I know, but so fantastic that they're not real either. It's like I stepped through a portal into another dimension." Annie sat cross-legged on the ground in front of Circe's small dugout cabin. A small fire had been lit to ward off the chill of the cool autumn air.

Circe', also cross-legged, sat on the ground across from Annie. She was busy stringing garlic bulbs onto a long string to hang from the rafters inside the cabin. She spoke without looking up, "You're stalling. Try again."

"I'm getting tired Eldest, can't I take a break?"

"You are trying to find something by looking for it where you think it should be, instead of looking for it where it is. Now again, you must try again."

"Do they call you Eldest because you are the leader?" Asked Annie looking for a distraction. "Or is it because you're so mean?"

"Hah, that's a good one. I'm mean because that's what suits me and the leader of what exactly?"

"You know, the sisters, the other witches, I don't know."

"Oh Annie, we don't need a leader. We are sisters. Sisters don't need someone to tell them what to do or when to do it or how much to do it. Sisters know what needs to be done, and they just do it. It's men that need leaders. Otherwise, with them it's all flexing and posturing. They will run around like chickens in a rainstorm unless someone tells them what they should do. No, child. I am known as Eldest because I am the oldest. Old beyond what you might possibly imagine. I am no one's leader, nor do I have one. And I am not mean either, in spite of how you feel right now. Now try again, please."

With a sigh, Annie followed Circe's instructions and gazed into the fire, watching the smoke curl and waver. Trying to listen to the voice of the flames as she had been instructed. In the ten days since Annie had saved her father's life, she had tried to find the power within her that had helped her do it. She had tried over and over to repeat the events that had saved her father's life. She had not been successful and Circe' had coaxed her relentlessly. She closed her eyes already feeling the futility of another try. As hard as she tried, she could not connect with that thing inside of her that had created it. Occasionally, she sensed it just at the edge of her consciousness, but it would run away. The harder she pursued it, the faster it retreated. It was exhausting for her, and Circe' seemed unconcerned.

"Do not try to hear with your brain just because you want to. And do not think you will please me just by succeeding either. It is not about you and your success or failure. It is not your ego or how smart you are. It is about listening to all that is around you. Recognizing that there is life in the flames as there is life in all things. That is the thing you call magic, but you are only as touched by the magic in this world as you want to be. You must reach out and touch it for it to become real. The more you try and think your way there, the less likely you will find the way to what you are seeking."

Suddenly, the fire flared up, the flames rising up above their heads as sparks shot up through the smoke. A sudden breeze whipped the smoke into a small cyclone that spun away down the hill.

"Hello the House!" Called Rafer Tate from below.

"They're coming!" Annie's face sprouted an excited grin as she jumped to her feet.

Annie raced down the hill to meet them.

"Oh Dad! You shouldn't be out running around. You should be resting." And then, touching his chest, "Are you okay? I've missed you Dad."

"I'm doing fine Annie, thanks to you really." He smiled weakly, "Although the stuff that Circe' is making me drink regularly is 'harshing my buzz' as you young people say." And then in a whisper. "It's awful stuff."

"He insisted," Rafer explained. "I didn't think he was up to it, but he just said we could carry him if it got to be too much. He really wanted to see you, Annie."

"Oh, I don't care, I'm really happy to see you. Can I

133

give you a hug, is that all right?"

"I'm doing okay dear. I'm not made out of Elspeth's fine china, but no hugs just yet if you don't mind."

"Greetings Eldest." All three men touched their foreheads.

"So? You think the potion that is saving your life is 'awful stuff'?" Circe' never raised her head from what she was doing.

"Forgive me Eldest, I meant no disrespect."

"What you mean is you didn't think I could hear you. Ah well, it is the burden of the healers to never receive credit for their efforts. That 'awful stuff' as you call it will mend you faster Guardian, don't complain."

She set aside her garlic bulbs and string.

"Greetings warriors. The sun will bring some real heat today. Michael you should not be out in it once it warms up. Although you are looking well, if I do say so, for an old man."

The four finished their climb and lowered Mike Abbott onto the bench. With a sigh he leaned back and smiled up into the sun.

"I know Eldest and I am grateful. Thank you. I am better every day."

Rafer smiled down at Annie. "So? How's it going?"

"She is a stubborn one to be sure."

"You don't have to tell me." Mike Abbott smiled, "I've had almost thirteen years of stubborn."

"I'm not stubborn in the least. How can you say that? I'm really trying Dad, I just don't..." She was suddenly holding back tears. "I just don't know what I'm supposed to be looking for."

"Easy now little one," Rafer reached down and touched her shoulder, immediately Annie

felt calmness rush over her. "You're going to get this; it's just wrong to try. It is like speaking a different language. You begin to recognize different markers, just like learning different words."

"Yes, that's exactly right," Gabe joined in, "the more you're exposed to the new language, you start to think in that language. It gets easier and easier."

"You guys talk about it. You even say that I've done it, even though I don't remember doing it myself, and I've seen you guys in my visions of you, but I've never actually seen it. You know, actually seen this 'magic'."

"It's not magic Youngest. It is the fabric of life. Life lived, and lives lived. It is a tapestry that is woven all around us in waves upon waves of lives, their passions, their loves, swirling around us caressing us with their beauty and knowledge." Circe' spoke with a radiant smile. "I think that is enough lesson for the day today. Raphael, I would like you to share your vision of the 'Dream Walker' please. The one that started this journey, if you please. I do not believe any of us have seen it in its entirety."

"Annie too?"

"Most especially Annie."

"Alright." Rafer stood up and faced Annie across the fire. "Annie, we are all descended from an almost endless line of ancestors. Some of them were wise beyond words, some were great leaders, some were warriors, and yet some others were none of those things. As one of the Three, these things that are remembered by them are handed down from one to the next. When the need is dire, they will often use us to carry a message. That is what I'm about to show you."

"What? Are you going to put it in my head like the other ones did?"

"No, I think a little, what you call magic, would be nice. Gabe? A little help please."

Gabe rose from the bench next to Mike Abbott, "Need some special effects?"

"That would be most helpful."

Gabriel didn't move, or change his expression, but suddenly Annie felt that the skies began to darken. Clouds rushed in from the west, and a cold wind raced down the mountain side, stirring the fire.

"Mike, how about you?"

"Okay, how's this?" Mike Abbott leaned forward, concentrating on the little campfire.

The fire that had almost died suddenly flared again, rising to the height of a man before sinking into embers and a thick smoke rose in its place. As the smoke rose a vision began to take shape within it. A hologram in the smoke took the form of a man standing before them. Slowly the spirit took shape looking down at Annie from within the smoke and flame. Tall and gaunt but with the face of Rafer Tate, he spoke to them in a deep haunting voice.

I am Talks-with-a-smile, and I am one of the first nations. I am old now, but it was not always so. Because I am old, I have many scars from when I was not so old. Because of my scars I know many things, but I also know that I do not know many other things.

I go out into the darkness of the morning and watch the rising of the morning star. When I see it many

136

things that seemed confusing during the time of the moon become less troubling, and I learn many new things.

It was in the time of the new grass and the snows had gone to the north that I went out to welcome the morning star. But when I looked to the east the sky was dark, and the light was slow to come. The sky was boiling and angry light danced inside of it. A light wind blew into one ear and then blew into the other and it whispered to me, but I could not understand the words for they were mixed up.

I thought that I must go to the top of the hill nearby and taste the wind where it blew stronger and I could hear the message that it told within it. I stood on the hill and faced the east, and the wind blew only a little stronger. It whispered and I listened hard. The wind told me that a storm was coming. It told me that it would be fierce and that it would bring danger with it. It told me that when the wind blew, I should stand tall against it. It told me when the skies poured its anger upon me that I should stand tall. It told me that when the lightning flashed that I should stand tall or I would become a part of the storm.

I told my people of the message that I had heard in the wind. Some listened and began to prepare for the fierce storm. Others laughed and told me that I was a foolish old man, but the storm came. It swept in from the east which was strange for storms usually were brought by the spirits of the west and are good for they bring the tall grass and the water to fill our streams and rivers. But this storm was stronger than any that I had seen before. It was so strong that many cried out, *and they made offerings to the storm to save them.*

I reminded them that they must stand tall and not be afraid or that they would become the storm. Some listened and stood tall with me. Others beat their breasts and lamented, not understanding why the spirits would punish them. One by one they became the storm and raged with it and were swept away. I stood tall, and although I beheld the storm all around me the storm had no strength against me.

The storm raged for days until all that lamented became the storm. Only then did the storm fade away. I stood tall.

Many things that I had known disappeared in the storm, and many things in my world were different after the storm than they had been before and I had many new things to learn.

The vision in the smoke faded and the smoke sank into the ashes of the fire.

"Now that's magic!" Annie was delighted with the little show. "Wow!"

"Or an illusion, maybe a bit of both." Mike smiled at her.

"What did it mean?" She looked around as the skies once again cleared and the sunshine returned. "What does it mean?"

"Well, that's a bit of a puzzler." Mike adjusted himself on the bench. "'Talks-with-a-Smile' lived at least a hundred years ago. He was one of the First Nations as he says, so probably a Cree. For him, the storm from the east was probably the push of the white men pouring across their lands. That storm, if it's what he was talking about was huge and heartbreaking. It engulfed all who opposed it, but many that didn't let those winds of change affect their inner spirits prevailed. Although everything about their world changed, they did not. Apparently, he was one of those. But why it matters today, is the question, and why was it important that we know it?"

"There is little doubt that there are changes being carried on the wind. I have felt it for some time now." Rafer added. "'Tis an ill wind that blows nobody to good', as the poet once said. It feels wrong this wind of change."

"Something has changed that's for sure. Just the fact that the Seeker has come of age while still so young in years is more than enough evidence to support that theory." Circe' added, "It would seem the time we have to prepare is short. Let's try something different, and maybe have a little fun too. Annie? Sound good?"

"What would that be exactly? I'm not sure I want to just say okay anymore."

"Please bring out your stones. Let's see if they have anything to tell us."

"I don't understand. Since that one time in the lighthouse at Raspberry Island they've just been pretty rocks again." It seemed like a very long time ago that she had stood in the lighthouse with Allegra and seen the power of the stones for the first time. Annie dug into her pocket and drew out the five little agates. "They don't light up anymore."

"We shall see. Let us have a look. Please throw them into the fire Annie."

"What? Why?"

"They may be ready to behave a little differently

with all of us gathered."

Still Annie hesitated, not anxious to give up the beautiful little rocks.

"Go ahead Annie. They were made in the fire a long time ago, let's see if they remember anything about it." Mike Abbott was curious as well.

Annie was still not too sure. She had become attached to the pretty little gemstones; she didn't want to lose them.

"Go ahead Annie, we can get them back once the fire has cooled."

Annie leaned forward and tossed them into the center of the hot and glowing embers. Nothing happened.

"Listen to the fire Annie, hear the life within it."

Annie narrowed her gaze, and focused on the wavering flames. Suddenly, she sensed something else that she hadn't felt before. She concentrated harder, looking deeper than she had before. Suddenly, a form began to take shape in the dancing heat.

"I see something!"

The flame grew, and the fire flared. Rising again, but without heat, the firelight bright as the noonday sun. It took shape again but this time instead of smoke it was wrapped in the flaming light.

"Greetings Circe', eldest of all. Well met my sister of old."

The vision of a tall woman stood before them, radiant in long robes of deep sky blue, trimmed in gold. She faced the old woman, touched her forehead and bowed slightly.

"And greetings to the Three assembled once again

in time of need."

Finally, the figure turned to Annie, and their eyes met.

"Hail Seeker. I have awaited your arrival for many ages." Again she touched her forehead and bowed. From beneath her flowing robes she drew forth a great sword. Raising it she held it outward with both hands. *"Seek the keeper who guards the Grimoire, the time of struggle is upon you, as in ages long past, the Black Prince will battle once again."*

The vision sank into the small fireplace, leaving only cold grey ash. The fire had gone out, the ashes dead and cold, in the midst, the five golden stones still shone in the morning light.

ISABELLE AND MICHAEL NELSON

The Black Prince

After the blaze of light from the vision in the stones, the sunlight seemed dim in comparison. Annie tried blinking away the blind spot it had created in her vision. All of the five sat leaning forward, all slightly dazzled by the vision they had just witnessed.

"What was that!"

"The better question Seeker is who."

"Morgan Le Fey? Right?"

"Yes, and from the appearance of her clothing, I would say from around the fourteenth century, if I was to guess. Right around the time of Edward of Woodstock's death." Mike Abbott couldn't resist the history in anything.

"The fourteenth century? Seriously, why so long-ago Dad?"

"Well pumpkin, as far as anyone knows, early accounts of the Faery Queen predate modern history. There are written accounts of her from the first century onward to contemporary times, but there are almost no actual encounters documented in the last millennia. At least of a verifiable kind."

"Wow! She was beautiful! I've never seen such a beautiful gown!"

"Not was, Annie, is." Rafer smiled at her.

"What? How is that even possible?"

"Because of you, Miss Annie, the Faery Queen once again walks the earth." Gabe had been silent until now.

"You guys keep talking about that, but I...I don't think I want the job. Can we just give all that stuff a rest?"

"Suit yourself, but you'll find out soon enough." Circe' said softly. The expression on her face spoke of fear and concern.

"Wait. What? Why'd you say that that way?"

"The Black Prince has been summoned. The battle approaches. We have no time."

"Who is the Black Prince?" Annie looked around like the danger was right behind her. "Is he one of the 'Others'?"

"It is time, I think. I was reluctant, but this has changed the need. They are upon us it seems. We must leave this place." Circe' rose from her place and hurried into the cabin. She returned shortly with a long object wrapped in burlap. Unwinding the swaddling revealed a beautifully tooled leather scabbard and the handle of an ornate hand-and-a-half sword. "The time for the Black Prince has once again come."

"Wait a minute! That's a sword; what the *heck*?"

"Yes, the Black Prince will be drawn forth again."

"I...I can't. I won't handle that thing. Circe' honestly, a sword?"

"Yes, a sword. Fear not little one. It is not your weapon; it is for the 'Three'. The formidable weapon of the ancients."

Annie was struggling to keep up. She looked from one of them to the next. Their faces were set in a grim countenance. This was not a joke. They were deadly serious.

"Swords? Seriously? They have guns! They've shot my dad already!"

"It is not just a sword Annie. It has a history as long as that of the Three. It is the sword of Alexander the Great, Excalibur of the Lake, and the sword of the Black Prince himself." Mike Abbott leaned toward and smiled a sad smile. "I am sorry that this has come to you my love. The time has come to a serious subject. Allow your old man, and professor of archaic history to elaborate."

"The Black Prince was actually Edward of Woodstock, eldest son of Edward III, King of England and Brittany, and heir to the throne of both England and France, because his mother was Phillippa, primary in the ascendancy of that country as well. He was also rumored to have a Druid mistress.

"He was fearsome in battle and undefeated in almost thirty years of warfare. And that was during the Hundred Years War, so quite a feat. During the later purges of the Druids, Edward took a more relaxed posture toward those that practiced the arts. As such, they gifted him with a wonderful sword, an enchanted sword that would never dull, that fought with the will of its master, and protected him from harm in battle. The Black Prince was feared across the continents—and respected and so Edward took the name of the sword as his own."

"What happened to him?" Annie was captivated.

"As time went by, Edward continued to consolidate his holdings and the business of diplomacy. His power and strength grew and those that had helped him in the beginning became inconvenient. He ignored their advice and wisdom. Finally, he turned on them and began to hunt them because he coveted their wisdom and the power of Morgan. The Druids went back into hiding and disappeared once again. Edward, the Black Prince, was never able to take the throne. Although he was never defeated in battle thanks to the enchanted sword of the Druids. However, he could not escape the times he lived in. He suddenly and mysteriously took ill and died of dysentery while still in his prime. He is buried at Canterbury Cathedral with his armor. All except for his sword, the Black Prince, which could not be found."

"Did they kill him? Is this that sword?"

"That first question is lost to the ages, but yes the sword is the same."

"When did he live?"

"The Black Prince died in the late 1300's."

"So? This thing is seven-hundred years old?"

Circe' laughed, "Oh child, this 'thing' as you call it, this instrument of justice is as old as I am. Truly, it was with Alexander in Mesopotamia; it was with the Hun that descended on ancient Rome, none other than Arthur, King of the Britains, carried it into battle after Morgan presented it to him herself, long before Edward of Woodstock walked the earth."

"Do we have to fight with swords?"

"Guardian?"

Mike Abbott rose painfully to his feet. Even as he reached for the hilt he began to change in appearance. Gabriel and Rafer stepped close, each reaching for the hilt together. All three hands touched the sword at the same moment. Again, the shock wave of their mutual contact resonated outward. Instead of the three, only one stood in front Annie. As the figure drew the sword from the scabbard there was a flash of light and the sword flamed alive. Before her stood a huge heavily muscled warrior, the flaming Hand and a half-handed sword in one hand and a long dagger in the other. A burnished shield hung down his back. His eyes glowed with an unholy light. Throwing his head back and raising the sword over its head it roared aloud, the deafening howl echoing off the distant hills and ringing through the valley.

"Aaarrgh! At last! The battle is joined!"

The figure's face was fluid first Michael, then the face of Gabriel and Raphael. Bringing the sword down he planted it between his feet, knelt and bowed his head to Annie.

"The Black Prince is drawn in defense and never again drawn in anger. Here Seeker, is the strength of the Three. The power of the sword and their own is too great to carry in only one man."

"Oh my god, where's my dad? This is too scary. I can't do this. I can't…I just can't do this." Annie felt like she needed to run away and run as fast and as far as she could. The anxiety and fear making her almost ready to jump out her own skin. She closed her eyes hoping it would all disappear.

"Return Guardian!"

When Annie opened her eyes, the warrior was gone. In his place again stood the Three, the sword rested safely in its scabbard on the lap of Circe' as it had before. Circe' looked at her with sad eyes.

"We have waited ages upon ages for your arrival Seeker, but it is not an easy road ahead and I am sorry that it has come to your door. You must prepare; you must try harder."

"I told you, I can't. It's not there, and I'll never find it. All this hocus pocus isn't making it any easier. I mean it, it's just not there."

"Maybe a little boost would help. Should we give it a try Eldest?"

"A boost? Why yes, that's a good idea Gabriel. Let's give her a little assistance."

"A boost?"

"Well sure Annie, wouldn't you like to let us give you a little boost?"

"That is an excellent idea. Guard your strength though Michael, do not overtax yourself." Circe' smiled and nodded.

"Yes Eldest." Then turning to Annie, "You're looking for something but at the same time you're not sure what it is that you're looking for. It's hard to find something when you don't know what it is, or what it looks or feels like. We can give you a little boost, so you might be able to look a little more specifically."

"Okaaay?"

"The kind of power that you are looking for exists

in a different place than your thoughts or feelings. Think of it as a bookshelf. Your body and how it works is used all the time so it is on a shelf that's easy to reach for your consciousness. Your thoughts then are on the next higher shelf, handy but you still have to reach for them. Then this 'thing' that you're looking for right now, would be on the top shelf. On a different level, a different plane. We can help you to know what you're looking for, or at least what it feels like. What d'ya say Annie?"

"I don't want to faint again, but okay."

"I think we can help you avoid that unpleasantness too. Let's see. Tell you what, turn around. Yes, now look up at Circe' and relax. Think about what you are looking for and don't be afraid for just a minute. Okay?"

Annie faced up the hill and looked at the old woman who returned the look. She tried to focus on the forces that she had touched. Three hands touched her shoulders in unison—immediately her eyesight seemed sharper, colors brighter. Then, her vision lifted, rising higher and higher until she was looking down at the ground from a great height. Higher and higher her vision rose into the air, turning from one horizon to the other. Below her the small cabin, with smoke trailing from the chimney and the old woman shading her eyes as she looked up at her. Just below the woman on the hillside, four figures, three men and a woman stood clad for battle. The men each with weapons drawn, the woman a burnished shield on her left arm, wearing a leather hauberk and brandishing a two-handed sword with both hands. As she watched, the warrior woman raised the sword in salute toward her. Her vision sank swiftly, approaching the warrior woman, and then her vision blended and became that of the woman's. Together their mutual vision looked out at the ancient crone standing near the cabin door as one.

"The Raven! The Raven flies again! Behold the Warrior Queen of the Druids! At last."

As the Three withdrew their hands, Annie's vision remained. She felt strength flow into her body. She looked all around her with different vision, seeing detail that she hadn't noticed before. Her thoughts were clear, without considering beforehand whether she should speak or not, she spoke, and when she did, she spoke with the voice of great authority.

"We must seek the Grimoire and find the keeper. Haste is needed. They are at our door. Eldest you must accompany us; we must find the keeper."

Circe' touched her forehead and bowed her head. "So mote it be."

Turning to the three men, she spoke again. "They are at our doorstep. Defend your queen; I so order it."

The Three turned as one and supporting Mike between them, raced away down the hill and into the woods below.

Circe' hurried into the small cabin. When she reappeared a few moments later, she was no longer the old woman of moments before. Before Annie once again stood the warrior Queen of Aeaea, dressed in a loose denim work shirt, stylish blue jeans, and heavily soled boots. Her thick black hair was pulled into a tight ponytail under a worn baseball cap. She carried an automatic pistol on one hip and had shouldered a knapsack over one arm. Snatching up her walking stick, she turned uphill.

Speaking over her shoulder to Annie, "Come my child, the race has begun."

From the woods below the sound of gunfire erupted.

Fire on the Mountain

As the sound of gunfire intensified in the woods below, a stiff, cold fog rushed down from the mountainside above on an icy breeze. Autumn leaves of gold and brown swirled about clattering and racing across their path making an unholy racket. Dark clouds began gathering over the early afternoon sun. Circe' moved quickly up the steep hillside and toward the tree line above the cabin. Carrying a heavy knapsack and climbing with a long walking stick. Her long strides had Annie struggling to keep up almost immediately.

Annie had often been frightened over the last few weeks, but now she was terrified. Everyone that she knew and loved was in danger for their life, and it was all somehow because of her. Worst of all, they were not the only ones in danger—so was she. The ones searching for her wanted to capture her, and make her their prisoner. They didn't seem to care that people might be hurt or even killed. What made it all the more frightening was that she had no idea who they were.

Once they entered the trees, Circe' stopped and crouched down. Looking back the way they had come.

"We are not followed—at least for now."

Once they reached the shelter of the trees and entered the dense forest, the cold wind calmed somewhat, and the air was alive with swarms of dragonflies and butterflies. They flitted back and forth in front of them, their gossamer wings rattling and buzzing. For Annie, who was trying to focus on what Circe' was looking and listening for, they were an annoying distraction and she waved her arms trying to shoo them away. Her efforts were rewarded by even more of them collecting in her vision.

"What is the matter with these stupid things?! They're everywhere here."

"They know our danger. They are here to help." Circe' spoke over her shoulder, never taking her eyes away from where they had just come.

"What? These dragonflies? How can they help us?"

"Remember what I said back at the fire. It is not your ego or how smart you are. It is about listening to all that is around you. Recognizing that there is life in the flames as there is life in all things. That is the thing you call magic, but you are only as touched by the magic in this world as you want to be. You must reach out and touch it for it to become real. It is time that you begin to touch the magic."

"Seriously?! We're running for our lives and I'm supposed to *'reach out and touch the magic'*? I can't think of anything right now except how scared I am and if my dad's okay. I can't even imagine magic right now."

"STOP YOUR WHINING!"

"What? Who said that?"

*"Look closely, it is time my queen. We must away, you **must** look more closely."*

Directly in front of Annie, a dragonfly hovered only inches away from her face.

"Look more closely."

Annie gazed at the hovering insect, and as she concentrated, its appearance began to change. Instead of the gauzy winged insect she had been seeing, a tiny figure was now suspended there floating on feathery wings.

"What?! How?" Annie stepped back to gain some distance. "Who?"

"I am Patch of the forest realm. We are here to help you. You are no longer safe here."

"What are you?"

"They are the fair folk, the fey of old times and called fairies today. They are part of your realm. They can guide us to safety." Circe' spoke from her crouch without looking back at her.

"Is that true?"

"Yes, my queen. We are here to serve you Morgana of old, Anne of present." Patch made a small hovering bow to her and touched her forehead.

"I'm afraid. I don't know what to do. I want to run as far away as I can, and I'm afraid for my dad, and Rafer and Gabriel. I'm so afraid."

"You must follow. We must hurry. There is no time."

Below them down the mountain side, a bolt of lightning flashed from the sky and struck the ground. The explosion of thunder only moments behind it.

"You must run Anne of Present, follow the glow to safety."

"Show us the way Patch." Circe' stood and unholstered her pistol, "We'll follow."

The small fairy turned gracefully in the air, within

moments she began to glow. Soon she was a bright blue light on fairy wings. All around her, other blue glows appeared in the air.

"Follow the glow to safety."

The blue glows moved away forming a line across the mountain's face.

"Hurry my queen."

Annie started to follow them but sensing that Circe was not behind her she turned around. Circe was crouched down in the dense brush, looking back the way they had come, her pistol drawn and ready.

"Aren't you coming Eldest?"

"You go—RUN! If they try to follow you, I'll give them something they will definitely regret! Now go, I'll catch up."

"They are coming, hurry Anne of Present."

Anne turned and started to follow the line of blue lights that disappeared deeper into the forest. She turned and looked one last time at Circe' concealed in her hiding place. She seemed to fear nothing, and Annie was almost paralyzed with fear.

"Faster Anne of Present, we must move faster."

Down the mountainside another bolt of lightning flashed out of the sky, followed by a deafening clap of thunder.

Annie followed the hovering fairies, afraid of what was in front of her and terrified of what was behind her. Running behind them as they flew faster and deeper into the dense trees. First, they raced across the steep slope, and then turning to her right they began a gradual descent downhill. Although, they guided her carefully, the dense underbrush pulled at her clothing and scratched at her face as she pushed through it. The effort had her panting, gasping for breath in the thin mountain air. Patch stayed just above her shoulder matching her pace and speaking encouragement.

"You'll be safe with us Anne of Present; we know of a place."

Behind her multiple gunshots erupted. Annie almost collapsed at the sound, knowing that now Circe' was also fighting for her own life as well as Annie's.

"Oh my God! This is too much; I can't do this."

"You must do this, and there is no time. The fey will help her. For now, we must flee my queen."

Breaking through a particularly dense patch of brush she beheld a gathering of the glowing fairies. They hovered together over a small opening in the side of a jagged cliff face.

"Here, you must enter here. You will be safe for a while. We will watch."

"What? In there? It's so small and it's dark in there! What if there's a bear or something?"

"There is no danger here." Patch came closer and touched her shoulder. *"We will stay with you. Come."* He dropped down and disappeared into the opening, then reappearing. *"Please hurry Anne of Present."*

Annie dropped down onto her knees and crawled through the opening. The floor of the small cave was dry and sandy. Within several feet she entered a wide room where several glowing fairies hovered, illuminating the space. The sounds from outside were distant and muffled.

"You must wait here until it is safe. You must be

brave."

Annie paced back and forth in the small room.

"I'm trying! Honest, I'm really trying to be brave. But this is insane, six months ago I was a 7th grade junior high school student. Since then, everything has gone crazy. First, we're digging up old gravestones, then they are actually speaking to me. That was nuts! But then it got worse, then there were witches and magic and visions and…and…I'm going crazy…or maybe I already am crazy. Now I'm sitting in a cave, in the mountains, in the middle of nowhere Wyoming with little glowing things that I know don't even exist, and my father and his friends are actually fighting for their lives—for real, fighting for their lives."

"We are all fighting to exist Anne of Present. And fight we will, but for now you must be brave." Patch again hovered facing her. In her hand she held a tiny sword. *"This is one dragonfly that has a sting. We fight for you my lady, and but we also fight for ourselves."*

The small warrior moved closer and touched her forehead. *"I must go for now, but will return soon. Some will stay and keep you safe, but be at peace for now."*

With that she turned and disappeared out through the cave entrance. Alone in the cave, Annie dropped to her knees and began to cry. Her sobs grew until she was crying with hiccups and gasping for breath between each one. The gathering of fairies drew close, each one touching her in different places. As they did, Annie's sobs gradually lessened, tapering off into a few sniffles. Suddenly deeply tired, she found it hard to keep her eyes open. Lying down on the smooth sand floor she closed her eyes and was instantly asleep. The glowing fairies found places to rest against her and on her. Surrounding her with peace.

Flight of the Heroes

Annie was roused from her deep sleep by a gentle touch on her shoulder. In the dim blue light of the stone-lined room Circe' smiled down at her, her wet hair clinging to both sides of her face.

"Come child, it is time to go."

"You're okay, oh my God, I was so scared. I'm so glad to see you. I was alone and afraid. Oh god, I'm so really glad to see you. Are you okay?"

"Fine. They'll have to try a little harder if they want to get past me. Unfortunately, they probably will next time. So, it's time for you and I to get away, before they do try again."

"But my dad, and Rafe and Gabe, what about them?"

"They have their tasks before them. We must trust in their strength. Gather yours now; we have another sprint in front of us."

"But they're out there, aren't they?"

"Not at this moment, but they will be soon. We have a small window of escape, and we must take it."

"But where?"

"Trust me for now, and Patch."

"Patch?"

"Yes, Patch. She is very brave."

The tiny fairy, appeared in front of her. She gestured toward the cave opening.

"We have stung a few, but alas it has come with a cost. Two of us will not return. But we slowed their advance. The Three fight on. Follow me my lady, I am ready."

As if to punctuate the little warrior's statement the sound of thunder reached their ears from outside.

"Who are they? Tell me please?"

"Most are human, one is not."

"I'm afraid she's right it would seem."

"Not human? What does that mean, not human?"

"That's a conversation for another time Annie. Right now we fly. Patch, you know the way."

"We will not be safe until we are away, far away."

"So then—let's go. Ready Annie? We've got this; we'll try the best we can to keep you safe."

She turned and dove into the small cave opening. Annie stood for a moment, hoping for a better solution. Patch flitted in front of her. Without words she scowled, pointed into the dark opening, and then shook her fist. Annie dropped to her knees and crawled out into freezing rain.

Darkness had fallen while she had slept and in the deep dark of the high mountains she could barely see her hand in front of her face. But she could feel icy rain as it pelted her face. Once again, a line of small blue lights disappeared down the slope.

She could just make out Circe' in front of her as they plunged into the darkness. Again, Patch followed with her, whispering encouragement.

"Not much farther. You are being very brave."

"Yeah? Really?" she panted, "I'm not brave like you Patch."

"I have fought many battles in my six-hundred years. I will fight many more."

"Really?"

"Yes, Patch is a warrior."

"No, I meant you're really six-hundred years old?" Annie had thought that Patch looked like a teenager.

"I have fought many battles in my six-hundred eighty-seven years, one month, and three days. I will fight many more."

Twenty minutes later, after a terrifying downhill run through the brambles and brush, Annie almost walked into the back of Circe'. She had stopped at the edge of the forest. Just ahead of them across an open field lay the small gathering of buildings where the healer's house was. One of the small homes was on fire. Circe' held up her hand to stop.

"Wait for it. Are you sure Patch?"

"Yes, any moment now Eldest."

A small but fiery explosion erupted into the air off to their left.

"That's it?! Patch? That's all?!"

"It was the best we could do on such short notice Eldest," Tiny Patch shrugged.

"Well, for better or worse, it's what we got. Let's

go!"

The tall woman broke from the trees and raced across the open space.

"Run Anne of Present!"

Annie had stopped trying to make sense of anything, but she knew Patch was right. She jumped from the trees and ran faster than she ever had. Ahead of her, Circe' reached the first building and leaned against it, beckoning Annie to more speed.

When she arrived, Circe' whispered, "Good job. One more will tell the tale."

She slid along the outside of shed and peeked around the corner. Turned the corner and disappeared into the dark. Seconds later she reappeared and beckoned, "Hurry."

Annie copied Circe's actions sliding to the corner and peeking around. Circe' stood holding open the door of the small shed and pointed Annie into it. As soon as she was inside, Circe joined her, both of them catching their breath.

"We are not detected."

As she stripped the water out of her hair and began to shiver in her cold wet clothes something touched her from behind.

Annie gave a shriek. "Oh my god, something's in here! It's trying to get me!

"It's okay Annie, it's Bracken. Just relax. Patch help me find the light switch in here, will you please."

Two dim incandescent light bulbs snapped on, illuminating the inside of the shed. In the center sat the bright red Maserati belonging to Elspeth, the White Witch. Directly at Annie's feet crouched a huge black wolf, bowing its head and slowly wagging its tail.

"Thank you, Bracken for keeping a watch. We must leave as quickly as possible." Circe' dropped to her knees in front of the huge canine. "I need you to take a message to the Three, if you please?"

The shaggy black animal rose to its feet, its shoulders reaching a height almost to Annie's chest, his massive head at the same level as hers. Turning away from Circe', the beast approached Annie. Annie could see that he was no threat, or danger, but the sheer size of him made her want to back away. Bracken's yellow eyes looked directly into Annie's, then he dropped onto his front paws in a deep bow.

"Bracken and his kind are also part of your realm Youngest. He answers only to you."

"That is true my queen." A deep voice rumbled across Annie's brain. "We serve the 'One', we rejoice in your rising."

"We must go, someone will see the light."

"Yes, we must. Bracken my friend, can you carry a message to the Three?"

"I will do the lady's bidding." The deep voice again echoed in Annie's brain.

"Tell them that we will make for the Hedge Witch in the Dell. They must try and rendezvous with us there if they are able. We will not wait for them until we are safely there ourselves."

"I will carry your message."

"Good. I thank the Lord of the True Brothers. Now we must make haste."

Circe' stepped briskly to the front doors of the shed and shoved them open. Then sprinted to the driver's side of the car.

"Quickly Annie, get in. They'll know where we are now. Get in and hurry."

Annie pulled open the door of the super car and climbed in. The door had barely closed when the mighty engine roared to life. Without waiting for it to warm up, Circe' shoved the pedal down and the car almost shot out of the shed into the dark night and into a sliding turn. Wheels spinning, grass and mud flying.

"Now that's what I'm talking about!" Circe' actually smiled in delight. "Let's see what this bad boy can really do!"

With the engine screaming with delight, and the windshield wipers flashing at high speed, Circe' turned the car toward the road out of the settlement. The tires threw up a rooster tail of grass and mud as the car fishtailed through yards and around the many small homes, before burning rubber when they hit the pavement of the road. Annie now understood why the seatbelts were made to be tight and the deep bucket seats were so soft as she was pressed back into the leather.

"Oh yeah, thank you Elspeth! I'm never giving this back to you; I love this thing!"

The powerful car hugged the curves and corners like a Grand Prix race car and flew down the straight-away as Circe' pushed its performance.

"Wow! It doesn't even feel like a hundred and twenty. I can't wait until we're off these mountain roads so we can really see what it's capable of."

"A hundred and twenty miles-per-hour?"

"Not consistently, the roads are too windy."

"We should hope to survive, perhaps a little safety would be good?" Patch had taken a seat on the headrest of Annie's seat. Until she spoke, Annie had momentarily forgotten about the tiny warrior.

"Patch! I'm ashamed of you. I thought you liked to go fast." Circe' said sarcastically

"I would like to live a few more minutes as well. Perhaps if you turned on the headlights so that we could see the road a little better, I would feel a little more safe."

"Oops, I totally forgot. Let's see, where is that switch, Ahh here it is."

The powerful headlight beams reached out into the night, turning the highway into daylight for a quarter-mile ahead of them.

"I can't believe you were driving one-hundred and twenty miles an hour, in the dark, with the headlights off and we're still alive."

"It's nothing really, if you're tuned in to your surroundings, and believe me I've had lots of practice, you know where the road is even if you can't see it."

"She is incorrigible. She was just showing off."

"Oh Patch, it's been a very long day and a longer night. Let's try and find some fun in it somewhere. Okay?"

The drive that had taken two hours the last time Annie had been on it, only took Circe' forty-five minutes to recover. As they approached the outskirts of Laramie, they drove out from under the overcast sky and saw the light of the new day growing in the east.

"We have to gas up before we can go any further.

This should be fun, hope I'm not too rusty."

"What does that mean?"

"Watch and learn little one, watch and learn."

They slowed and pulled the sports car off the road into an all-night service station. Several cars and trucks were in the lot, as early workers stopped for a quick breakfast or cup of coffee before heading off to work. Circe' pulled up to the gas pumps and shut down the engine, but not before it had caught the attention of most of the men at the counter inside.

"How do I look?"

Annie looked across at Circe' and blinked her eyes. Seated in the driver's seat was again one of the most beautiful women she had ever seen. Her thick black hair cascaded down over her shoulders, her denim shirt was neatly ironed and open at the throat, and somehow her makeup was suddenly perfect. In place of her lugged hiking boots, she wore stylish boots with a two-inch heel.

"What? How did you do that?"

Circe' gave a small smirk. "It's just an illusion, young one. But it's a fun one, so watch and learn."

She threw open the door and setting one heeled shoe on the ground. Inside the restaurant, every stool at the counter had swiveled to watch who or what was getting out of the amazing super car. When Circe' stood up they were not disappointed. She dropped the wing door of the shiny super car, and strode to the entrance. Everyone at the counter swiveled back pretending to not be interested, but there was no conversation going on when Circe' entered.

Striding to the counter she took a seat at the far end

away from the men. The waitress, was in no hurry to see what she wanted, but Circe' remained patient. Eventually she wandered down with a coffee urn in her hand. A name tag pinned below her left shoulder announced her name was Charlotte.

"Coffee?"

"Yes please, with cream if you don't mind."

"Coming right up, would you like a menu or just coffee?"

"Just coffee, I've been getting a little sleepy." The coffee splashed into a cup and

stopped just short of running over the rim of the cup. "I'm driving down from Casper and I have to be in Denver before noon today, so I can't take too long a break."

"Oh, you goin' down for business or pleasure?"

"If all goes well, both I hope."

"It's still quite a way down there, hope this coffee's strong enough for you."

"I've got a little boost, that I carry with me."

"What do you mean." Charlotte's eyes narrowed.

Circe' reached into her shirt pocket and pulled out a small vial. She opened it and

dropped two drops from it into her coffee cup. As the level of the coffee adjusted itself, she stirred in cream from a small cup into it as well, she set down her spoon, and making eye contact with the waitress she took a sip.

"Ah, that's just so good! I love this stuff. It just makes everything better."

"Oh? What's in that? It didn't look like you put very

much in there."

"It only takes a couple of drops and it changes the taste. It makes it taste like you're putting something delicious in your mouth and just makes me feel so good about the day ahead. Would you like to try it?" Circe' made eye contact with Charlotte. "I'm sure you would, wouldn't you?"

Charlotte's eyes went blank, and for a second she didn't respond, but eventually, "Yes, yes I want to taste your coffee. Let me taste your coffee." She stated almost robot-like.

"Certainly, here you go. I'll just have another."

Charlotte picked up Circe's cup and took a large mouthful. As she swallowed a look came over her face that spoke of a complete revelation.

"This is amazing! I don't think I've ever tasted any coffee like this. Absolutely amazing."

The men at the other end of the counter had not taken their eyes off of the exchange for a second.

Charlotte wandered back down behind the counter with her coffee urn still in her hand. One by one she refilled the cups of the three men.

"I gotta say boys, you've never tasted coffee anything like what I just did. One of the best tasting things I think I've ever tried."

"Yeah?" One of the big guys spoke up, interested, but still glancing down at Circe'.

"Oh my yes."

"Would you like to try it?" Circe' spoke up from fifteen feet away, swiveling on her stool, she rose and walked down to the three men. "I have plenty."

"Sure."

"I guess."

"If'n I don't like it, can I have a fresh cup Charlotte."

"Sure John, but you're gonna like it, I promise."

Circe' leaned across and carefully dropped three drops from the small vial into each cup. "If I put too much in, it spoils the taste, but three is just right."

In unison, the three burly men sipped the coffee suspiciously. Then as their eyes widened and their eyebrows rose, they took much bigger sips, and finally a full mouthful of the hot and tasty coffee.

"By gosh, that's about the best tasting coffee I have ever put in my mouth!"

"I'll say, can I have some more?"

"Yep, really amazin' is right!"

"Sorry boys, I've gotta get back on the road." Circe' looked at Charlotte. "Check please?"

"No charge." Said Charlotte, "just tasting that coffee was more than worth it."

"Really? Thank you. Can you tell me how to turn on the gas pumps outside? I'm afraid I don't know very much about that sort of thing; I've never pumped my own gas before."

"Let me give you a hand miss. It's my pleasure."

"Yes, let's see if we can help."

"Well, I was in such a hurry to leave this morning because I have to be in Denver before noon today for an important meeting. I rushed out of the house without my purse, and now I don't have any money for gas."

"Let me help you ma'am, how much to you need?" One of the men spoke, his eyes a little glassy.

"I can help too, if you need it. My name's Jake." Jake was already reaching for his wallet.

"Yeah, mine's Tom, let me give you some money just so's you can get by."

Circe's eyes teared up. "Oh thank you, I didn't know what I was going to do. It's too far to go back home without gas, and now I'm stranded."

"Nonsense, we'll be glad to help you," I'm Jim, by the way."

"Oh, how can I ever repay you, thank you so very much. I just didn't know what to do."

"Here's some cash, so you can get some gas for the return trip. Maybe you could stop back in, and we could have a coffee when you come back home."

"That would be so nice. I'd like that. There just aren't very many nice men around anymore, if you know what I mean."

"We know ma'am, but we're nice guys."

"You don't have to call me ma'am. I'm Megan, and now we're friends. Right?" She reached out touched his forearm. "Thank you, boys."

The three men not only pumped the gas, but cleaned the windows, wiped down the head and tail lights, then checked the tire pressures. Finally, they emptied their wallets and gave all the money to her.

"There you are Megan; you're all set."

"Thank you so much. How will I find you when I come back this way?"

The one called Tom reached into his shirt pocket and drew out a business card. This is our number; we all work at the same place. I own it though."

Circe'/Megan took the card and after looking at it,

slid it down into her shirt pocket.

"I'll get in touch as soon as I return. Thank you again."

Back on the highway, Circe' chuckled while she dug the business card out of her shirt.

"That was amazing!"

"She has absolutely no shame." Patch was scandalized.

"Oh come on, we don't have any money, or credit cards. How else are we going to get where we need to go? Besides, I don't get to do that as often as I used to in the old days."

"In the very old days." Patch was still pouting. *"At least you aren't turning them into farm animals like you used to—in the very old days."*

"Okay smart-aleck, next time you take a turn."

"No thank you. Nobody's going to want to give a dragonfly any money."

"Not even one as cute as you?"

Even in the dim light of the dashboard, Annie could see Patch blush.

"Is that true? Did you turn people into farm animals once?"

"Only trespassers, and then I just turned them into pigs specifically. It sent a message to other trespassers, but that was ages upon ages ago. They wrote a couple of popular books about it."

"She was not the nicest person in the world once upon a time."

"And I'm still not when the circumstances call for it Patch, but I've learned better ways to gain what I want." She reached in her pocket and pulled out the small vial and held it up. "I am still the greatest potion and spell master of the past and the present.

"We have somewhere near eight-hundred miles to cover, and cover fast, so lean back and try and get some rest Annie. I can't take the interstate because I don't plan on going the speed limit, so it's going to be a while, but we'll be there before dark. Patch will keep me company, won't you Patch?"

"I'll also try and keep your speed below one-hundred."

"Party pooper."

The Hedge Witch in the Dell

Annie dozed fitfully as Circe' drove, the whine of the powerful engine somehow soothing. She roused occasionally to bright sunshine and long stretches of straight road that ended at the horizon. She doubted that the car ever dropped below a three-digit speed or that Patch minded. The autumn sun was lowering in the western sky when Circe' turned off the road and into a long lane leading down into a thick wood. An ornate wrought iron gate and archway stood at the entrance. As they approached the gate in front of them slowly opened.

"Awake at last?"

"Not entirely. How long have I been sleeping?"

"Almost eight hours Youngest. We couldn't come directly, so I took a few wide detours. But you needed the rest. Things were a little unsettling recently, and I'm sure it was very tiring."

"Unsettling isn't the word I think I would use."

"This is as safe a place as any other in these times. We are at the home of Olivia of the Dell. One of the finest practitioners of herbology and divination that I've ever met. She was also very close with your mother at one time."

"Really?! She knew my mother?" Annie sat forward in the seat, peering ahead now with anticipation. "How is it possible that I've never heard her name mentioned before?"

"Your mother and she had a falling out many years ago, and as far as I know never spoke to each other again after that. I'm sure she'll be very excited to meet you again after so long. Very excited."

"Why is that?"

"Well, she and your mother were extremely close until they weren't. You look very much like your mother. I think you will find you have a lot in common."

"You said she was a 'hedge witch'? What's that?"

"That explanation is a lot longer than this driveway. Let's take it a step at a time and let her show you what it is. Shall we?"

"Yes Eldest."

"That's the spirit. Now in the little time we have left before we get to the house, see if you can do something with that hair of yours, please. I don't think it can find any more directions to fly than it already does."

While Annie struggled to try and arrange her long and tangled hair, the car reached the bottom of the lane and followed a curve to the right where a small cut stone cottage came into view. The roof appeared to be made of lush green sod, and to Annie's amazement and delight several goats grazed on it. In the front yard a riot of flowers in every color bloomed vibrantly behind a snow-white picket fence. To one side of the house, a well-tended garden displayed rich black and weedless soil between the rows of healthy vegetables. The surrounding dense forest grew up to the edge of the property and gave the impression of country comfort and safety.

Leaning against the cottage doorway, an attractive woman of mid-years stood stirring a teacup and watching the approaching car. She did not move as the car stopped near the front gate, nor did she move when the door opened and Circe' stepped out. When Annie climbed out, she smiled and hurried down the stone path and out through the gate.

"At last! Hello Annie, I'm so very excited to see you again. My goodness, look how tall you've become! Come in, come in. I've made a pot of stew and the kettle is on. There's plenty of hot water so that you can get cleaned up if you like as well." When she stood in front of Annie, she touched her forehead and tipped her head, "Well met little sister."

Turning to Circe', "Greetings Eldest. It has been many years."

"Greetings Olivia, we are not pursued as far as I can tell, but they were almost upon us at Wind River before we knew of it. It would seem that they have learned to somehow cloak their activities from us."

"The gate will keep a watch for now."

"We appreciate your hospitality sister. It is only out of dire need that we intrude upon you, but I for one am starving."

"Come in, come in. Annie, I've laid out fresh clothes, and there is a shower out in back. Why don't you get cleaned up and changed while Circe' and I get caught up a little?"

Annie was old enough to recognize that what Olivia was really saying was 'go keep yourself busy while the grownups talk'.

"If you don't mind, um, Olivia; I think I would like to stay and 'get caught up' too."

The two adults exchanged glances, and Circe' nodded.

"That's fine Annie, come on through to the kitchen. I'll make some tea and we'll all catch up for a little while. Circe' I'll fix you a bowl of stew and then we'll see about sleeping arrangements."

Inside the little cottage the walls were gleaming white. Shelves filled with books, jars, plants and candles hung on every wall where there wasn't a window. Comfortable chairs faced each other across the small living room, and a warm fireplace took up an entire wall. Annie's eyes were attracted to a handsome crow that sat on one of the high shelves. The bird, motionless, regarded her with shiny black eyes. It was so realistic that Annie expected it to move at any second, and then it did.

The sleek bird dropped down from the shelf and took a perch on Olivia's shoulder. After arranging its feet, it bobbed its head a few times and then ignored the two guests.

"Don't mind Percy, he's pouting."

"Percy?"

"Yes, this black reprobate is Percy. He's spoiled rotten and is showing off his bad manners."

"What do you mean?"

"Percy, that's enough. We have guests and you must be polite. I mean it. Or you can sleep outside tonight."

The black bird rotated on Olivia's shoulder and turned its back to the guests.

"All right then, out you go. And just because you're being so cantankerous, I'll make sure it starts to rain."

"No! Please don't Olivia! I'm sorry, but you didn't tell me we were having company, and I look a mess!"

"Then mind your manners, and be polite."

The crow had a deep mellow voice when he spoke. He turned again on Olivia's shoulder, bobbed his head again and spoke. "Greetings, ladies of renown, I am Percy and I am most honored to make your acquaintance."

"He doesn't really mean it. He just doesn't want to go outside." Patch laughed.

"Patch! Honestly, I didn't know you were coming too! Oh, this is a special delight. I haven't seen you in…in a very long time."

"It has been seventy-two years, three months, one week and three days. Yes, we had some high times back then, didn't we?"

"Well, time flies doesn't it." Olivia bustled to the stove and began to warm stew and put the kettle on for tea. Annie quickly counted out seventy-plus years on her fingers, shock and incredulity in her expression, shaking her head in disbelief. While Olivia bustled, Percy balanced expertly on her shoulder all the while. And Patch found a convenient shelf nearby to sit and watch.

"I could use a good cup of chamomile, if you've

any?"

"Of course, and even better, Thomasina was here only yesterday and left her teacup. I'll fix one right away. I'm sure once she knows you've arrived, she'll be back quite soon. Her work in the forest seems to keep her quite busy these days. Oh, what a treat for you to see her again."

"It has been a very long time indeed, one-hundred and fifteen years, one month, two weeks and two days. When did Thomasina come to the forests near here?"

"I don't actually know, before my time here certainly."

"I came after the last battle, at Verdun, during the great war of the mortals, WWI. I had had enough of war, and death."

Another small fairy zoomed in through the open window and now hovered in front of Patch. She was dressed in deep forest green from head to toe and wore a leather buckler across her chest. A long bow in one hand and a quiver of tiny arrows slung over one shoulder. With a great smile, she embraced Patch.

"Greetings sister-kind!"

The two hugged, waltzing in the air around the inside of the house, laughing with delight. Percy cawed in unison and everyone for a moment forgot their cares as the two rejoiced in their reunion.

"Come away with me Patch. You must see what we have accomplished here in so little time."

And with that the two disappeared out the window.

"Well, wasn't that unexpected, and fun?" Olivia was still smiling. "They have an entire village farther down the glen. The wood and the greenery are so lush it is almost impossible to get through unless you know the secret ways. It is so wonderfully pleasant having the fairy folk for neighbors."

Filling a large China teapot, she placed it on the table after adding two different tea balls. Opening the oven door, she drew out fresh bread and set it beside the teapot. It had been more than twenty-four hours since either of the travelers had eaten and until then Annie hadn't realized how hungry she was too. Olivia lifted the large stew pot from the stove and set it and three bowls on the table also.

"Come let's break bread, we have much to discuss and it's better done on a full stomach."

For the next ten minutes, no words were spoken while they worked their way through the delicious hearty stew, fresh herbed bread and drank cup after cup of the hot tea. Only when fresh cups had been poured and the bowls and plates had been cleared was it time to talk. Annie watched in fascination as the dishes began to wash themselves and then place themselves in a small drainer next to the sink.

"So, it's the Others again?" Olivia looked across at Circe'.

"Yes, and this time there has been an alliance. The mortals have gained a dangerous ally and I suspect also a leader. They are much stronger and apparently more determined. The Three had their hands full, and there has been no word."

"No, I've had no signs either. They would not allow themselves to be taken, I'm sure."

"They would not allow it, but the silence bothers

me. They are dear to me."

Tears sprang into Annie's eyes, "That's my Dad! Nothing can happen to him, can it? He's too powerful—right?"

"If anyone has ever met Michael Abbott, they cannot help but love him," Olivia met Annie's pleading gaze. "He is also, the most powerful of the Three, and the most powerful Guardian that has ever walked the earth—ever."

"Then you know my Dad?"

"I knew him very well at one time, but that seems a long time ago now."

"How did you know him?" Annie couldn't contain her curiosity.

Olivia looked at Annie with a sad smile, "I was his wife."

Memories of Loss

"What!? How is…how could that be true?"

"Yes, we were a couple for a time. I loved that man completely."

"That can't be, can it? How could that be?"

"That is another long story, and one that it's time you heard little sister." Olivia covered Annie's hand with hers and looked deeply into her eyes. "Look into my eyes, and concentrate, think of your father and look at me."

Annie had no trouble thinking about her father. She thought about his kind face and ready smile. She suddenly had a vision of him in pain. She saw him standing with his back to a stone wall, his face drawn back in a grimace as he fought an unseen foe.

"Do not go there sister!" Olivia called her back from the vision. "Think of the pleasant things, his love for you and his great strength."

Again, Annie pictured her father. She imagined him standing in sunlight and laughing.

"That's the way! Good job, Annie. Now look at me

while you hold that image in your mind."

Annie tried to do two things at once. She found herself hopping from her thoughts of her father, to trying to concentrate on Olivia's face. She jumped back and forth, trying to do both. Then, she was looking past Olivia's face, into the depth behind her eyes, and an awareness of things past.

"Look deeper and know the answer to your questions."

Annie looked at the vision in her head. Her father stood laughing in the sun but was no longer alone. Two women had joined him, one on each side and he held the hand of each of them. One woman was a slim and comely beauty with long flowing strawberry blond hair and radiant smile, laughing up at the handsome face of her father. On the other side of Michael, a raven-haired young woman leaned against him, holding his hand and smiling across at the other woman. The dark-haired woman resembled a young Olivia.

"Who is the other woman?"

"It is your mother Annie. Roison McQuinn, the Rose of West March."

Annie beheld the two women. She looked deeply at the image of Roison, hoping to remember her, to find an image in her own memory, but there was none. Turning her thought to the young Olivia, she regarded her critically. An image of Olivia burst into her mind. She saw her smiling at her from above. She saw her talking and laughing, and she felt that she must be laughing as well. It was a happy memory.

"Do you remember?"

"You are in my memory. You were with me once."

"Yes, I was."

"Where is my Mom?"

"Come back Annie. We have much to tell you." This was the first time Circe' had spoken and Annie blinked her eyes and once again was sitting in the cozy cottage, a cooling cup of tea in one hand.

"I don't understand. You're not my mother, but I saw you when I was a baby. Where was she?"

"Little one, Roison was a wonderful person. Indeed, I'd say she was almost perfect in every way and the dearest thing to me that has ever been, but she was very stubborn. Headstrong wouldn't even cover it. When she became pregnant with you, she fell ill almost immediately. It was a difficult pregnancy, and she suffered greatly but refused any assistance from me or anyone else. She would not take the medicants that I proposed, afraid that it might somehow harm the life that grew inside of her. As a result, she grew steadily weaker. Michael suffered right alongside her. As did I.

"When it came time for you to be born, she had weakened to the point that she didn't have any strength left. And as you came into the world, she left it. I still mourn that moment but was also very angry with her because I believed she would not accept it when I might have helped. I knew better; she had been stubborn and headstrong her entire life, this was no different, but I miss her to this very day."

Annie had never heard an explanation before of what had befallen her mother, other than that she had died during childbirth. She felt the sadness in Olivia's words and recognized that it struck a chord inside of her as well.

"How did you become friends with my mom?"

"Honey—we were more than just friends; she was my sister. My twin sister."

Annie's eyes opened wide with surprise. She looked across the table at the woman who was sadly smiling at her. There was something about the shape of her shockingly blue eyes, the curve of her mouth. There was a resemblance that she hadn't noticed until just then. It was a resemblance to the girl that peered at Annie when she looked in the mirror. Across the table from her, was her aunt, and there was little question about it.

"You look so much like your mother that it's almost painful. She was a beautiful woman, smart and an amazing hedge witch in her own right. But in this one instance, she was blind to what she needed. She made her own concoctions to alleviate her troubles, but as they say, 'you cannot give what you haven't got'. She couldn't self-medicate because she wasn't healthy enough herself. All magic has a cost, and you must put a little of yourself into anything you create, or it is not going to be effective. Roison made her own medications, and unintentionally a little bit of her illness spilled into each one. The effect was dire nonetheless. I'm afraid I let my anger fuel my response and I refused to watch her disappear by inches. I left her alone when she would no longer listen to advice and I only returned when it was time to help bring you into the world. I was the first person you saw when you took your first breath, even before your father. Your mother held you close as she took her last. My tears that day were both joyful and filled with sorrow and despair."

Annie had been looking at the woman in deep wonder as a tear slipped down her cheek and she smiled back through misty eyes.

"I was so angry with her, that I left her when she needed me most."

"But you said you were married to my dad."

"I was, and I actually may still be."

"I don't understand?"

"Your mother, Roison, was your father's wife until the moment she passed through the veil. Your father is and was a warrior. There were times when he would need to be absent for long periods of time. He is clever and smart but with no talent or skill at raising a little girl. As I grieved the loss of my sister, I began to care for you. My affection for you and my natural attraction to Michael made us partners in your raising. As you grew, our deep sorrow for Roison brought us closer, and eventually we admitted our love for each other openly. When the solstice occurred, we pledged our troth before the druid.

"When the power of the Three began to rise, it was clear that the Druid Queen once again had appeared. As your seventh birthday approached, I began to see your 'gifts' emerge, and understood it was time for me to go away. A hedge witch has many powers; one of them is the ability to communicate with those on the other side of the veil. I feared the risk of letting you communicate with your mother at such a young age and knew that I would want it too. So, I went into exile to avoid that, after doing my best to erase myself from your memories. Your father has done a remarkable job in my absence. He is an amazing man."

"You just left me? Walked out and left us both?"

"Yes my love, and no. Michael and I discussed it a long time, we argued with raised voices and thunder, but we both knew that you were not destined to become another hedge witch as your mother and I. If I had stayed, and if you had been shown my talents at such an impressionable age, you might have been diverted to a different path than what your fate line had predicted. It would have torn you apart, and we both knew it. In the end, we agreed, and we parted."

There had been one life-changing shock after another in Annie's young life recently, but this news shook the very foundations of it. She looked from one of the women to the other, their faces regarding her with concern and affection. This was not what she had hoped for or wanted. It was more than she could process. Jumping to her feet, she ran out the door, down the stone path and out through the gate. She ran down a grassy path and into the woods, running and sobbing. Blinding tears filled her eyes as she pushed through the trees and brush, paying no attention to her direction.

Finally, emerging into a small clearing where a clear running stream flowed between grassy edges. Annie collapsed into the tall grass, covered her face with her hands and wept.

"Are those tears for me?"

"What? Who said that?" Annie looked up in surprise. In front of her stood a young woman, dressed in pastels of rose and yellow.

"I did my dearest love." The woman, did not move but gave a soft smile. Her red hair glowed with golden highlights in the evening sunshine.

"Mom?"

"Yes my love."

"How…?"

"Olivia, of course. She can help you my lovely child. She can show you the way to who you are. Trust Olivia, and believe in Circe' as her time draws near."

"I don't understand. What does that mean?"

"Trust Olivia." The vision of the woman faded back into bright sunlight."

"Wake up sleepy-head, the hour is late."

Annie sat up quickly, for a moment unsure of her surroundings. "Patch, I must have fallen asleep."

"I have watched over you while you slept." The little fairy smiled at her. *" I have something to show you. Will you come with me Anne of Present?"*

"What?"

"Come, follow me, I will show you."

The tiny fairy flitted off into the trees. Annie got up on her feet and followed. In a short distance they came to an impenetrable wall of shiny holly bushes and bright red sumac where Patch patiently waited for her to catch up.

"It's a dead-end Patch."

"Is it? Follow me."

Patch turned and flew directly at the sharp-edged leaves of the nearest holly bush and disappeared into it.

"Wait! Where did you go?"

"Follow me."

"Where? How can I follow you through that?"

"Follow me."

Annie stepped up to the bush and extended her hand to try and push the branches aside. Instead, her hand disappeared as it approached the bush.

"What…"

"Follow me."

Annie leaned forward and extended her other hand. Both of her arms disappeared up to her elbows into the bush that looked like it was there but was not. Stepping forward she moved into the space and took another step, then two, then another. The tight space opened out into a large clearing. Inside the space, the air was springtime fresh and the sound of trickling water filled the air. Everywhere she looked fairies bustled through the air. The trees and shrubbery surrounding the small clearing were neatly pruned and trimmed. Hanging baskets of woven grass hung from branches everywhere festooned with tiny lanterns that lit the clearing with twinkling lights in the darkness that had fallen. Fairies carrying bundles and baskets went in and out of these constantly. There was busyness everywhere. When Annie appeared at the edge of the clearing, all work stopped and as one, the fairies gathered in front of her. Annie had never imagined there could be so many of them in one place.

"Greetings my Queen, welcome to our home." The fairy Thomasina hovered before her eyes. *"We have prepared a place for you. We are honored that you have joined us. Come and take your rest with us, and be at peace while you are here."*

Several other fairies flew near, all of them chattering a welcome. Delighted at their good fortune. Together they gathered at her shoulders, arms and hands and pulled her forward.

"Come with us." "This way Anne of Present."

Walking through the small glade, she was assailed by sights and sounds that she could never have imagined before. Several rabbits moved out of her path, only to turn and bow before scampering into the underbrush at the edge of the clearing. A young doe approached and matching her pace, walked beside her. Near the end of the open space a massive bower made entirely of woven vines and the last roses of autumn beckoned invitingly.

"Your home while you are with us." Thomasina beamed with pride.

"But I need to be at the cottage with Circe' and… and my Aunt. It's getting dark…the sun has already set."

A shadow momentarily passed overhead. Looking up Percy fluttered to a landing on a nearby tree branch. He bobbed his head and then spoke,

"Here you are, and here you must stay, in the secret glade, in the secret dell until the witches deem you safe. Here you are safe and can be hidden. The gate keeps watch; the sisters will defend."

The Sanctuary of the Fey

The sound of running water and bustling activity awakened Annie. It had been more than a week since she had entered the glade. In that time, there had been no word of the Three. The women had visited, but only briefly.

In spite of all that had occurred over the weeks, she slept soundly in a bed of sweet grass and flower petals, under a warm soft blanket of hemp fiber dyed the color of midnight sky. The light of day had not fully penetrated the small glade as yet, but tiny shadows already flitted back and forth in the air outside of Annie's bower.

As soon as she sat up and rubbed her eyes, Thomasina appeared, *"Greetings Anne of Present, the new day has arrived. Welcome Helios!"*

"Good morning, Thomasina. What time is it?"

"We do not track the course of the sun, but only give thanks for it."

"So? You don't have clocks?"

"Time does not exist, it measures nothing. Worth in

accomplishment, love, honor and friendship are much more telling of the value of a life."

Annie thought about that statement for a moment and then shrugged. She realized that it actually didn't matter what time it was, what day it was, as long as she woke up to meet another one.

"I don't remember hearing water running last night Thomasina, did it rain last night?"

"No, although the dew of nightfall was heavy last night, there was no rain." Another fairy had entered the bower, then another and then a dozen. They all smiled and looked at each other with a shared secret look.

"Okay…I'll bite. What are you all up to?"

"Come with us Anne of Present." "Follow us, come see." They began to chatter. *"Oh you must come."*

Like every day since she arrived, they gathered around her urging her to move more quickly. Instead of leading her out the opening at the front of her little home, they took her to the back of it where a narrow opening led out and under the shelter of a great willow tree, its weeping branches gently stroking the grass underneath.

The ancient tree stood rooted at the edge of a small clear pool of water. A small nearby waterfall spilled over a rock outcropping, disturbing the stillness of the pool as it fell. Around the pool, flowers still bloomed in the late autumn. Water lilies in full bloom floated on the surface.

"We worked through the night to restore the water flow to the falls. Many years ago, it moved away from the stream. Ancient Willow has missed it and wished

for its return. It is now restored to its proper place, and Anne of Present has a place of solitude to bathe. It is most pleasant. Yes?"

"It is most pleasant, YES! Beautiful." Annie whispered voice was filled with wonder. "You did this last night?"

"Yes, many hands were busy. But not all. There is more, please take pleasure in the fall and the pool; speak with the Ancient One if you can. There is soaproot and aloe at the pool's edge. Then come back inside. We have other notions to be shared."

Thomasina shooed some of the fairies away, and then with a wink and a wave left Annie alone. Annie walked to the pool's edge admiring the natural beauty of the setting. The troubles that had brought her to this place seemed far away in this peaceful setting. She wondered if the water was too cold to bathe in. Reaching out one foot to dip a toe and test the water, she placed a hand on the trunk of the great willow to steady herself. She was immediately aware of its consciousness. Her hand recoiled from the shock.

Looking up into the spreading branches, she plucked up her courage and reaching out again placed her open palm on the tree.

"Thankful." The voice echoing with wisdom and depth.

"Wait! What? You are thankful."

"Thankful."

"Why are you thankful old one?"

"My water has returned; I am thankful."

"It is beautiful. I am thankful too."

"Only by thankfulness is anything accomplished."

"That is a deep thought. I wonder…is it true?"

"My roots are deep; my thoughts are my own."

"Thank you, old one. May I share your water for a moment."

"All that come, all that are, are only for a moment."

"You speak with the old one!?" A fairy had approached, combs and brushes in her hands. The fairy's voice was filled with awe.

"He spoke to me first. Why, is that a strange thing?"

"The old one only speaks with the Red Witch or the White Witch. No one else hears his voice."

"I have met the White Witch, but she is far from here. Who is the Red Witch?"

"Let us prepare you for this day Anne of Present. Soon you shall see, soon you shall see."

The small fairies guided Annie into the pool. The bracing chill of the water on her skin was only a shock for a moment, as she swam under the waterfall. Standing up the water reached her shoulders. The fairies swooped in their arms filled with soaproot and lavender balms and immediately began to shampoo her hair, filling the air with the heady aroma. Annie closed her eyes and tipped her head back under the falling water, enjoying the bliss of the moment as the tiny fairies rinsed her hair.

Long minutes later, she emerged from the pool feeling clean and refreshed. Other fairies brought soft towels of the brightest gold and wrapped her warmly. Then with fragrant oils and fine combs they swept the tangles from her hair. In spite of the riotous thickness of her hair, it dried in minutes, cascading in waves of the red gold, for once behaving itself. Entering her bower, she found clothes of fine linen arranged neatly on her bed. A blouse of white, slacks of amber and soft slippers.

The fairies hovered on all sides, expressing approval in sighs of encouragement. Annie caught a glimpse of herself in the small mirror they provided and smiled. The clothes were amazing, and her normally unruly hair was more perfect than she had ever seen it.

"We have a gift for you Anne of Present. Please come outside, we must show you."

Anne stepped out into the early morning sunlight. Across the glen a small table had been set up with four chairs. Three of the chairs were occupied. Facing her directly across the table sat Circe' in a hooded robe of the deepest green. On her left sat Elspeth resplendent in robes of the brightest white. On her right sat Olivia in a richly embroidered and hooded robe of the deepest red. They each smiled their greeting but did not move.

Several fairies approached, carrying a large bundle.

"For you my queen, your new robes Anne of Present."

They unfurled a long, brocaded swallow tail coat of the lightest blues and white. Gold filigrees of celtic runes and the pointed septagram, the Elven Star adorned the front placates. The fairies held it open for her and she lifted her arms as they draped it onto her shoulders. Floating backward they admired the finished product from a distance; then a collective gasp escaped them all. The three woman's eyes widened in surprise, their lips all making an 'O' where their mouths used to be.

"What!?"

No one spoke. The fairies drew further back in shock. The three women sprang to their feet immediately, spreading out across the glade, hands raised palms outward.

"What?"

Again, no one spoke.

Looking down, it was Annie's turn to gasp. The beautiful sky-blue coat and the rest of her once beautiful outfit were no longer pale pastels of beauty. Instead, she stood dressed in black from head to toe. Her new slippers had changed to heeled black boots with toes of silver. The Elven Star on her chest blazed fiery red. Around her waist she wore a baldric and a two-hand sword hung from the belt.

"How...how?"

"The Black Queen! It is the enemy of old flee!" The fairies as one shouted in panic. *"Flee for your lives! It is the Black Queen the 'Taker of Souls'!"*

The Colors of Battle

The three women, white, red and green spread themselves across the glade, faces set in angry determination. They approached, right hand palm outward and left hand brandishing their staffs. Together they chanted;

"Namhaid sean, laoch trom; begion minion de na Fomorians
Fuil ar an gcarraig, fuil ar ghaineamh, harry tú ar ais go dtí an cúlchríoch
Trodaí dána, namhaid na sean; ar ais thú ar ais sa fuar
Ravens ar aer, bás sa talamh, a fháil ar ais go dtí an dumha bara"
('Enemy of old, warrior bold; begone minion of the Fomorians
Blood on rock, blood on sand, harry thee back to the hinterland
Warrior bold, enemy of old; return thee back to the outworld cold
Ravens on air, death in the ground, get

thee back to the barrow mound.')

Annie recoiled. Slowly she backed away.

"Stop, please! What is going on, I don't understand. Stop! You're scaring me."

The staffs of all three witches began to glow, as they brandished them, aimed directly toward Annie's chest they chanted again:

> ***"Trodaí an cháil, anois cuirimid síos thú;***
> ('Warrior of renown, now we put thee down;)

A flash of blue light burst from all three staffs and streaked toward the Black Queen. But before they could strike, they were blasted aside by the bright sword she now brandished in her hands.

"Whoa! How did that happen?" Annie looked at the sword in her hand, "No, not this, not this!"

Annie looked up. The witches continued to advance, staffs aimed in attack, faces determined. Annie backed away.

They began to glow again, their color this time; blinding red.

> ***"Namhaid sean, laoch trom; begion minion de na Fomorians***
> ***Fuil ar an gcarraig, fuil ar ghaineamh, harry tú ar ais go dtí an cúlchríoch***
> ***Trodaí dána, namhaid na sean; ar ais thú ar ais sa fuar***
> ***Ravens ar aer, bás sa talamh, a fháil ar ais go dtí an dumha bara"***

"Stop! Stop now!" Annie's hand came up, and a thrum of vibration burst forward. It struck the three women forcing them back and turning their staffs away. In a voice of power and authority, she commanded her hand raised palm outward: "Enough!"

Annie dropped her sword to the ground and fell to her hands and knees.

"No, please. It's me; it's just me, it's just Annie. Please—please don't kill me." Tears dropped on the grass between her hands.

A hand touched her head, stroking it lightly.

"It is alright child, we had to know. You have passed the test. You are safe and so are we, for the time being."

Looking up through the tears in her eyes Annie beheld all three of the witches smiling down at her.

"I think we could all use a nice cup of tea." Smiled Olivia.

Once the four were seated around an ornate wrought iron garden table, the three witches smiled at Annie again and held her gaze.

"This has started to get out of hand! I, for real, thought you were trying to kill me a minute ago, and now I'm supposed to enjoy a 'nice cup of tea'! Seriously?"

"I'm sorry dear," Olivia leaned over and touched Annie's wrist, "we actually **were** trying to kill you I'm afraid."

"Yes," Elspeth chimed in from the other side, also touching Annie's arm, "but we couldn't do it, you wouldn't let us. It is as we feared—and as we had hoped."

Annie's impulse was to jump up and run, but the women lovingly held her arms. As she looked into each face, her own thoughts betrayed her: *'They want to tell you, their story. It is safe. I know this to be true.'*

"How is it that I know I can trust you right now?"

"We are your sisters; we cannot lie to each other. Even if we wanted to."

"Seriously? Wait! I actually knew that; how do I know that? Oh, wait…now I get it."

"Good because we need to tell you some things that we all wish we could lie about, but cannot."

"Should I be afraid?"

"What! You mean different afraid than you've been for the last six weeks? Or just more of the same kind of afraid?" Elspeth couldn't resist trying to lighten the mood at the table.

In spite of herself, Annie smiled, "I guess, just more of the same."

"Okay, so we'll tell the story backward to begin. With what just happened." Elspeth began the narrative; "What happened was a necessary test. It had to be done that way, because we had to be sure that we would get a completely honest response from you. Everything since you rose this morning was designed to relax and rejuvenate your spirit."

"What! The pool, the bath? The old willow?"

"No, the 'Old One' was real. We would gladly have done all the other anyway, but this particular time it had another cause to serve."

"And…?"

"It worked."

"Annnnnd…"

"We have reason to believe," Circe' began, "that

your ancestors may not have been all of the Tuatha Dé Dannan. That perhaps you also carry the blood of the Fomorians."

"The who!? Who's Pomeranians? And the What!?"

"Fomorians."

"Okay, who are Fomorians?"

"They are and were the bad guys. If you think of it that way, the Tuatha De' Dannan were the good guys in the old days. Over the ages they have battled. Sometimes one side would win and there would be times of peace," Elspeth frowned, "and sometimes the other won.

"The Fomorians rose from the underworld and the sea. They, like all of us, are descendants of the Elven races. But they are not like the elves or fairies, witches, or warlocks though. More they appear as demons, sprites sometimes, and giants. Some are unfathomably evil, others just like to make mischief."

"So, they're mean and apparently really ugly. I don't get how I might have inherited any of that." Annie sat forward, her arms folded and resting on the table.

"Not all Fomorians were bad. Not all of the Tuatha were entirely good. There were great periods of peace and comradery. During those times the races mixed freely; some even married." Olivia began her part of the story. "The arranged marriage of Cian, a Fomorian prince and Ethniu, a Tuatha De' Dannan princess, who were both the children of kings, ended all war in our world for a very long time.

"We appear to be at the end of this last long peace. Most hoped that it would last forever, but it did not.

Fourteen years ago, events took place that altered the future for all of us. Many of us were there to witness it and feared the eventual outcome. In four days time, it will be thirteen years to the day that the peace was shattered. We have worked to revive it. We were successful until recently, and now we watch for help and prepare for danger. We look to you Morgana."

Annie recoiled, her eyes wide in surprise.

"Your mother and I were young, practically girls. We were children of privilege, of royal blood, and we chafed under everyone's observation. We were determined to show our independence, so we moved away from our kind and into the city. We practiced our craft and were doing well.

"Then in the time of 'The Water Bearer'," Olivia paused looking for the correct reference, "No, Aquarius, oh um January, that's right January. Our home was invaded. At first, we thought it was just clumsy burglars or some other riff-raff that we could have dealt with easily, but it was not. Instead, it was a true demon, the son of Balor himself. He sought our power of craft. His evil was so hot it burned from across the room. He came for me, as I was the elder twin, but then he saw the lovely Roison and he would not be deterred. She fought him, and so did I. But in the end—he prevailed.

"When we were defeated, he roared a great laugh. It was that roar, that evil voice that summoned the Guardian to appear in all his strength at last. Although we had suspected Michael for some time, we could not anticipate his true ferocity. He came with the force of the storm itself and they battled. Our home was destroyed. Much was laid in ruin. In the end, Michael of the Three had won, and the demon was returned to the underworld, but it was a bitter victory. Almost immediately, Roison's health began to fail. Michael did everything he could, so did I, but we could not help her. Nor would she allow it. Within days we knew she was pregnant."

"With me! She was pregnant with me, from that beast!" Tears again appeared in Annie's eyes. "So, I'm not good at all—I'm a monster?"

"No, my dear, and you proved it only minutes ago. But we did fear that it might be so."

"But you suspected it from the very beginning, didn't you?"

"Yes and no. Your father, Michael Abbott had been close with Roison for a while. We were all young and full of life. You could tell they loved each other immediately. We were a trio of youth. But the return of Cian, the son of Balor had been foretold and we watched for signs of it. Michael was especially cautious, but the actual Guardian did not appear until the demon also did.

Within days of the attack, Gabriel and Raphael also arrived. Together, they have watched over you and protected your every move for almost thirteen years, always close but never nearby. The fact that their power and strength have not diminished in that time supports our fear that there is still trouble on the horizon."

"Is that why you left me?"

"Yes. When your immense power began to appear, we feared the worst. We feared that the horror of that night and my hatred of all things Fomorian after that night could influence how I treated you. How I taught you. I would not have done it consciously perhaps but we all suspected that I might hesitate to reveal some of the inner secrets and pathways to someone who might eventually become my enemy. And to be honest, I probably would have done just that.

"Michael disagreed, and we argued. We parted in anger, and I have not seen him in seven years, but I am praying; we all are praying that we see him again very soon."

"I don't feel mean. When I look in the mirror, I don't think I'm very pretty, but I don't look like a monster either. What is it that you guys see, that I don't?"

"What color are your eyes?"

"Blue, light blue. With little flecks of color."

"Correct; the Fomorians all have something in common. Their eyes are red; the iris is completely red. It makes them capable of seeing very well in darkness. The flecks of color in your eyes are all bright red. When an infant is born, it usually takes some time for the true eye color to emerge. Yours were bright blue one day, and then the next day totally red, then back to blue. Eventually, the colors blended with blue being the dominant color."

"How tall are you Annie?" Elspeth leaned forward.

"I'm not sure, maybe five-eight or five-nine?"

"A little hard to find women's pants with that inseam I bet. Isn't that a little tall for a thirteen-year-old girl?"

"I was the tallest kid in my class, lots taller than any of the boys."

"Odd, don't you think, that you would be so tall at

such a young age? I'm pushing it at five foot six and I am your closest blood relative." Olivia stood up to demonstrate, "The Fomorians are unusually tall, and so are you."

"There are other things too Youngest, but they can be explained in a variety of ways." Circe' began again, "What is clear is that you have become a woman, without your even noticing. You are tall, athletic and really quite beautiful, if you need to know. Those are all things that your mother was. What we didn't know was what gifts you have that you inherited from your father and if your father was actually Cian.

"Your thirteenth birthday is in four days. I'll bet you've forgotten that haven't you?"

Annie nodded.

"On their thirteenth birthday, woman of our sort come into their full powers. It is both a timeline and a doorway. On that day, the sisters welcome you into the council, and we acknowledge you as an adult. As such, you would be free to make your own decisions, exercise your gifts as you see fit, for good or evil. Our fear was that considering what glimpses we have had of your power and potential, once you came into your adulthood, you would be too powerful for us to stop, if it became necessary. Even if we worked together."

"As it was, we couldn't do it even now. Your gifts are starting to expand, we might have defeated you in the end but the cost, to us and to the world around us, would have been unimaginable."

"Who is the Black Witch then?"

"The easy answer to that is—you are dear. You just proved it. That's not really what you wanted to know though is it?" Elspeth leaned forward. "The Black Witch was the wife of Balor of the Fomorians, and a feared warrior who was rivaled in evil only by her cruel husband. In an age past, she was wounded in a battle with the gods. The wound was mortal; with a last effort she speared Dagda before she fell. Dagda, was dealt a wound that killed him slowly. Actually, he suffered for almost a hundred years before he finally died, but the wound from the Black Witch was the cause of his and our grief. His…"

"Wait! Who was Dagda?"

"Dagda was King of the Tuatha De' Dannan and the father figure to our order. He was also the husband of Morganna, whom you know of as Morgan Le Fey. Not her first marriage or her last, but definitely his last."

"What became of the Black Witch?"

"Her name was Ceithlion Chaisfhiaciach, or *Kehlen of the twisted teeth*, in today's speech. She was carried from the battlefield. It is said that she escaped by swimming to a lonely island where she then died, but no one has ever been able to prove the tale. It is one of the many mysteries of our times."

"Before, when you were *testing* me, how did you know she would appear?"

"The Elven Star is all we had dear. Its ability to draw out your identity was what we used. We were even more surprised by the appearance of the Black Witch than you might have been. We were expecting a minor Fomorian, not the 'Taker of Souls' herself."

"But I'm not the 'Taker of Souls'!" Annie looked around the table at the serious looks that were returned. "I'm no warrior."

ANNIE ABBOTT AND THE DRUID STONES

"Very soon, young one —you will be."

The Battle in the Wood

Ever since the appearance of the Black Witch, there had been no fairies in sight. They had fled at the sight of their most primal enemy—the Taker of Souls. But now one streaked into the glade and approached the garden table at speed. Keeping one eye on Annie, Patch addressed the witches.

"One of the true brothers has arrived. He is badly injured but says he brings a message from the Wind Warrior to the 'One'. We have stopped him at the cottage. We do not allow their kind into the glade until we are sure of their intent. What would you have us do?"

"Patch? It's me. Just me. You know, Anne of Present. I'm not the Black Witch, I'm just me, don't be afraid."

"Patch is not afraid. I am not afraid of you or anything else, why would I be? I am a warrior. But I am cautious."

"I think that you can trust Annie again my friend.

She has passed our little test." Olivia smiled. "How badly is the wolf injured."

"The wounds were not mortal, but the journey has weakened him. His message may be lost very soon."

"Leave him at the cottage then. Annie, for now stay in the glade. If Bracken or one of his kind have found the glen, he may have been pursued. We must keep you safe until we are sure. Rest up, things are heating up and this is as good a place as any for us to make a stand." Circe's face was grim as she looked across at Annie.

"Stay here? By myself?"

"Yes, we will come back for you when it is safe, but for now be patient. There is no better place for us to hide you than right here."

"I don't want to be alone, and I don't want to be hidden away either."

"Go and speak with the Old One. He will assure you."

"If Bracken will not give us the message, we will need you to ask him for us. He only answers to the 'One' so we may be back very soon."

"No! No, I'm afraid already. I'll be more afraid if you leave me here by myself, especially with all the fairies hiding from me now. No, I'll be afraid either way, so I'm going with you. You said he's bringing me a message. I'm going with you."

"But Annie…"

"I'm going! Everyone is risking their lives. Everyone is battling except me."

"Annie?"

"I don't know how to fight, but I know I'm too scared to sit alone. Take me with you. Take me to Bracken. I want to go."

The three women exchanged glances, then Circe' looked at Annie with a wry smile. "We will keep you as safe as we can but after the events of this morning, we might be asking you for the same."

"Let's go then, but slowly. Okay Patch, take us to the wolf." Olivia's face was determined as she hefted her staff.

The four followed the fairy as she flitted from tree to tree, carefully stalking the cottage and watching in all directions. The forest was totally silent, no birds sang, no small creatures moved out of their way. The bright sunshine beamed down through the bare trees of early winter, creating stark shadows of black on the golden leaves. The three witches advanced slowly, walking carefully in the rustling leaves, trying to be as quiet as possible. Side by side but several feet apart, they formed a formidable line, keeping Annie behind them as they, like Patch, watched in all directions.

Annie walked behind, terrified by the decision that she had just made. She tried to look in every direction at the same time. The silence of the woods made every sound that the group made seem explosive.

'What am I doing? Honestly, I've lost my mind. This is such a bad idea.'

'Relax sister. Breathe in, breathe out. Reach out with your feelings, touch the life that surrounds you. Sense danger, sense safety. Reach out; prepare yourself."

Annie was no longer shocked by the mental

messages she received. She took a deep breath. She tried to focus on the three brave women carefully stalking through the trees, trying to imagine herself as one of them. They appeared fearless, gazing forward and to the side, taking each careful step. Guarding each other and protecting her.

"Run!" The voice in her thoughts screamed.

As Elspeth peered around a trunk of large tree, bark and splinters exploded just above her head. It was followed by the report of a firearm. The speed of the bullet faster even than the sound of the shot. Elspeth dropped to her knees, blood streaming down her cheek from a cut above her eyebrow.

"Run Annie!" Olivia yelled as she dropped into a crouch behind the safety of the nearest tree as more shots rang out.

Annie stood rooted in place. Without thinking she raised her hands, palms outward. Sudddenly, she could feel the approach of their assailants, she could feel their hate and anger. She looked at the three women who had sworn to protect her, now in danger for their lives, pinned down, hiding behind trees. She could sense their determination, frustration, and their fear for her safety. Her own fear was almost a living thing, fighting for control of her mind and her body, freezing her in place. And then she sensed the silent forest, watching, hoping for justice, hating the violence. The emotions and energy of the moment swirled in the air, thick with dire implications. She took a deep breath and let it out, clearing her mind, settling her heart and then she knew what she had to do.

She took another deep breath and let it out, reaching

out with her senses. She felt the great strength of the old forest and its watchful impatience. She knew how many tiny creatures moved in the leaves under her feet and how many birds watched from the trees above. There was a breathless moment when it seemed that time had stopped. Every living thing seemed to be waiting. That moment of breathless anticipation, waiting for the plunge from the high dive, tinged with the fear of the high place and the shock of the cold water to come. She knew that their attention was not directed at the enemies concealed in the underbrush ahead; they watched her, wanting her to do something. Hoping she would respond. They were waiting for her.

All of the fear she had been feeling evaporated, replaced by anger and determination. Her vision changed; the colors of the autumn forest brightened and were tinged in scarlet red. She scanned the area ahead of her and could immediately make out the attackers as they advanced, dressed in camouflaged clothing, but still obvious to her.

As she focused on them, her sight changed and she watched them from higher and higher. Now she was looking down on them from above the treetops. Their intent and attention focused forward on the women as Annie's vision descended, returning to the ground. Annie was now looking at the four men from behind them as they crouched in the bushes.

"That is enough! You will leave this sacred place now, for your consequence is upon you!"

The quartet of attackers turned as one, surprise on their faces, their weapons raised in defense from the fearsome visage they now faced.

The Warrior Queen of the Druids advanced on them in a rush. Her speed a blur. Using only the heel of her open palm, she struck one across the bridge of the nose. In a pirouette she spun to the next striking a blow behind his ear and on to the next. So quickly did she move that the men were all lying on the ground, rendered senseless from the skill of her blows before they could make a move in their own defense. Annie stood over them, breathing heavily.

"That's enough," she whispered, "We have had enough."

"Goodness! You are having a *very* busy day Annie." Elspeth waded up through the fallen leaves. "First the Black Witch, then a raven on the attack, and finally the Druid Queen herself."

Circe' approached and put a hand on Annie's shoulder, turning her so she could look directly into her eyes.

"It is a gift and a blessing to be a changeling. You are doubly blessed and doubly cursed. It is difficult to be one, but two distinct personalities is a challenge we have no experience in. You harbor both the good and the evil. Two queens of equal power, but with different goals. Guard yourself against them Youngest or you could lose yourself in them. Be Annie always, if you can. That is where your true power rests."

"They'll have heard the shots fired. Let's deal with these four, but then what?" Olivia posed the question that they had all been thinking.

"Don't kill them!" Annie yelped.

"Oh honey, who do you think we are? If the tables were turned, they would not hesitate. We have adequate

ISABELLE AND MICHAEL NELSON

reason to dispatch these rabble with prejudice, as they have already tried to kill us once."

Annie shivered as she continued.

"But no, we're the good guys remember. We don't have time to re-educate them properly though, so we'll have them experience a few days of mental confusion instead."

Circe' walked to the four figures lying senseless in the deep leaves. Straddling the chest of the first one, she grabbed a handful of his shirt and jerked him into a sitting position. Where he sat, his head wobbling on his neck, a blank look on his face.

"Hey you! Dumbellina! Hey!" She slapped him on the cheek. "Hey!"

"Yeah…where's…where's my lunchbox?"

"Hey Dumbellina! It's not lunchtime yet! Now listen up buster."

"Ahh…ye..yes..ma'am." He tried to focus on her, but it didn't seem that his eyes could concentrate.

"There was no devil woman, understand?"

"No devil woman.'

"Right. Good boy. Now instead you got jumped by an alien that zapped you before you could defend yourselves."

"Space invaders…got the jump on us."

"Very good! You go to the head of the class. Next."

She did the same with each of the other three as they slowly revived. At last, they all sat on the ground rubbing sore spots on their head. Circe' stood in front of them, flanked by Olivia and Elspeth.

"Ok boys…you should know that we space aliens

eat rats. If you keep pursuing those women, we will come back and you will be very sorry."

"Aw…we ain't afraid of no girls."

The three women, their faces set with malice, approached the men, who scooted backward on the ground.

"You have been warned earthman! Don't be fooled by our disguises. Here is what you will see the next time we meet. Elspeth if you please?"

Even Annie was horrified at the visage that appeared in place of the three witches. Three hideous beasts stood on hind legs, with long snouts, their jaws filled with sharp teeth, slavering as they pawed the ground. The vision lasted only seconds and the women returned to their normal appearance.

The effect it had on the three men, now cowering on the ground, was profound and immediate.

"We won't! We won't tell nobody. Holy cow…we promise…we didn't see nothin'!"

The four soldiers, terrified, continued to scoot backward on their bottoms.

"Yeah." "Yeah, me too. We didn't see nothin'."

"That's good boys. Now, you fellas do a one-eighty and don't stop walking before the sun goes down. Do you understand? We'll be monitoring your progress from the mother ship, so don't test us. Understand?"

"Y..y..yes ma'am!"

"Now git!"

The four hapless would-be assassins struggled to their feet. They started off into the forest, their balance not yet trustworthy and rubbing the sore spots on their heads.

"It's the little things." Elspeth smirked as she watched them stumble off.

"Yep, you gotta find the fun where you can, and that part at least was kinda' fun." Olivia stood next to her watching the progress of the staggering men with a bemused expression.

"Let's go find Bracken and hear his news. Time is shrinking." Circe' was back to business.

"We shall have them followed, the defeated ones, to make sure they leave and cause no more trouble." Thomasina and Patch floated in front of Annie. *"We are pleased to see you are a capable warrior Anne of Present."*

"Oh Patch, I'm so glad you are speaking with me again. Thank you."

"Your mystery has resolved itself. Light has been shown into the darkness and yet the darkness did not overcome it. Now Patch understands the struggle that is within you."

"Wait! What did you say Patch?"

"Patch understands your struggle."

"No, the other thing. What did you say?"

"I said that the light had been shown into the darkness and yet the darkness did not overcome it."

"Where did you hear that Patch. How do you know that phrase?" Annie's focus was so strong that the other women were watching intently.

"It is written on the stone of the woods." Thomasina continued, *"Its meaning is unknown to us. I have shown it to Patch. She does not know its meaning either."*

"It is a wisdom. That much we understand, but why

it is on the stone we do not know." Patch finished *"I see now that you struggle against the darkness, but in the first battle you did not succumb. You are Anne of Present."*

"Circe'! *'Seek the stones, and feel their life. First before all things, feel the life in all that you see and touch. Only then will the steps to the great mystery become clear to you. Seek the stones, that bear the mark.'* We have to go to the stone. It might be one of the ones we seek."

"We'll have to see this stone, but now we must find Bracken." Circe' remained focused.

The Message of Bracken

"He is here." Thomasina pointed into the woods near the small stone cottage.

"Where? Where is he? I don't see him."

"He is right here," Thomasina pointed again. *"Here."*

The fairy hovered near the base of a great oak tree. "Here." She flew down and moved some of the leaves away that had collected around the roots of the tree. A bundle of shaggy black fur appeared under the leaves. *"Here he is hidden."*

The women rushed forward and pulled the rest of the leaves away. Gradually the great wolf emerged. The massive canine was lying on his side, panting rapidly. Along his side, from his shoulder to almost to his right hip, a long gash was crusted with gore. His ear on the same side was ruined, torn and bleeding.

"Bracken my friend, can you hear me?" Circe' leaned over him and spoke into his ear. "Do not leave us. We are here to help you."

The wolf's lips drew back from his teeth and he

snarled, "I fight for the One, I die for the One. I go to join my kinsmen; I have fulfilled my tithe to hell." The once great rumbling voice, now a painful whisper.

Annie stepped around Circe' and knelt next to Bracken. The sheer size of the beast still frightening to her.

"Bracken, it's me. The Seeker. I can help you; I am the One. We have to leave here. You need to help one more time, can you come with me? They are coming; we must go."

"I cannot. I am spent."

Annie looked up at the women with a look of desperation. Elspeth gave her a look and thrust her chin forward, arching her eyebrows at the same time. A gesture that meant, 'Do what needs to be done.' Then she spoke as well, "Reach out to him Seeker. Bring him back. Find his life."

Annie looked down at the wolf and thought.

"Sisters, I must help him. I must find his strength."

"You do not need us Seeker. Find the life."

Annie was panicked. The women looked at her expectantly. The wolf's chest rose and fell slowly, each painful breath escaping through his clenched teeth. There was no help; they were depending on her. She struggled to become calm. She took a deep breath and let it out.

Leaning over she spoke into the wolf's mangled ear.

"You must find the strength true friend. You must come with us, but we cannot carry you."

The wolf struggled to rise and then collapsed back into the leaves, gasping.

"Rise True Brother, I so command. Take my

strength, take all of our strength. We must flee and you must rise and follow. Rise Bracken."

The great black beast again struggled to his feet. Annie placed her hand on his shoulders.

"We will help you. Lean on me brother."

Annie listened to herself with wonder. Her voice sounded strong and confident; she felt her own strength and was amazed. The great wolf leaned against her as they began walking away from the cottage.

"I follow the One. For one last time—I follow the One." He gasped as he put weight on his right leg.

"We will help you. Circe' help me help him."

Circe' stepped forward and also put her hand on his other shoulder. "Here is my strength as well brave one."

With Olivia in the lead, watching in every direction, they started out slowly supporting the courageous warrior as he limped between Annie and Circe'. Elspeth took the rear position, backing slowly behind the small group. Her eyes on the trail behind them.

Passing back through the fairy's glade, they arrived at the base of the old willow tree.

"Rest here brave friend. Water is life. Drink from the pool. There is magic in the water for you." Circe' gently spoke in his ear.

The wolf dropped to the ground with a groan. "I carry a message for the One. I must give my message."

"Tell us Bracken. What is the message?"

"Cian approaches; he holds the Grimoire but cannot open it. He seeks the One; she is the key. The Three retreat. The Fire Warrior is weakened." Bracken's eyes closed panting from the effort. "Beware the traitor in disguise; their reach is long.""How can Cian fight the

Three, and for so long?" Circe' wondered.

"He brings an army from the Underworld. Their magic is strong together; they bring evil and cruelty with them." Bracken whispered without opening his eyes. "He uses mortals as expendable pawns."

The women exchanged serious glances, knowing what the message meant.

"Rest now Bracken. Ask the Old One for his strength to heal." Circe' paused and took a moment to make eye contact with each one of the women. "It is time—we must summon the rest. The thirteen must come together once again, perhaps for the last time. Here is where we will stand and fight against the ancient evil of old. I will run no further. Here we will make our last stand."

The Fate of Bracken

"They must come together. We must provide a united front. Only then will we have the power to resist the onslaught of Cian and his minions. The mortals are clumsy and untrained, it won't be like that when the Fomorians attack."

"But is it wise to put all of our eggs in one basket Circe?" asked Olivia

"If we do not come together and combine our power, he will hunt us down one at a time. Alone he will be too strong to resist, as you well know having fought him once before. We must summon the sisters, and we must tell the Druid."

"So mote it be." They each bowed their heads in turn, the seriousness of their decision heavy on their minds.

Annie watched with fascination, "What do you want me to do?"

"Care for Bracken; ease his suffering if you can. He is of strong heart and undoubtable courage. Help him for now, while we await the council of the thirteen."

"I don't know how to heal him."

"Reach out. The answer is on the wind, in the life around you. Listen, and know Youngest."

With that they left her and the glade. Gradually, fairies began to appear. They approached slowly, their confidence thin. Several of the first vanguards brandished various weapons as they drew nearer. Patch and Thomasina were in the lead, Thomasina with an arrow fixed to her bow, Patch her tiny sword drawn.

"We know you well Anne of Present. We also know the Killer of Souls. We learned of her at great cost. The witches have tested you, but we see the shadow of Kehlen within you. We are loyal to the One, but we remain watchful of the other." Patch gave Annie the honest assessment without frills.

"I know Patch, but you are my friend. I've seen, you've seen what I can do with the powers I know of. I am doing my best, but I could use a friend right now— please?"

"I have survived and fought many battles in my six-hundred eighty-seven years, one month, and eighteen days. It is not because I took foolish chances. I will trust you for now, Anne of Present. That is what I want, but I will remain cautious."

"That is fair I guess. Thank you Patch. Do you have any healers? I must help Bracken, but I don't know how. Can you help me?"

"We can help, and we will teach you the hidden ways Anne of Present. If we have your pledge of secrecy." Several fairies moved forward.

"I promise. I want to help him. I'm pretty sure that's

the only thing I'm trying to do right now."

"He is a great and powerful warrior. He is Bracken of the True brothers. We must heal him; we will need his strength and skill in battle."

"Do you think it will come to that Patch?"

"The battle is already joined. The Three are retreating. They are doing what they can to delay the onslaught of the unclean, but they are coming and none can stop it. The thirteen must come, and soon or we will all perish on the spears of our enemies."

"Will the witches come Patch?"

"They will come, but some are at a great distance. The minions of Cian will attempt to delay them, there is no doubt. They will have fought many battles to make their way to our assistance before they arrive. We will have to fight with or without them."

"How long Patch? How long do we have before the thirteen can arrive?"

"Some will come with speed; others may be weeks for they live across the waters in many other countries."

That did not sound very good to Annie as she considered the implications. As she thought about it, she remembered that it was only a mere six months since she had been in seventh grade and complaining about having to study for math tests. Now she was one of the most powerful people in a world that until very recently, she hadn't even known existed.

"Then I guess we're gonna need all the help we can get." Turning to other fairies, "help me with Bracken. If this is the only thing I can do to help, then that's what

I'm going to try to do."

The tiny healers gathered over the great wolf, each one touching him in different places.

"He is in great pain from his wounds," said one.

The great slash to his side has become infected, and his shoulder and leg are badly damaged," said another *"He has injuries inside as well, but the infection has taken hold of his spirit,"* said Thomasina.

Annie heard what they said but had never learned the science of what their assessment might mean. She knew that what they were telling her was not good, but what she could do to help, she didn't have a clue. She reached and stroked the noble head, like an electric shock she knew the answer.

"Help me get him in the water! He must be in the water. The water is life."

Slowly, with the help of the many fairies, they dragged the huge beast down the bank of the pond and into the pool. Annie waded in beside him, supporting him so that he did not sink below the surface. The shaggy warrior turned his head to her and sighed, "Thank you, my queen, I will drink the water." Then he slept.

"Can you help me?" Annie looked around. "I can't hold him for long. He's too heavy. Can we make something that he can rest on, but stay in the pool?"

"We will make him a resting place, but it will not hold in the water Anne of Present. The Old One may help if you ask."

"I can't ask him while my both of my hands are full."

"His roots run deep, you can touch him as he drinks from the pool."

"Is that right? No, I'm sure it is. Let's see." Annie felt around the sand at the bottom of the pool until she felt a root of the great tree. "Will you speak with me Old One?"

"I rest, my thirst satisfied."

"Old One, I bring a great heart to you. I want to heal him. Can you help me?"

"All walkers of the earth are fragile."

"Fragile? Yes, they are. I agree."

"Your agreement is not requested."

"I agree."

"As you must."

Annie moved her feet so that both of them were firmly resting on the root. She felt she had nothing to lose. This time she spoke strongly.

"Old One, it is with great respect that I come to you. It is I, Morganna of old, old before you were a sapling. I respectfully request your help, your green life for this a worthy being, a being of great power and honor in his short time on this earth."

"Morganna of old? Greetings. The roots of the many speak of the Morganna. They speak of your love for our brothers and sisters. Can it be that you again walk this earth?"

Annie reached out with her feelings until she could feel the very spirit within the heart of the aged willow tree.

"I feel you Old One, but I am older. I honor your wisdom and knowledge. I ask your help and respect your decision."

"Well spoken as of old. I will help. What is your wish, Morganna, wife of Dagda, assassin of the Black Prince."

"Wait. What, how can you say that? No one knows what killed the Black Prince."

"The roots of the Old Ones contain the history of the world. They witnessed your justice on the evil one, the killer of trees, the lover of death. The roots remember."

Annie's arms began to tire, her shoulders to ache. She would have to wait to think about what the Old One had just told her.

"Please Old One, I ask you, can you help me?"

The root under her foot moved, the water stirred, more roots moved and rose. Tangling as they rose from the bed of the pool, they formed a network beneath the wolf supporting him as he floated in Annie's arms.

"You grow tired ancient one; let the dog rest in my arms."

"Old One, he is no dog; here lies the king of the true brothers."

"One of the great? Of the Dire Wolves of old?"

"Yes, Old One."

"The roots say they passed from the earth ages ago, how does one exist?"

"I don't know, but here is the proof in our arms."

"So it is. I will do for him as I can. He is a worthy ally for the Ancient One."

Within days, the sisters of the thirteen began to arrive. Arriving under cover of night, their faces hidden within the deep hood of their capes. Some had already fought the minions of Cian to complete their journey. They appeared out of the darkness without warning, gliding like smoke across the ground, through the trees. They made no sound as they moved through the glade and toward the stone cottage. Passing Annie without a word, nodding a slight bow before moving on.

Magda, guardian of the 'Slow River' arrived first, her long staff flashing silvery in the pale moonlight. The next to appear were Celene and Ardus traveling together. Sisters in real life they were the keepers of the books of lore. Each new arrival another member of the circle who kept secret the mysteries and magics of the ages past. Each one concealing her power, swathed in robes of black, watchful and wise. They passed through the glade and the fairies marked their passing.

"It is Marcella, the young, keeper of the keys of Dagda. Warrior of the Sioux nations. Now we are seven."

"Here has come, Isabella, scholar of the books of Wisdom, pupil of Merlin. Now we are eight."

Events had been bad enough lately Annie thought. The arrival of these women of power was testament to the universal seriousness of the struggle. That these women would travel at great risk, in order to face an enemy that they could not hope to defeat. Knowing that in defeat their lives would be forfeit at the end of the struggle. They came none the less. They came to make their last stand together. Annie could not imagine the courage that such a decision would require. She was in awe of each one as they stepped out of the woods.

One after another the robed figures floated past.

Some tall, some bent with age and wisdom. Each one with unique gifts and responsibilities of the order. Each one an essential part of the whole, the circle of thirteen.

In ten days' time, nine of the ten remaining women had arrived. Some had needed medical care, some were immeasurably old, and two were very close to Annie in age. Only the last, Hua, warrior Queen of the Han dynasty, eldest of all save Circe' herself, had not arrived. Her journey from China the longest, and most dangerous. There had been no word from her.

At first, Bracken had shown no improvement. He slept on his makeshift bed of tree roots, suspended in the water of the pool. The fairies brought him food, but he would not eat. His breathing had steadied and the wounds to his side and face had been mended with due skill, but as time passed, he slowly sank deeper and deeper, drifting farther and farther away.

Annie fretted over him, whispering into his ear, urging him to come back. But he had not responded.

"Old One, is there anything else that I can do?" Annie asked the great willow in frustration.

"The life force has departed."

"What does that mean?"

"His spirit longs for death." The great tree's voice was deep and morose.

"No, that can't happen. I need him. I need him to get well."

"A selfish wish."

"No! Well maybe, I guess. But he shouldn't die in vain, not someone who has battled so bravely for so long. He shouldn't die like this."

"The battlefields of man are littered with those that

deserved a better death."

"Old One, how can I help him?"

"So that he may serve your need?"

Annie consulted her feelings, "No. I want to help him. If his wish is to pass through the veil then I will try and make him comfortable. But if I can spark his spirit to live again, then I wish for that. I want what is best for him."

"Heartfelt?"

"Yes."

"I will help. Tell the brave one, your deepest desire. Then ask his."

The great tree shifted his roots and the great wolf descended deeper into the cool water.

Annie leaned over the great Dire wolf, "Bracken, please hear me. My greatest desire at this moment is to see you restored. To see you again in all your strength. I have a lot of allies right now, but what I need and want more than anything is a friend. I need you to be my friend." Annie surprised herself when she recognized that that was really what she was hoping for. "What is your wish? I'll do my best to help you accomplish it, my friend."

For the first time in several days Bracken opened his eyes, "You wish my friendship?" he whispered.

"Yes, I do."

"I have no friends of trust, only allies in battle."

"I would be your friend if you desired it."

"That is a kindness." He took a deep breath, "a friend is a treasure but carries its own burden. I must become stronger to deserve such a responsibility. I must earn such a gift. I will be your friend for one hour, one day or perhaps a lifetime."

Bracken closed his eyes and his breathing steadied. Annie smiled, happy for the first time in what felt like a long time. Climbing up the stone staircase, she emerged from the pool. Looking up she beheld Circe' standing at the top.

"The council has convened; you must stand before them."

The Council of Twelve

"Right now?"

"Yes, right now."

"I'll go and change my clothes; it'll just take a second."

"Right now means, 'right now' Youngest."

"But I'm not ready, don't I get to think about it? Get prepared or something?"

"What would you prepare for? You have never stood before the council before, so you can't know what it will be like. Come along. They're waiting to be introduced."

"Why didn't they just say hello when they passed me in the glade?"

"It is a mistake to trust a shape-shifter when you meet on the wooded path. They may be friend, they may be foe, it is best to wait if waiting is available. You are both shape-shifter and enemy. They guard their gifts against such as you. It is time to introduce you and decide your fate."

"My fate?"

"Yes. Now don't try and delay the inevitable with more questions. They are waiting."

Annie plucked up her slippers from the grass and hurried along with Circe'. Hopping on one foot she managed to pull them on over her feet. Her wet clothing clung to her, making them feel tight and chafing under her arms. Her long red hair hung wetly down over her shoulders and face. As she hurried along, she tried to rearrange it with her fingers. She thought to remember her manners, should she curtsy she wondered? Did she stand in the middle of a circle and recite her history? *'I am so out of my league here. I wish my clothes at least weren't such a disaster.'* she thought.

As they approached the clearing where the cottage was Annie could see that a great fire was burning. The pleasant fragrance of the wood smoke floated on the air, and even at this distance the light through the trees was easy to identify. Several fairies approached, carrying bundles.

"Here Anne of Present, here is your wardrobe to go before the council. You must be robed. Here is your coat of the Elven Star. You must wear it before the council."

"I don't think so. You all know what happened the last time I put that thing on."

"This time you know what to expect Youngest. The council will wish to see the effect as well. Put the coat on just before you exit the woods, and put up the hood. Your head must be covered when speaking before the council." Circe' had stopped and stood, arms folded blocking any further progress to the clearing.

Annie was skeptical. She was terrified to put the

coat back on. She remembered the flow of energy that had burned through her senses and the way it had changed her vision and thoughts. The first time she had been shocked and terrified as the three women tried to kill her. This time she would not be surprised, and she didn't know if she would be strong enough to resist the call of the Elven Star.

When they reached the edge of the clearing the fairies held the coat open for her and she put her arms into the sleeves. Nothing changed. She looked down at her clothes which were suddenly dry. Whereas the deeply hooded robes of the others were long and dark, Annie's was the lightest blue, the filigree glowed in red gold tones and the swallow-tail coat was a perfect fit. Reaching her hand to brush her hair back, she found it dry and in perfect order, cascading down over her shoulders in both front and back. As she stepped into the clearing, silent hooded heads raised as one and watched her approach.

Circe' took her place in the circle and the rest rose to their feet facing the fire and spoke first.

"Sisters, we gather tonight in dire times. Often, we have met in celebration and joy. This time we meet with our existence challenged and evil on our doorstep. Our fate and the fate of many will be determined by what we agree upon this night. The winter solstice is only days away; the full moon is tonight. May we have discourse that is both constructive and creative."

"Who is this young one that stands before us?" Davida, of the Highlands, asked.

"This youngest, wishes to be recognized by the council as one of us." Olivia spoke, acting as Annie's sponsor.

"This wisp of a girl has many gifts it would appear. What of her heritage?" Another asked.

"She is the daughter of Roison of the West March, daughter of Felicity, Queen of the Highland Shire, and sired by Cian of the Fomorians."

All of the heads turned as one to Olivia. Two rose to their feet, staffs upraised. Olivia continued.

"She is my own niece by heritage. She has been tested we three of the colors and found to have profound gifts. Since the rise of the Three, she has manifested these gifts for good. She is the incarnation of the Morgan Le Fey, the Druid Queen."

"We shall see. We shall see." Marietta, guardian of Chichan Itza, reflected.

"I see your mother as you stand before us. Roison was my friend, but what are you young one?" Davida asked.

"I am Anne Marie Abbott, my father is Michael Abbott the Guardian and one of the Three. I have no knowledge of who you say is my sire. I've only recently discovered that this world, your world, exists."

"You do not introduce yourself as Morganna?"

"I am Anne Marie Abbott, I've felt the presence of another and even used some of the power there, but I choose to remain as I am. The fey people call me Anne of Present."

"The spirits have identified you as the Seeker. We have waited time on end for the appearance of the true seeker and the hope of the lost secrets. Do you think you are this Seeker that we speak of?"

"I don't know what a Seeker is, but everything that I

am doing these days seems to be guided by fate." Anne fixed her gaze on Circe'. "I only know how to be Annie Abbott, so I want to remain Annie Abbott, and not try to be what I imagine someone or something else might be."

Circe' gave a small smile and nodded.

"It has been witnessed that you also harbor the ancient enemy, the Taker of Souls," this from Magda, "this we cannot allow in our midst."

"Agreed, it is too great a risk." Celine added.

"What does that mean?" Annie looked at Magda in shock and fear.

"The devil behind you, is far more dangerous than the one you are facing. We hope for an ally, but cannot risk an attack from behind." Magda pressed.

"I'm not an enemy. I'm trying really hard to be an ally, but circumstances have made it all very confusing. I know I'm not your enemy. Didn't you guys already test me?"

"Not enough; the test was too thin. Olivia is soft, and Elspeth has taken a liking to you. I do not trust them to be entirely objective."

"What then sister?" Ardis asked. "Do we eliminate the threat before there is one?"

"I believe it is prudent. We cannot risk a powerful enemy that is also the daughter of our most despised foe. We must act with an eye to our future and safety and await the next seeker in time."

"Elimination then? Let us join hands, we must have a vote."

As one the circle rose and joined hands around the fire.

"Namhaid air thoiseach oirnn, no nàmhaid air ar cùlaibh.
Toradh breith, dàn le dealbhadh.
Urras no marbhadh, feumaidh sinn ar toil a cho-dhùnadh.
Stiùir ar breithneachadh, eòlas no gearan,
a-nis feumaidh sinn breithneachadh.
(Enemy before us, or enemy behind.
Consequence of birth, fate by design.
Trust or kill, we must decide our will.
Guide our judgment, knowledge or grudge,
now we must judge.)

A fairy appeared, flying swiftly into the circle. She stopped in front of Olivia, demanding attention, breaking the concentration of the group.

"There is an injured one in the forest. We have found her, gravely wounded. She is one of the thirteen, and calls for assistance. She is hunted."

"Where? Where is she Thomasina?"

"To the north, we have concealed her, but the minions are searching."

Gathering their staffs, as one the council moved forward in haste. Leaving Annie gaping near the fire.

'What should I do? Should I stay here and wait for them to come back and decide to kill me? Oh, this is so screwed up.'

She didn't want to follow them, and she didn't want to wait. Finally, she decided to hurry back to the pool. Maybe the Old One could offer some wisdom, or tell her to run for her life.

ISABELLE AND MICHAEL NELSON

Stumbling through the dark, she was almost back in the fairy's glade when a voice stopped her.

"Where do you think you are going young one?"

"What? Who said that?"

"I did." A light flickered and then grew brighter. Standing in front of her was a tall, hooded figure. The figure held a ball of blue light in its outstretched hand. "I've finally caught up with you."

Captured

"Don't come any closer! I'll scream for the others!"

"They won't come." The voice was male, deep and mellow. "They're busy elsewhere."

"I can defend myself! Don't come any closer, I mean it. You don't know what I'm capable of!" Annie continued to back away as the figure advanced.

"It is hard for them to trust you." He spoke quietly, punctuating each sentence with another step forward. "Their memories are long. They remember the bad times. They fear the darkness that you hold inside, but I do not. Some mean to kill you when they return. I have distracted them for now, but they will soon return and finish their business. Thumbs up, or thumbs down. I wonder which way they will decide."

"How do you know that? Who are you? You're one of the Others, trying to confuse me. I'm warning you, stand back."

The figure laughed a low chuckle, "Oh, I daresay, I would like to see your defenses little one. It would make quite a reveal I would imagine. But for now, let's just say that I've delayed your fate for the time being. Their mission right now is one of importance, and you and I will have some little time to become acquainted. Doesn't that sound nice?"

"No! It most definitely does not."

"Well, it appears we have a bit of a standoff then. You can't go forward, and I don't think you want to turn your back on me, do you?"

"No!"

"How about I turn and walk back to the pool. You can follow if you wish. There is an old friend there that I have wanted to speak with for some time. He you trust, although his judgment has been skewed as of late. Perhaps we can ask him his opinion of your current dilemma?"

"Who? You wish to speak with the Old One? He only speaks to the witches. You're not fooling me; you're trying to trick me."

In answer the dark figure turned and walked away, carrying the orb of light in his hand.

"I'm not falling for this," Annie called at his retreating back.

The figure continued to retreat, the light in his hand fading in the distance. Annie hopped from one foot to the other. What should she do? The hooded figure was mysterious and radiated danger. The fairy had said that the Others were pursuing the wounded one in the forest, so they could be nearby. This one was much smoother and conducted himself very differently than the minions of the Others that she had come in contact with so far. She stood in the blackness of the early winter night, with no direction that she could go safely. She couldn't consult with the Sisters; she was on her own with the consequences of any decision she made.

'I can defend myself, right? I'm powerful. I beat the three sisters once. I can do it again can't I?' She coaxed herself. 'I'll go to the Old One; he'll help me decide what to do.'

Annie stumbled the rest of the way through the darkness and into the secret glade. She wondered how the stranger could find the secret entry. He was obviously not to be trusted. As she approached the pool, she slowed and moved as quietly as she could. Trying to avoid detection if it was supposed to be a trap.

"It's awfully dark for you to be stumbling all over the place Annie. Come on out, I have something to show you."

Annie froze, no way he knew where she was. She peeked around the corner of her bower and gasped.

The small area around the pool was lit by several of the blue orbs. The hooded figure, sat comfortably on the ornate bench of wrought iron near the water. Standing next to him, as high as his shoulders stood Bracken, his fur coat dripping water as his tail waved in the air.

"You see? Here is an old friend that I have not seen in many a year. Truly the best of friends is this one."

"What did you do to him? How is this even possible?" In spite of her caution, Annie rushed forward and touched the dire wolf. Almost afraid he wasn't real.

"Here is my last friend and my newest friend together my Queen." The great beast's voice rumbled again with its former strength. "Here is the descendent of Brian Boru', last great king of Ireland, and Druid to the order of sisters and the Fey. He has healed my heart, as you have healed my soul my Queen".

"What? You're the Druid? I don't believe it; let me see your face."

The man stood and faced Annie. Reaching up he pulled the hood back from his head and smiled. "I am Colm McQuinn, and I am pleased to meet you Anne Marie Abbott. The Old One speaks well of you, and you have helped my friend. Shall we sit and talk?"

Annie was gob smacked. Whatever it was that she had been expecting, it wasn't the sight that greeted her. Standing three feet away from her was a young man. A man in his late teens at best. He was inches taller than her and deadly handsome. His shaggy dark hair and beard framed a bright smile and his dark eyes twinkled with merriment. He was simply gorgeous. The fact that he knew it did not hinder the effect at all. Annie found herself blushing in spite of herself.

"Please sit with me Annie. We have a lot to talk about before they come for us. In just a little while they are going to need both of our gifts."

Annie found herself rooted in place. Unwilling to admit the effect that he had upon her, wanting to trust him, and fearful that she shouldn't.

"Let's talk with the Old One together, shall we?" He placed a hand on the great smooth trunk. "C'mon Annie, it will be fun. We can learn much from each other, but we have to trust."

Annie moved around the tree to the other side, away from and out of sight from the new stranger. Reaching out she touched the smooth bark of the Old One.

"You have brought the shield."

"What?"

"The pendulum swings both ways. Action/reaction."

"I still don't understand Old One; what is the shield?"

"He stands before you."

"He is the shield?"

"Asked and answered."

"What does that mean?"

"The spear and the shield, they stand together."

"He is the shield? What's the spear?"

"The Ancient One is the spear."

"What does that mean? I don't understand."

"Understanding is the beginning of wisdom."

"But, what does it mean, this shield/spear thing?"

"The dark and the light, each needs the other."

"But…"

"Darkness shields, Light penetrates. One cannot be without the other."

"So I am light? And he is darkness?"

"Darkness conceals malice within; Light shines truth on all things."

"Malice?"

"To hide potential, to create doubt is a powerful weapon."

"So, they will underestimate me. I understand, but where does the shield fit in?"

"Darkness is the absence of light. Much can be hidden in dark places."

"And so?"

"When the light shines, potential is revealed."

"Why can't I just keep it a secret? Why do I need

him?"

"You are woman; he is man. The shield and the spear, ever to face the enemy together."

"What! I don't want that. I don't need a man telling me what to do."

"For every effort, there is a compliment."

"So I'm just there to give him compliments?"

"Every action must have balance." You could almost hear The Old One sigh in frustration. "It is a greater thing that is done, if done with two. The leaves of summer pass through the winter and are no more, but the tree does not do that. Those that dwell in the ground and the air remove the leaves. They are returned to the tree in due time, but the trees do not labor. There is balance on this earth as each life form supports the other. For every spear, there is a shield."

"So, I'm stuck with him for now, is what you're saying."

"The strength of the many rests in the two."

Annie pulled her hand away in haste. She didn't even know if the witches wanted her dead now. It seemed that some of them at least did. For sure, the Others wanted her dead and now she was supposed to be partnered with a complete stranger because some old tree wished it. She didn't want any of it. She was caught in the web of intrigue. Captured by a war that spanned centuries, and the only weapon she still held was her wits and she was beginning to think that she was losing those too.

In the distance, thunder rolled.

Uncomfortable Alliance

"That's strange. It's almost the solstice. It shouldn't thunder in the winter. The moon is out; there are no clouds." Colm McQuinn looked in the direction of the sound.

"It's the Three, the fighting has found us!" Annie had heard the thunder once before and knew what it was. "The storm is upon us; what should we do?"

Colm stood, looking to the west, his hands clenching and unclenching. "When others run from danger, we must rush to it. Come on little one, it has come to the very edge. Our time has come."

"I'm not ready to be your shield while you hide behind me."

"Is that what you got out of the Old One's wisdom?"

"Yes."

"We fight together, as the Three fight. Our strength together is greater than the sum of us apart. There are times when I must be the shield, and you the spear, and there must be times when the opposite is true. I must be spear to your shield. But right now I have an idea that should serve. If you're brave enough."

"I'm brave, but brave enough is a different thing."

"Being brave doesn't mean not being afraid you know. Being brave is being afraid and going anyway. C'mon Annie of Present, time to show our true colors."

"I'm a coward."

"No you aren't." He paused as the thunder rolled again, and this time the flash of the lightning could be seen in the distance. "Your friends are out there. Your father is out there. They may be dying. We can't leave them to it. They are fighting for you."

"I know." She took a deep breath and looked at her shoes.

"We fight together my queen; I fight beside you once again. I ache for the fight against the evil of old." Bracken his hackles raised, and teeth bared pushed up against Annie, almost knocking her over. The very sight of him terrifying.

Annie thought, if he is ready, then I am as well.

"Let's go then." Together the three struck off toward the west.

"They do not know that I am here. We have a moment to surprise them. If you show yourself, and get their attention perhaps I can do a little damage before they recover."

"Easy for you to say, I'm the one that has to show myself."

"Well, you're the shield in this one I guess, after all." He joked but the truth was, it was a good plan and they had no other.

"Just don't leave me hanging, or I'll kill you myself."

"Oh, you probably won't survive. I'm pretty safe there." Again he joked.

"You better hope so."

Pushing through the brush beneath the winter bare trees, they tried to be as quiet as possible. Bracken ranged out ahead of them, scouting for danger. They needn't have tried. The closer they approached, the louder the sound of a fight raging at a high pitch and the shouts of pain and anger. The reality of what they were going into suddenly struck both of them. Colm stopped and bent at the waist, his hands on his knees.

Taking a few deep breaths, "I am scared stiff, I know I have to do this, I hope I can. Thank you for being with me Annie. You're really brave."

"Me brave. You've got to be kidding. I'm trying to keep from peeing myself."

Bracken rushed up. "They are at the edge of the next clearing. They have numbers against us. One of the thirteen is on the ground. The Three have stopped their advance, but just. The fight hangs at the balance point. It is time for us to tip the scale my queen."

"So be it." For some reason, she felt the urge to touch the Elven Star on her chest. Immediately it flamed red hot and her vision shifted to red. Her night vision sharpened. Reaching down she unsheathed the great sword that suddenly hung at her waist and brought the bright shield from her shoulder.

"Lead on true brother. I will give them something to regret." She now spoke in the voice of the One.

"Holy crap! I wasn't expecting anything like that."

Colm took a few steps back, "You look awesome! Well, no time like the present." He touched the silver star that hung around his neck.

In his place, instead of the handsome man/boy a warrior rose up. In his right hand was a massive war hammer, in his left a white staff, the head of which glowed fitfully.

"Let's go then Bracken. Lead us to them."

The great dire wolf sprang away. The two behind him as fast as they could follow.

As they reached the edge of the clearing, the full moon had risen and lit the scene in front of them. The Fomorians stood at bay, their appearance hideous. Their eyes bright red in the darkness, their bodies bent in grotesque ways as they brandished weapons of all types. They shouted their anger and spite. Beneath their feet the ground was littered with many of their comrades who had already paid the price for coming against the combined force of the Three and the thirteen. As one they sprang forward for one last charge. The Three stood their ground, but their strength was weakened and the fatigue showed in their postures.

Colm hung back in the undergrowth as Annie the Druid Queen raced forward. With a great cry she raised her sword high, and a brilliant beam of the whitest light flashed from it. The front line of attackers were leveled as one. Blasted to the ground, writhing in agony. The others fell back as Annie moved to the front of the resistance.

"Begone evil spawn, or die on this battlefield without honor."

The throng began to slowly back away. Gabriel and

Raphael stepped up beside her.

Michael's left arm hung useless at his side, Raphael had a scar down the right side of his face to match the one he already had on the left.

"Where've you been little sister. You've been missing all the fun." Raphael, spoke out of the corner of his mouth, his eyes fixed on the enemy before them.

"I've been on vacation."

"Well, welcome back, nice ta see ya'. Shall we have at it."

They stood together in defiance. The ranks of attackers continued to retreat, backing away slowly. From behind their ranks a great noise erupted as the ranks were pushed aside. A great figure bulldozed through them.

"Well daughter of mine. It is good to see you at last." The giant Cian broke through the front ranks of attackers. "You are as beautiful as your mother once was. Pity that she had to die. I'll be happy when I send you there soon enough, but first I shall finish with this rabble of crones."

"Hello Daddee! I don't think so; what my mother lacked I have ten-fold. Take not one step further."

"Whoa! So, you truly believe you are the Seeker, spirit of Morganna. Well, this will be doubly satisfying. I have killed you twice already in times past daughter-mine. Three's the charm as they say. Maybe this time you'll stay dead. That is once I have what I need from you." The voice of the odious leader of the Fomorians was deep and haunting. "You are no match for us. You appear as Morganna, but I see the child within; you cannot hide behind a hallucination from me."

"We shall see father, shall we."

"TAKE HER! KILL THE OTHERS!"

The line of disgusting rabble surged forward. From the side a black figure in the moonlit night streaked into the line. His roar fearsome, Bracken attacked. Wherever he went screams of pain and agony followed him. As soon as Bracken had appeared Gabe and Rafer raced forward, a great wind behind them, lightning flashing in the moonlit sky. Behind them the witches advanced, their staffs glowing unearthly light in the moonlight darkness.

Annie found herself racing forward, a great battle cry erupting from her lungs. She launched herself into the air and descended into the front line, her sword flashing as she swung it in every direction. The lines fell back, the fury of the defense too strong for them to continue the attack. The defenders pushed forward, the snarls of Bracken providing all the motivation they needed.

"That's enough!" Cian stepped forward and struck out with his great war club. Bracken was thrown into the air and fell to the ground, where he lay motionless. Swinging again, he caught Rafer in the side knocking him to the ground. The evil warrior stepped closer and raised his club, ready to finish Raphael where he lay.

"No!" Annie screamed in anguish. "No!"

Again, from the side of the ranks a white streak flashed. Moving with the speed of lightning the glowing figure struck Cian with all the force and speed of the storm itself. Colm McQueen crashed into the captain of the underworld knocking his club from his hand. In a furious onslaught the druid raised his war hammer again and brought it in a wide arc, catching Cian on the side of his great knee.

Cian screamed in anger and pain as he fell to one knee, groping for his weapon. But before he could raise it, the war hammer swung again and caught him in the chest, knocking him over backward, gasping for breath. As Colm advanced, he raised the hammer for one last stroke.

From his back, the great demon swung his club in defense. It caught the druid with only a fraction of its usual strength but still knocked him several feet and landed him hard on the ground, his hammer flying into the darkness. Working to catch his breath from the blow of the club, Colm searched the ground for the weapon as the demon rose slowly to his feet, a growl escaping his lips.

"Well, I must say, this is a night of surprises. Now the magician appears, and all my enemies stand before me. How convenient."

Standing with his weight mostly on his uninjured leg, he limped toward the druid, raising his club over his head.

"I hope you are the last in the long line of spawn sired by the useless king of old. I will now end you, as I did your father and your father's father, all the way back to Brian Boru' and your line will vanish from the earth at long last."

Standing over the young man, he raised his club for the killing blow. A shadow moved through the darkness. Leaving the ground it leaped high into the air and a great sword flashed in the moonlit night. Swinging in a full arc it struck the fearsome demon high on the shoulder. Howling with pain, Cian dropped his club and clutched at his nearly severed arm. A vision of terrifying ferocity dropped to the ground and stood before him, brandishing the bright sword, eyes blazing red.

"Back to the abyss evil child."

Cian's eyes opened wide and he gasped. "Mother? How…how is this possible? How?"

With an otherworldly voice, the Black Queen spoke, "Leave this place, and return to your dungeons, or die on this night never to return."

As one, the ranks of Fomorians dropped to their knees bowing their heads in obeisance.

"Go from this field of battle and do not return. This is a last warning."

Stepping forward, she raised her sword over Cian.

"And so; this ends now. The sand of your hourglass has run out my son."

"Stop!"

The druid shouted from on his back as he lay on the ground, 'Stop".

She looked at him, puzzled her ferocity unabated.

"If you do this thing, you will forever be the Black Queen. You cannot go back. Your strength and gifts lie in who you were and are. Do not let the heat of this battle or your hatred of this opponent change you, or you will carry it with you for the rest of your life, to haunt your dreams and steal your rest."

"Why should I listen to you, insignificant wizard?"

"That's what I'm talking about, Annie. Let me see Annie, and we can talk again."

The Black Queen paused, hesitating.

"Anne Marie Abbott, let me speak with Anne of Present."

The Taker of Souls took a deep breath, and then another. She shook her head and paused. The red in her eyes faded, she stepped back from the downed Fomorian. Raising her sword that dripped the black blood of her enemy and son, she regarded it as if seeing it for the first time. She shivered and then was Annie once again.

"I wouldn't put that sword down just yet." Colm said, "He is still deadly as a snake."

A keening wail broke the silence. A group gathered around a dark figure lying motionless on the ground. Soon it was joined by others, the incredible despair evident in the cry.

Without thinking, the two ran to the spot. There on the ground, broken and motionless lay Circe' the Green.

The Naiad of the Stream

"He is escaping. You must stop him!" Patch hung next to Annie's ear. But looking down she saw what they all saw. *"The Eldest? She is gone?"*

Behind them, the vanquished Fomorian had risen to his feet. Glancing over his shoulder, he limped away into the darkness. His life, his own for the time being.

"She is still alive, but barely." Elspeth knelt beside the fallen witch. "Gabriel, bring her to the cottage. I must have light."

Gabe stepped forward and gently raised the woman into his arms. No longer young and vital, Circe' now appeared as she was, an aged crone pale and limp. The battlefield now empty; the group turned as one and moved slowly back into the darkened forest. Any joy in their victory lost in the tragedy of Circe's injuries. The women walked first, for once not having to be watchful of enemies. Behind them, huge Gabriel gently carried the limp form of Circe'. Michael and Raphael came next, both supporting the other. A host of fairy warriors surrounded the throng as Annie and Colm brought up the rear.

Once they reached the little cottage, the women gently took Circe' in their arms and carried her inside. The druid followed, but before entering he turned to Annie.

"The circle has not recognized you as yet Annie. You cannot come in without their permission. Wait here. If I need you, I'll send for you."

One minute became one hour, and then two. As the night passed, the light began to grow in the eastern sky as Annie waited with the throng of fairies and the impatient Three. Michael and Raphael, injured, rested on the ground while Gabriel tended to their many wounds. Each keeping his own thoughts, silent in their worry and grief.

Still there was no word from the stone cottage. As the sun began to rise, Annie's patience finally gave out.

"What can be taking so long? Do you think she's going to be okay Patch?"

"The spirit of the eldest is valiant and formidable, but her body is not. Age is not her ally. She has given much of her strength in resisting the evil of the world longer than any of us."

"What does that mean?"

Patch came close, and with a serious face she spoke directly.

"The longer we wait for word, the worse that word is likely to be. Until then, we pass this time honoring the memory of a great warrior and being thankful for her mentorship."

"I know you're right Patch, but I'm about ready to

jump out of my skin here."

Another hour passed, and still there was no word. Shortly, several fairies brought food: warm biscuits and the last of the summer's strawberries.

"We must break our fast, whether the news be bad or good, we must be prepared. The mortal minions of Cian will seek revenge for their defeat. They may return at any moment; our strength must be maintained." Thomasina said to Annie when she at first refused to eat.

Annie tried to eat, but her mouth was too dry. No amount of water seemed to make a difference. At last, she decided to go to speak with the Old One at the pool to see if he could offer her solace.

As soon as she approached, Annie placed her hand on the bark of the ancient tree, and spoke.

"Old One, the battle is won, but the price was high."

"The price of war is the cost of pure spirit."

"I know that now. I almost lost myself in the hate and anger. I wanted to kill. I wanted to hurt."

"Violence of war steals the joy of youth."

"I understand that now. I will never forget this night. I think, I feel like I can never be completely happy again."

"Death and suffering become the smoke of nightmares."

"I want to forget, but I know that I won't."

"To forget is to deny the lesson."

"But it makes me so sad."

"The pendulum must swing; without the bitterness of remorse the heights of happiness cannot be felt."

"Do you think that I will be able to be happy after this Old One?"

"The roots of memory hold many lessons of old. The roots know happiness; the roots know the pain of loss. The tapestry of life is woven with both threads."

"I understand, but I'm still sad."

"It is the end of innocence."

Annie sat on the bench and put her chin in her hands, gazing at the waterfall, listening to the sound of the falling water. The sunlight dappled the water, sparkling as it fell into the pool below.

"Come to the water Anne."

"What?" Annie sat bolt upright, looking around.

"Sooth your aches, calm your heart. Come into the water and rest."

"Who? Where? Where are you? Who are you."

"I am Daphne."

"Where are you, um…Daphne."

"Here, look more closely. Here in the water."

Annie looked into the pool, and then watched the water as it fell. Slowly, as she focused a face appeared within the water itself. As she watched, the small graceful form of a young woman gradually became evident. Her hair waving gently in the water, with bright eyes and ruby lips.

"Wow! You are beautiful Daphne. What are you? How can you stay under the water like that?"

"Many have said I am beautiful, as I know. I am the naiad Daphne, daughter of Helios, water nymph of the springs and brooks. Come into the water Morganna of old, rest and heal your heart. I can ease your pain."

"The Old One says that my pain is permanent."

"The wise one knows much. Pain is many things, a hurt to the body, a disappointment of the heart. A moment of sadness. Forever a memory bathed in bitter wisdom."

"Everyone but me seems to be a philosopher. I am seriously out of my league."

"Come into the water, and find solace. I will sing to you so you may find your way to the memory beyond pain."

As Annie listened to the hypnotic voice of the naiad, she found herself wanting to step into the pool. Rising as if in a dream, she moved down the stone steps and into the pool. The coolness of the water on her skin was refreshing after the vigorousness of the battle.

"Leave your worries behind you on the earth, come under the falls and bathe in the peace I offer you. I will sing the song of forgetfulness. You may rest in your innocence and never be troubled again. Rest young one, and sleep."

Annie drifted to the waterfall. The naiad smiled, "Come under the water young warrior, soothe your heart in the life that is within it. Come under and rest." The haunting voice continued to soothe.

Annie stepped into the waterfall. The cool water pouring over her was relaxing. She closed her eyes and sighed.

"Yes, young one. Sleep. The water will wash your hurts away. The pain of your body, the hurts of your heart. Rest. Rest now, and forever."

"Forever! What does forever mean."

Strong hands gripped Annie, forcing her down into

the water.

"Now you die fowl witch! The price of war is death and only death." The naiad, no longer beautiful but now hideous in her appearance, forced Annie's head down beneath the water of the pool. **"I serve my master, Cian rightful king of the Underworld. Die young one and be free at last."**

The naiad began to sing a wordless song while Annie struggled against her, fighting for air. As the song continued, she struggled less and less, her consciousness drifting as she began to weaken. Finally, she closed her eyes, a feeling of calm settling over her and breathing did not seem so important. Fighting the incredible strength of the beautiful naiad slowly became less and less important, and suddenly, living didn't seem important at all. She stopped fighting. She no longer cared. The song of the naiad soothed her as she relaxed, giving Annie a feeling of safety; a feeling of sanctuary.

Her world narrowed to a small spark of light—and then— went out.

The Passing of the Torch

Nothing but darkness surrounded her, as she opened her eyes. Cries of anguish, screams of pain and suffering filled the air as Annie tried to look about. Her vision was unable to see in impenetrable blackness. Rising to her feet, she stumbled forward feeling her way with her hands.

"Hello? Is anybody there?"

The only answer was a crescendo of screams in the darkness. Her hands touched a cold wall of jagged rock. Turning to the left, she followed along feeling her way with her right hand. She arrived at a corner where two stone walls converged; she followed the new wall. Within a few short steps she arrived at another corner. It only took a matter of minutes before she realized that she stood in a stone cell only a few feet square.

"Hello! Can anybody hear me? Help! Somebody…?"

From above her, erupted hyena-like laughter, screams of delight. As the laughter increased, Annie put her hands over her ears, deafened by the volume. The demonic sounds were terrifying enough, but then ice-cold water came pouring down from above, chilling her to the bone. The laughter became more hysterical.

"Stop! Who are you? Why are you doing this to me?"

The only answer was more demented laughter and more icy water pouring down from above. Annie was soon drenched in foul smelling, icy water. She dropped to her knees, her shivering legs no longer capable of supporting her. The water continued to cascade from above. She couldn't get a breath as the cataract poured over her mouth and nose. She put her head down and bent to the floor in order to breathe.

"Annie? Come back Annie..." The voice, familiar but far away.

"No please, no more water. I'll be quiet. Please."

"Annie, come back Annie." Again, she heard the voice call, but closer this time.

"I can't...I can't come back. I can never come back."

"Annie, come back. I'm here, open your eyes, Annie."

She tried to open her eyelids, but they resisted. She struggled against them; they seemed glued together. She was ready to give up. She tried to give up.

"Come on Annie, you can do it. Come on, come back."

Almost against her will, her eyes opened into bright sunshine.

She was lying in a grassy clearing, evening light filtering down through the waving branches of a great willow tree. Above her floated the gentle concerned face of Colm McQueen. Over his shoulder Gabe MacDonald breathing hard, his face set in anger, dripped icy water which fell onto both of them.

"Annie it's alright. You're going to be alright. Gabe got here in time. He defeated the sprite."

"I don't understand," Annie's voice still trembled with the cold of the water and wintery air. "She told me she was a naiad. She said she was Daphne."

"No Annie, she was a sprite. A mischief maker, a Fomorian. She disguised herself as Daphne." Gabe spoke, his voice still tinged with anger and fear. "She almost succeeded, but she'll fight no more for the evil one—she will no longer fight, ever again."

Annie struggled into a sitting position. "She was a sprite? She was so beautiful; I thought she was beautiful."

"No honey," now that she was out of immediate danger, Gabe stepped back so he wouldn't drip any more cold water on them, "she was not beautiful. A hideous creature from the depths of hell is what she was. She fought me like a tiger. It was a close thing at the end; she almost had us both. But it will be a cold day in hell indeed when a water sprite can defeat the Mariner, but it was a near thing before I could snatch you back from her clutches. I'm sorry Annie, I'm sure it was a horrible experience."

"Was I…was I dead?"

"You had passed through the veil, yes."

Annie's eyes widened in horror.

"But not to be the usual death of peace and rest, they wished you to suffer first." Colm said gently, "You were in the 'Well of Misery'. You were there for their sport, and they meant to make you suffer. I'm sorry too Annie. I came as soon as I could."

"You came…you came after me?"

"Yes," Colm rocked back on his heels, "it's not my favorite place to visit."

Annie shivered; she couldn't imagine going to that place on purpose. "How do you even know how to do something like that?"

"It is the blessing and curse of my house. Once there, most have already given up. They refuse to return. It is difficult to maintain my focus and purpose while I am there. It steals one's strength, your will to live. You fought me at first too. You put up quite a fight."

"No!"

"Yes, but let's just let that go for now okay. We need to get you into some dry clothes. The Eldest calls for you. We should hurry."

"The Eldest! She going to be okay?"

"Come on Annie, she's already waited too long. Let's hurry."

Ten minutes later the trio approached the stone cottage in the glen. Evening darkness had begun to deepen and inside of pristine white picket fence in the front yard was filled with ten of the thirteen witches of the council gathered around a small fire. Raphael sat on a small stool, his arm in a sling gazing at his feet beyond the light of the fire. Michael was pacing up and down the stone pathway, but when he saw Annie, he threw open the gate and rushed to her.

"Annie, my love. Are you alright? Patch told us what happened. I'm so sorry. We're going to have to doubly guard you from now on." In spite of his injuries, he grabbed her in a one-armed hug, "God, if anything was to happen to you, I don't know what I'd do. I love you so much Anne."

He was pushed aside by the muzzle of a huge wolf. Bracken looked at Michael and leaned his great shoulder against Annie. "She will never be alone again. I will give my life for the One, as she has already saved mine. I pledge this with my life," he rumbled.

Michael grinned a great smile and pulled Annie into his chest. It had been so long since Michael had held her close that tears sprang into her eyes. She buried her face in his chest and sobbed. "Oh Dad, I've missed you so much. I...I...I've just missed you so much."

Michael pulled her back and held her at arm's length and smiled at her, his eyes misted. "It's been a long time, in both events and in time. You look all grown up Annie. I almost don't recognize you. So beautiful! Like your mother, so beautiful." He took a deep breath and his face became serious. "I saw what you did; I saw you fight. I wouldn't be able to resist such malevolence." Then he winked, "I'm so proud of you!"

"Oh Dad."

"But for now, Circe' asks for you. You can go right in."

Annie looked into his eyes. She didn't understand what she saw there. Michael looked away before she could look deeper. She turned and started toward the doorway. Magda, who had previously questioned her admission to the circle smiled a sad smile of greeting. As she passed, Magda reached out and gently stroked

Annie's sleeve, the others came forward and did the same. Each one touching their forehead and bowing their head.

Stepping over the high threshold of the small house Annie was greeted with a sight she certainly hadn't expected. She wasn't sure what she had expected, but it wasn't what she saw now. The single room blazed with dozens upon dozens of candles on every surface that would hold one. Strings of colored ribbons drifted from the rafters of the ceiling in the rising heat of the candles. A teakettle bubbled and whistled quietly on the stove, and the smell of fresh bread and cinnamon filled the air.

Olivia, resplendent in robes of blazing scarlet smiled as she approached. "Greetings, sister-niece. Welcome. The Eldest asks for you." She placed a hand on Annie's shoulder. "I am so happy to see you. Come in, and enjoy our time together."

At the back of the room, a large raised spindled bed rested. At its side, Elspeth aglow in the brightest of pure white robes stood holding the hand of the ancient woman who lay on the bed. They appeared engaged in a light conversation, sharing a private joke perhaps, with smiles on both of their faces. As Annie approached, Circe's expression showed her pleasure.

"At last, my child. You are hopelessly tardy… shame, shame," she quipped in a whisper. "Now that you are here, we can begin!"

"Begin what Eldest? What are we going to begin?"

"Why the inevitable my dear. That which assures that the circle is complete."

"I don't understand?"

"Why, it is time my dearest child. It is time that I step through the veil. The end of this earthly experience, on to joyously embrace the next."

"What? NO! No, Circe' you can't go Circe'! No."

"I cannot stay child." The old woman gave Annie a pained looked and whispered. "My body is broken. No longer can it contain the spirit that is Circe'. The spirit must live on, but this body has done its diligence, and a good body it was, but alas—is no more."

Annie fell to her knees next to the bed. "No, you'll be fine. Elspeth can heal you, or the Druid can. You can't go Circe'. I need you."

A hand reached out from under the coverlet and stroked Annie's head, "Oh don't be sad Annie," Circe' smiled, "you're 'harshing my buzz' as you young people say. This is my party, I wanted you to be here for it." A cough escaped from her lips, and then another; soon she was coughing uncontrollably. Elspeth cradled her in a half-sitting position and dabbed the blood away that seeped from her lips. Slowly the coughing abated and Circe' collapsed back onto the pillows gasping for breath. As she regained her composure, she nodded at Elspeth who stepped away.

"You see little one, my circle is complete. Another must begin. As it is written so mote it be."

"I don't have to like it though."

"Silly girl, I'll always be with you. I am entwined within your very soul." Turning to Elspeth, she looked up through her eyebrows and whispered, "It is time."

"No!"

"It is time. Bring her." Circe' repeated.

Annie jumped to her feet. Elspeth raised her hand

and gestured as Olivia took a position on the other side of the bed. As one they reached and took one of the ancient woman's hands.

"It will take three Anne of Present." Elspeth spoke gently. "Place your hand over her heart."

Annie looked at Elspeth, terrified.

"Don't be afraid Annie, it has been foretold. Your place is foretold."

Annie reached out her hand and placed it on the chest of the old woman. Circe' smiled at her and nodded.

"We are not properly attired. One is not robed." Circe' croaked through tight lips, gasping for air. "We must see you as you are Morgana of Old, Anne of Present."

The two women nodded their agreement, and Annie understood. Stepping back from the bedside, she wasn't sure how to do it, but she knew what she had to do. Looking down she thought of the power she had touched and recognized. She felt the approval of the women and the life that filled the small cottage. As she watched, the clothing she wore fell to the floor in a puddle of linen at her feet. In their place, she now stood in a long robe of the deepest midnight blue. She gasped.

"I have to admit, I was a little curious." Elspeth smiled.

"I was too," Circe' gave a slow smile. "Neither blue nor black, but both together. Sisters, let us begin," Circe' whispered.

Tears streamed down Annie's cheeks. The two women smiled into Circe's eyes.

"Farewell true heart."

"We will see you on the other side, my oldest friend."

"Bring her forward." Circe' whispered

From the corner of the room, until now bathed in shadow Allegra, daughter of Gabriel, the Mariner and Elspeth, the White Witch stepped forward. Robed entirely in grey, she stepped to the bedside and placed her right hand on the forehead of the ancient one.

> *"Thàinig irisean gu crìch, thòisich irisean. Bidh mar ether an-màireach spiorad an-dè. Tòisich às ùr. Spiorad an-dè, spiorad an latha an-diugh. Fare gu math air do shlighe, an dà chuid sean agus ùr.*

Annie's eyebrows raised in surprise. She understood the words. When they began to repeat the chant, she joined in.

> *"Thàinig irisean gu crìch, thòisich irisean. Bidh mar ether an-màireach spiorad an-dè. Tòisich às ùr. Spiorad an-dè, spiorad an latha an-diugh. Fare gu math air do shlighe, an dà chuid sean agus ùr.*
>
> (Journeys ended, journeys begun. Become the ether of tomorrow, the spirit of yesterday. Begin anew. Spirit of yesterday, spirit of today. Fare thee well on your path, both old and new.)

Circe' closed her eyes, the muscles in her face relaxed. She took a great breath and let it out. As they stood around the bed, Annie felt the courageous heart slow, each beat a little farther apart, and then, at last—

there were no more.

The lights and candles as one went out, and the room was plunged into darkness.

§§§

In the shadows of the room, the form of Circe' began to glow with a bright iridescence. The glow slowly increasing, coalescing as it gathered and rose into a form in the air above her.

"Hold steady Annie! Do not move," Elspeth spoke without raising her eyes.

An image began to form within the glittering glow and became clear, the image of the young Circe', vibrant and alive, with a gleam in her eye and a smile on her face as in times of old. She turned to each one and bowed her head.

The image faded and glow shrank into a small bright ball that spun suspended above the form of the great witch. Then as if making up its mind it streaked toward Allegra and exploded into her chest.

Allegra, her eyes closed, took a deep breath. The lights and candles about the room flamed into brightness, as she opened her eyes. A great cheer erupted from outside the cottage as Annie gaped in wonder. Before her appeared the beautiful Allegra, tall and blond, now with a long streak of black hair within the strands of gold. A crystal head chain held a star of diamonds on her forehead. Allegra stood before them robed in colors of deepest forest green, a staff of the alabaster in her hand, smiled at her.

"Hello Annie—once again."

ISABELLE AND MICHAEL NELSON

Alliance of Need

For December, the weather had been more than pleasant, but in the days that followed the passing of Circe' it had finally decided to act like winter. The temperature dropped below freezing, and several inches of snow fell overnight. The forest and glen became a landscape of pure white. The oaks, with their unfallen leaves, provided an additional hue of rusty brown and sporadic spruce trees contributed their deep blue-green.

The silence of the great wood was broken only by the cheerful call of chickadees and nuthatches as they flitted in and out of the few evergreens. The deep woods spread up the surrounding hills of the deep glen until they disappeared into the distance. The boles of the great trees, black against the background of white snow, created a three-dimensional view that spoke of vast depth and distance—unbroken calm. The forest was asleep, content to wait for the warmer sun of spring, still months away.

The two sat on the bench next to the pool. The waterfall still chuckled over the rocks and fell into the pool disappearing beneath its frozen surface. As they sat they watched and smiled as dozens of fairies skated and slid on the icy surface creating a havoc of grace and epic collisions. The noise of the chaos and laughter was a welcome relief for a change. At their feet the huge black dire wolf shook his head at the mayhem on the pond but rumbled his approval.

"For the time being, I am both," Allegra spoke in answer to Annie's question.

"How can you be more than one person at the same time?"

"I could ask you the same question."

"I know, I just want to be my old self, not all this other stuff. It's like…It's like I'm starting to forget me."

"When you robed before, you could have been any color you chose. The sisters believed that at your age, a pastel would be better than a solid color. A soft blue is such a perfect color for your blue eyes and strawberry-blond hair; you seemed to resonate with that color. You could have been light blue easily, but the Black Witch is also in there. When you blended the two, without willing it, when it came to you naturally, without consciously deciding, you became both. The blue of your innocence, the black of your potential. The incarnation of both Moganna, Queen of the Fey, and Kehlen, Queen of the Underworld. Forever, to be midnight blue. And something we had never imagined could exist."

"So, I could be a 'good witch or a bad witch' like that line in the movie?"

Allegra laughed a light laugh and put her hand on Annie's arm, "The Wizard of Oz. Yes, sort of. But it would seem that you can be one or the other as you see fit. It's very confusing, isn't it?"

"That would be an understatement. How are you going to do it?"

"Well for me, it will be different from your experience. Circe' and I both had/have the same goals in mind. I was raised to understand the need and the fight that continues against the powers of evil. Circe' did the same. With each incarnation, she continued, true to her purpose and never wavering over the ages. I am that latest incarnation, and for the time being; days, weeks, months—decades or centuries, it will be my time to continue."

"Did you ask to take the job—you know—apply?"

Allegra threw back her head and laughed heartily. "Absolutely not! Oh my goodness, that's a good one."

"What's a good one?" Colm McQuinn, robed in solid brown, his hood thrown back, shaggy black hair and beard combed and trimmed, appeared wading through the deep snow.

"Annie asked me if I had asked to take Circe's place." Allegra continued to smile.

Colm smiled, "I can't imagine anyone who knew what that sort of decision might require would actually ask for the job."

"But everyone respected and listened to her. She was really important and powerful."

"That she was, and will be again." Allegra fixed a serious look on Annie. Reaching up she twirled the thick long streak of black hair that had appeared within the shining gold. "Gradually, over time she will once again appear. I will slowly become the Eldest as the time passes, and I will be both Allegra, keeper of the light and Circe', Queen of the Aeaea. Eventually, only Circe' will remain."

"That's really sad. Where will you go? Will you just disappear?"

"No Annie, that's not how it works. At least not in the past. This is how it has passed down over the ages. What little knowledge we have of the lore of the druids, kings and wizards, their science, their mathematics and even their philosophies have been maintained by the passing of the consciousness of the elders to the next generation as it steps into place." Colm explained. "My own skills once belonged to another and I have added my own as I learned new ways to do things."

"But don't you want to be Allegra anymore?"

"But Annie, I am Allegra. I will be Allegra until I can no longer be Allegra. I can choose to live a full life, or I can choose to accelerate the transition. It is difficult to be both, so at some time, I will choose completely. But for now, I am Allegra, Keeper of the Light."

"And dear to my heart, and more beautiful than the rising of the sun on a springtime day." Colm stood in front of Allegra, smiling down at her.

"You think you can seduce me with your sweet words and handsome face boy?" She fixed him with a haughty stare, looking down her nose at him. "You're going to have to do better than that."

Without another word, Colm swept her up into his arms and kissed her on the lips. Annie almost swallowed her tongue she was so taken by surprise. Even more surprisingly, Allegra returned the embrace and the kiss.

"Good morning my love." Allegra broke the kiss and gazed into his eyes, Annie forgotten was speechless as she gaped at the two. "How did you sleep my love?" Allegra inquired.

"Excellent! It has been a quite a while since I last slept in a real bed. The Fey are excellent hosts. Am I interrupting anything?"

"No, you can actually add your own thoughts. Annie is confused."

"Annie is confused about more than one thing right now," Annie let out a breath she didn't realize she had been holding. "Are you two…boyfriend and girlfriend?"

Allegra gave a long musical laugh. "Oh, I'm sorry Annie. We didn't mean to be rude. It has been many months since I've seen Colm, my love. My imposed exile on Raspberry Island was necessary. Two powerful personalities under the same roof had become difficult, and the White Witch is a hard taskmaster. I enjoyed the freedom but it came with the price of separation from Colm."

"For my part, I had to be at the well of Tam Lin for Samhaim. He still rides the white horse on that night."

"What, who's Tam Lin?"

"Tam Lin was a fearsome knight of Scotland. He was of great renown, merciless in battle, but kind to others, but he was also mortal. He fought for justice against evil for he was a true heart. At one battle, long ago he was struck from his horse and would have been killed by the Fomorians in one of the epic battles of that age. Mortals and the Fey fought together against the great evil that threatened to end our ways. At the last minute he was rescued by the Queen of the Fairies. Guess who that was?" He winked at Annie.

"She kept him and loved him for a time, but the next year she owed a tithe to hell that she had to pay. She could not bring herself to part with any of her people and as a mortal, Tam Lin became expendable. Unknown to Morganna however, he had fallen in love with another mortal. On the night of Samhaim, the great vanguard of elven knights rode against the forces of the underworld. Tam Lin because of his great renown and because he was, as before, a formidable warrior, believed that he was to be the tithe, to be sacrificed to appease them.

At that time, the Fomorians were much stronger than Tuatha De' Dannan. The task of Tam Lin was ride on the side closest to the town and protect against their entry. Again, he was driven to the ground by the massive forces of Balor, the evil one. His true love pulled him from under his horse and held him tight while the fairy queen turned him into all manner of beasts hoping she would let him go and she could then pay the tithe. In the end, she gave up and Tam Lin became a mortal man again. The well of Tam Lin is a sacred place to our people and a crossover point to the other world. I needed to speak with him and learn more of the ways of the dead."

"You needed to learn the ways of the dead?" Annie was incredulous, "Why?"

"Yes, Annie. Those that have passed through the veil have taken their history with them. Their experiences, the wisdom they have gained. They have taken the legacy of a lifetime of experience, no matter how long that life might have been. They loved, they grew, they learned. At death, they took all those things with them."

"So you go there? Through the veil of death? To speak with the dead."

"Yes, Anne of Present and it is a skill that I must teach you. It is one of your gifts of old, and one which you must learn again."

"No stinking way! I'm not going into—what do you call it —that place."

"It is called many names in many different civilizations. Purgatory for the Christians, the Well of Souls by the Muslims, the Holy of Holies by the Knights Templar. Believe me, you go anywhere in the world and they have a name for it."

"So, isn't it scary?"

"Yep."

"Then I'm not going."

"You enter at your own peril. That is something that Tam Lin learned almost to his undoing."

"But you are returned to me my love. Welcome into my arms once again." Again, Allegra embraced him and he returned it, their joy with each other evident.

"But I don't want to learn how to go there."

"When the time comes, it may be the only answer that you can find. Many answers lie within the 'Well of Souls'. Don't be too quick to judge."

Annie wasn't too sure about that. Just another thing that she wasn't too sure about.

"So, what are we talking about today?"

"How long before Allegra becomes Circe'."

"That's easy. It will be about the same amount of time before I become Merlin."

"What!?" You're Merlin? You mean Merlin the Magician?"

"Merlin was not a Magician. He was/is a scientist, a student of the arts, a scholar."

"How is that possible?"

"I've got an idea, my story is complex but as long as we're here, ask the Old One. He can simplify some of the toughest questions."

"Ask him what?"

"Ask him, let's see...oh I know, ask him who he is?"

"Ask him who he is? What will that tell me? He's an ancient willow tree—isn't he?"

"You should ask him."

Annie rose from the bench and pushed through the snow to the ancient willow. Placing her hands on the cold bark, "Old One, who are you?"

"Many." The deep sonorous voice sounded sleepy.

"Many?"

"The roots of many, become one in memory."

"They are all in your memories?"

"We are one."

"Your memories are all together?"

"I am the one; I am the many."

"You are all of the others."

"Their roots are my roots."

"They became you?"

"I became them; I am the many."

Annie removed her hand from the tree, processing

the information.

"So the memories become the memories of the next one?"

"Yes Annie, the lore of the ages is passed to the next. The next are free to be who they are, but when the call of necessity rises, they can respond with wisdom and strength."

"But what if you don't want to *'respond'*?"

"It happens; more often than not. There are those that lack the strength of character to assume such an incredible burden of integrity in times of conflict. Those who cannot pass from the earth rather quickly. Usually by their own devices. That is why you Anne of Present are so unique."

"Why? What do you mean?"

"The muses have waited centuries upon end for the next incarnation of Morganna, Queen of the Fairies, to rise again. Many have been tested, many have not been able to assume the mantle, their strength failed, and they declined the position so to speak."

"So why me? I haven't done anything special."

"You must be kidding. Really you don't think you've done anything special? Really?"

"Well, okay some really weird things have happened and somewhere inside of me I've done some things but I didn't consciously think about doing most of them."

"You see? The power of the wise already exists within you. No passing of the knowledge and wisdom is required. You are already Morganna Le Fey without even realizing it. The only challenge for you is to find it, to manifest it when you need it. You are indeed the

One that we have waited for." Allegra explained.

"In addition, for the first time in recorded time. The Druid of Merlin, the Queen of Aeaea, and the Queen of the Fairies are joined in alliance."

"And the king of the True Brothers." Bracken had almost been forgotten.

"And the great king of the True Brothers, united again."

"So? What do we do now? Because I'm not sure I want to do anything. This is the first peace that I have felt in almost six months. I'm too tired to jump into any more adventure."

"What is your wisdom, druid-mine?" Allegra smiled at the handsome man.

"The wisdom that was passed on to Connor Abbott many years ago. The wisdom that was passed to many before him, those that ignored the call and delayed the return of alliance. We four that sit here on this most pleasant morning."

"And what is that pray tell?" Annie was getting impatient with so much flowery talk and no information.

Colm McQuinn stepped in front of Annie and took her hand. When she looked up, his electric-green eyes held her focus completely:

"Seek the stones, and feel their life. First before all things, feel the life in all that you see and touch. Only then will the steps to the great mystery become clear to you. Seek the stones, that bear the mark."

"Well that was weird. How did you make your voice do that?"

"That is the voice that has come down through the

277

ages. It is the voice of the nephew of Uther Pendragon, King of Camelot and father of Arthur. Arthur of the Round Table was the first pupil of the teacher, Merlin the Wise. I am he."

"Like I said, weird."

"He had only one other pupil. That pupil he loved with his whole heart, and he passed to her all the knowledge his spirit contained."

"Don't tell me, Morgan Le Fey?"

"Yes." Colm and Allegra both smiled down at her. "So you see? We are entwined together, we three. Fated allies, in the secret struggle against ignorance and suffering."

"So, you are tasked with seeking the stones. We cannot seek the Grimoire because, at least for now, Cian has it in his possession, but if there are stones that may contain the key, we should find it if we can, before they do."

"Where should we look? Great-great grandfather Connor Abbott's diary was destroyed in Lake Superior. I don't have any directions to follow."

"First of all Annie, it is your quest but not ours. We can support you and advise you, but the quest is yours and only yours."

"You're going to abandon me? I don't know what I'm doing; you can't do that."

"Each one of we three have different quests. I must convene with the thirteen, Allegra is now part of the council. You have been admitted to the sisterhood circle, but not of their council. For now you will be on your own, but we will circle back to you as soon as we can. For now, we're going to consult the others and rest.

You should do the same. When the time comes to seek, we will know if we keep our hearts open to the signs."

"You have me, my queen." Bracken rumbled from where he lay at her feet.

"What about me, I'm not staying here. There's no excitement here anymore. Just young people hugging and kissing." Patch making a face had been silent until now. *"I'm ready for a quest."*

"You're welcome, Patch, my first friend." At her feet Bracken huffed out a jealous breath.

"So, the three of us are supposed to find stones that we don't know where they are or how many." Annie's voice echoed her frustration, "by ourselves."

"I know where one is," Thomasina hovered into view, *"I'll show you, but I want to go with you on your quest. I am a warrior and a hunter. I have had enough of planting pretty flowers and trimming shrubs. At least for now."*

"Why not? The more the merrier I guess."

"The Guardian will not be happy," Patch reminded her.

"Then we better get going before we are missed," growled the great wolf.

"You mean like right now?" Annie was more than a little reluctant.

"Right now, is always the answer, except when it isn't," Colm smiled at her. "Only you know the answer, Annie. Besides, Thomasina said before that this stone is in the wood very near here. You won't be going very far and we'll be close if you need us."

"I'll change my clothes." Annie rose from the bench

and went to pack her knapsack.

The Stone of Lilith

The snow under the bare trees was deep and undisturbed. Bracken in the lead pushed through the snow seemingly unperturbed by the inconvenience. The story was different for Annie; even walking in the track that the dire wolf left, it was difficult making her way. The two fairies ranged ahead and to the sides, keeping watch for intruders and enemies.

"Can we stop for a minute?" Annie panted, short of breath.

Bracken immediately stopped and sat down but facing away from her, watchful. Patch returned and fixed her with an inquiring eye, *"You are fatigued Anne of Present?"*

"I know how to walk in deep snow, but the ground is uneven here and I haven't had any practice lately. I just need to rest for a minute." Annie was also thinking that no matter how far they walked into the woods, they also had to walk all the way back to the grove no matter what they did or didn't find. "I wish I could fly like you guys can. That would make things a whole lot easier."

Bracken turned his head and fixed his gaze on Annie. Patch looked at her with an arched eyebrow and a smile, and a sidewise wink to Bracken. *"Really? You wish you could fly?"*

"Yeah, that would make this a lot easier."

"Yes, imagine that. If you could only think of an easier way to travel through the forest, wouldn't that be wonderful?"

"Boy, it sure wo…oh!"

Again, Patch raised his eyebrow, *"Well?"*

"I can…I think I can. I'm sorry Patch. This is all kind of new to me. Do you think I should try?"

Bracken rose to his feet and retraced his steps. Looking directly into her eyes, "You are the One."

Annie smiled at him, "I wish I had as much confidence in me as you do my shaggy friend."

Annie closed her eyes. She didn't know where to look for the thing that she called magic. At all the other times when she had felt it, there had been others around her that not only knew how to find it, but knew how to use it. They had made it seem effortless. This time she was alone, and there were no enemies, no stress to trigger her defense response. She would need to find it on her own, without any help.

She tried thinking about what Gabe had told her about finding it on the top of a bookshelf, but that idea didn't seem to work for her. Beside her, she heard Patch give a little huff of impatience.

"If you keep thinking about it, pretty soon you won't need it. The snow will be melted and the flowers will have returned; winter will have passed."

"Patch! That's just mean, I'm working on it."

"Less working, more flying if that is your wish, or just keep walking."

Annie looked into the distance. She was looking at the trees as they marched away out of sight. Suddenly, she was looking down a long tree lined tunnel as she sped through them. Ahead, a hooded figure stood waiting for her. She raced to meet whoever it was.

"Hello my love. You called to me?"

Roison of the West March pulled back her light blue cowl.

"Mother? Mom? How…how is this possible?"

"I am your memory; we are one."

"The Old One, said the roots of the many are the roots of the one."

"And so it is, what do you seek my little one?"

"I was trying to see if I could fly."

The image of the beautiful Roison laughed heartedly, "Fly? Really?"

"Well, it sounds silly when you put it that way, but I was trying."

"But child, the memory of the gift of Morgana le Fey resides within you. All you need is to ask her. She, I, all of the many are in your memory of heritage."

"So, I should try to contact Morganna?"

"You are Morganna, you do not need to 'contact', only recognize your identity. And then you will fly!"

Annie opened her eyes. She hadn't realized she had closed them. In front of her Patch and Thomasina hovered, concerned looks on their faces.

"Anne of Present! Are you alright? We could not

reach you, you were speaking the ancient language—aloud. Are you well?"

"Better than okay Patch, let's try this again. Shall we?"

Annie looked down at the wolf as he slowly shrank in the distance. From above the treetops, he looked up at her and then turned and began to race ahead into the woods. The two fairies zooming ahead of him. Annie soared in a great circle, gliding on the vesper of a breeze, exhilarated by the freedom and the joy of experience.

'Thank you Mom.' She thought.

As she circled above the trio below, she looked ahead. In the distance a faint trail of smoke rose through the trees. She was immediately alarmed. Looking down, it appeared that Bracken was heading in the direction that would bring him to whatever was at the base of the smoke trail.

She spiraled down through the trees to get the attention of the fairies, her raven voice croaking in alarm. The two tiny warriors turned and came back to the black bird as Bracken arrived as well. The need for Annie to warn them was enough for her to return to her earthly form.

"There is smoke ahead. There's someone there."

"Stealth is called for." Thomasina pulled an arrow from her quiver; Patch drew her sword starting forward.

"Yes, I smell the smoke now," Bracken rumbled. "We shall take them by surprise."

"What? No, that's not what I meant. It's just the four of us. What if there are a lot of them?"

"We cannot allow a force to attack the glen from

behind. They must be delayed, the council must be warned." Patch was looking into the woods ahead as she spoke over her shoulder.

"Agreed. Who will warn them, which of us must go?" Bracken asked.

"I gotta say, I wish it was me," Annie frowned, "but I guess I know better than that, don't I? Patch it's gotta be you. Thomasina knows these woods, and I need Bracken for protection. It's gonna have to be you."

"I am a warrior, not a messenger."

"Well for this one time, you are a messenger. Hurry and warn them, then come back. We will need your sword."

At that, Patch smiled and, in a wink, she was gone.

Again, Annie's vision rose into the air and she turned and silently approached the faint trail of smoke. Slowly, she narrowed the circle as she scanned the ground below. In the distance but closing fast she could see the dark form of the wolf racing to conflict. Thomasina was nowhere to be seen.

Below, under the spreading branches of an ancient oak tree, five figures squatted around a small campfire. They appeared to be eating their morning meal. Their packs and weapons were leaning against the trunk of the tree. Annie had never seen creatures that resembled what she was looking at.

They appeared to be manlike, but their facial features were sharper. Their fingers were long and slender, and their ears rose from under their long hair to a point. As she watched one of them laughed and slapped another on the shoulder. There was general good humor. Another of the group scooped up snow and quickly fashioned a snowball which he then threw at the laughing partner. Within moments, all five were engaged in a furious snowball fight. Yells erupted when someone was hit, and laughter filled the silent forest. Annie thought they looked rather old to be behaving like children.

Before she could plan her strategy, the huge dire wolf burst through the underbrush into the midst of the fight. With his hackles raised he dwarfed any of the group of five who now stood frozen, their snowballs forgotten, their weapons unreachable.

"Stand and identify!" Bracken's rough voice brooked no nonsense. "Who are you and why are you in my wood?"

"Bracken? Can it be? Bracken it's me, Micah. Micah of the mountain folk. You remember me, don't you?"

"Micah? Yes, yes I remember you well." Bracken's hackles lowered and his angry voice softened. "You are a long way from the 'Mountain of Smokes' Micah."

"We seek the One. Her rising is foretold, and the signs tell of the battle of the Three. The healer of Wind River told us to seek the Red Witch. We're going to the Red Witch to pledge our aid. It is said that the Glen of the Woods is where she resides among the woodland fairies."

Annie dropped to the ground next to Bracken, becoming Annie once again as her feet touched the ground.

Placing one hand on the shoulder of her great protector, she asked, "Who are these people Bracken, and can they be trusted?"

"My lady, these are Micah and his kind, elven folk. Their home is far from here, the journey of many miles. I have fought alongside Micah in the past."

"Elves? She rolled her eyes, "This just keeps getting better and better."

The one named Micah, his slanted eyes snapped open as wide as they would go. In awe he spoke, "You are the One, the spirit of Morganna!"

"Yes, and you should watch your words and your manners." Thomasina swooped in front of the quintet, her bow drawn back, an arrow at the ready, "We will have none of your elvish nonsense here."

As one, all of the elves dropped to one knee and bowed their heads. "Greetings! We bring a message from the Queen of the Smoke Mountains for the Red Witch. We meant no disrespect my lady. We come to serve the One, for better or worse—to the death if need be."

"You guys don't need to kneel in the snow. C'mon, stand up and introduce yourselves please. I am Annie. The fair folk call me Anne of Present and apparently, I carry the spirit of Morganna within."

"The signs told us of this. We rejoice that the time has come in our lifetimes. This news is of the greatest pleasure. Now, at last, the oppression of evil will be ended."

Each of the elves rose to their feet, their height matching Annie's. Each of their names, musical in a way, and Annie seemed to be able to remember them immediately. There was Micah the leader, Ash, and Mink, Raisa and Link. Standing shoulder to shoulder they appeared strong, their muscles bulged at their shirt sleeves. They turned and began to dress, putting on hauberks and leggings of finely tooled leather each carrying a different hand weapon.

"Where will you go this fine morning, our queen?" asked Micah, pulling on his boots.

"Thomasina is taking us to a stone in the woods. We need to examine it to see if it holds a secret that we seek."

"We will accompany you if it suits your wishes."

"That will be fine with me. What about you Bracken? Is that okay?"

"We will always accept an alliance of those that carry weapons on our behalf."

"Well then, let's go. I'm going to walk now. How much further Thomasina?"

"Not much further, at the base of the next ridge. You will see it before you arrive."

The band struck out moving more quickly with so many more eyes to watch for danger. The elves did not appear troubled by the deep snow as they easily moved through without seeming to leave tracks behind them. As they approached the steep ridge ahead of them, they saw a strange sight. Scattered about an overgrown clearing, several broken buildings pushed up out of the drifted snow. The roofs had caved in long ago, and the stone walls and foundations had cracked and collapsed in places. The signs of a house, barn and sheds were unmistakable, but there had been no one living here for a very long time.

The group picked their way carefully through the clearing looking in every direction. Ahead Thomasina waited at the edge of the trees pointing to a spot on the ground. Micah arrived first and stood looking with his hands on his hips. One by one as they arrived the rest did as well. The snow was more than half-a-foot deep everywhere except on this one spot.

In front of them, a rectangle roughly six feet long and three feet wide was clearly defined. There was no snow on it and the ground was bare of any plant growth. At the far end of the rectangle a grey headstone faced out across the clearing.

Crouching down Micah brushed scattered snow off of the face of the stone, revealing worn carving. In the bright morning sunshine, the mark of the druid was clear for all to see at the top of the stone. Brushing further, a name and a quote appeared just above the ground, "Lilith," Micah read.

Underneath the engraved quote, almost hidden in the ground, another rune appeared. Annie didn't recognize it or its meaning but immediately the elves and the fairy drew back. Even Bracken, usually stolid and steadfast, retreated several steps.

"What? What's going on?"

"Do not read the stone aloud, Anne of Present! Step away!" The tension in Bracken's voice was almost palpable.

"Why? What does it mean?"

"It is the grave of an evil one, you must not approach Annie." Colm McQuinn, accompanied by Allegra, Elspeth and Olivia with Patch in the lead, approached moving as fast as they could through the snow. "Don't touch anything, please."

The Path into Darkness

Colm turned to Olivia, "How did you not know that this was here Olivia? I can feel it from here."

"I had never heard of the stone before just a few days ago when Annie asked about it. In the seven-plus years that I've lived here, I've never ventured this far up the valley before. For some reason it never interested me." Olivia said gazing at the barren rectangle on the ground. "Now I understand why. There is still power here though, you're right, but it is masked. I can feel it as I stand here."

"So can we all," Elspeth stood with her right palm out, touching her thumb to her little finger to ward off any evil.

"You are the Red Witch?" Micah asked.

"I am the Red Witch, yes, but who are you, pray tell?" Olivia spoke like she had just noticed the group of elves. "And where did you come from?"

"I am Micah, from the Mountains of Smoke far in the south. We slept in the forests here last night, but we have traveled many weeks under cover of darkness to bring a message from our queen for the Red Witch of the Glen."

"The Queen of the Mountains of Smoke? I have not heard from Garnet in years upon years. Does she still rule the elvish folk then?"

"The Lady Garnet is our Queen for almost two centuries. She, the Red Queen, bids greetings to the Red Witch."

Colm was still looking at the stone, but spoke to Thomasina. "How long have the Fey known of this settlement and the stone of Lilith?"

"It was here when we traveled here after the great Peshtigo fire burned our homes. We do not go here often, nor do we wish to."

"That would be something like one hundred and fifty years ago then?"

"One hundred fifty years, two months and six days ago, we left the forests of the north pursued by the flames."

"The grave, if that's what it really is, has been salted so thoroughly that after all this time the ground is still sterile. Whatever is buried here, and whoever did it, they really didn't want it coming back. The rune at the bottom of the stone binds them to the grave. It is a triquetra, a rune of protection, but a strange one. It is usually used when there is a family to protect. There were children here once, and they must have felt they were in grave danger."

"But where did they go?" Annie asked.

"And when? It was more than a hundred and fifty years ago and they were already gone."

"The stone houses were in ruin even when we arrived."

"So, even before that. The mark of the druid is clear enough, so we can assume that he played a role in the burial, but I have no memory of that or this place The triquetrum carries a strong spell so it was no joke. I cannot read the inscription aloud lest we suffer the consequence of a possible summoning, but we can all read it ourselves. It speaks of something of legend, lore, and evil. I cannot imagine what might have brought it here.

Annie read the carved inscription silently, *'The book of light, calls out the demon of night.'*. "What does it mean?"

"Lilith is mentioned by name in almost every sacred writing in almost every civilization. The Old Testament of the Bible speaks of Lilith as Adam's first wife, and so does the Hebrew book of Isaiah. She left the Garden of Eden because she did not wish to be subservient to Adam. She wanted to be free of any rules and pursue her own pleasures. She became a succubus, a demon of the night. The legends are clear about this and that she stole children from their beds, although I'm not too sure about that one. Supposedly, she used them to keep herself youthful. In most ancient writings, the bible is referred to as the 'Book of Light'. This inscription comes dangerously close to that tale of lore." Colm had not taken his eye off of the stone since he arrived. "I feel there is something here, but I cannot place what it is."

"This is one of the stones for sure, isn't it? One of the ones we're supposed to find, to seek, right?" Annie was puzzling over the message of the stone; it made no sense to her. "Why would the bible call for the demon of night?"

"Not exactly call for, but warn us of the danger, for certain," Olivia said.

Annie looked around the small clearing. The stone foundations of a small house, a barn and what might have been a shed rose up out of the snow; their mortar cracked; the ground below them littered with broken stones. The trees had slowly reclaimed most of the snow covered clearing and some even rose up from the inside of the ruined structures. Beyond the gravesite of Lilith, a gigantic lightning-blasted oak stood in ruin. Severed limbs lay about its feet, and only one massive branch retained its leaves of summer. Giving the blackened grave a wide margin, she circled to the tree. Wading through the tangle of fallen branches she placed her hand over the shaggy bark.

"Greetings friend."

"The touch, is the touch of our friend," a slow and tired voice replied.

"I am trying to be a friend. The Old One has been kind to me."

"The roots have told that Willow speaks to the One of old."

"Yes."

"At last, wash my feet."

"Wash your feet?"

"Evil is in the ground; it poisons the root."

"Evil is in the ground?" turning to the group she repeated, "He says evil is in the ground."

"Yes, touch that kills, dealer in death."

"Lilith?"

"Say not the name!" This time the oak spoke strongly.

"She is the evil, the evil in your roots."

"The evil of the world, dealer of death."

"Do you know what happened here? To the family. The mortals?"

"They slumber."

"Asleep, they're asleep?"

"In the house of brick and stone, they sleep."

Turning to Colm, she whispered, "The family sleeps in the house."

Taking her hand from the tree, she started for the largest of the stone foundations. The rest followed behind, careful to avoid the barren grave. The elves moved swiftly ahead and vaulted inside the ruined building. Only to return and run back to meet the others.

"The dead sleep within."

"I'll go ahead, Annie, you wait here. Allegra you too." To the other witches he waved them forward before approaching the building himself.

"I don't think I want to wait here," Allegra spoke up. "I'm coming with you. I'm not some little fancy-pants you put up on a shelf. Don't even think about it."

It took Annie less than ten seconds to admit that she felt the same way.

"I'm coming too."

Inside the ruined house was a riot of fallen roof

rafters and the remnants of broken furniture. Although it had been a large structure, it appeared that the house had been only one room. As the group carefully moved through the wreckage of someone's life, it became clear that there was no one still alive within. Along the wall in one corner, a set of rough bunk beds leaned against the wall, the only thing still mildly intact.

On the two beds, moth-eaten remnants of woolen blankets covered the forms that lay on mattresses of corn stalks. With two in the top bunk and three in the lower one. Lying on their backs lay five small forms, perfectly preserved, appearing ready to awaken at any moment, asleep not dead—five young children.

"This is an abomination!" Bracken sniffed and backed away.

"It is certainly something," Colm said solemnly.

"The spell of containment again. They have been preserved with a spell of containment. They have been kept on this side of the veil by it, but why?" Elspeth, her right hand still warding against evil, spoke with wonder.

"Someone just wouldn't let their spirit cross over you mean?" Annie was horrified by the sight.

"What evil is this? What wickedness could do this?" The elf Ash, spoke with a tear running down his long face.

"Evil of the world, the touch that kills, the dealer of death', that's what the oak told me."

Colm looked out over the stone wall toward the grave of Lilith. "There is a story to be told here. I feel it is important that we know what it is, the power that wrote it still exists or we couldn't all feel it. Just to have visited this wretched place, we have scratched its consciousness, and the danger of re-awakening it is real. We cannot fight a war on two battlefronts. We must read the story that is here to be read."

Having said that, he stepped to the bedside and placed his hand on the amulet that rested on the chest of the nearest child.

"No! Don't!" Annie reached out and clutched his arm; her world plunged into darkness.

For a moment, Annie felt as if she had accidentally closed her eyes, but when she blinked, the darkness remained. Near her a glow began to grow in brightness.

"Ah, that's better." Colm held a glowing blue orb in his outstretched hand. "Don't you have one of these Annie?" He gestured holding out his hand, seemingly unsurprised by Annie's presence. His voice echoed hollow in the emptiness.

"Until a little while ago, I couldn't imagine needing one of them." Her voice too echoed in a vibrant whisper.

"Well, here take this one, I've got plenty." Handing one to Annie she almost giggled; it felt like she was holding a lump of gooey glop that glowed. As the blue ball touched her hand it immediately changed color to a glowing red.

"Hmm, well that was unexpected." Colm mused. "Oh well, shall we go?"

"Go? Go where?"

"Why Annie…welcome to the path into darkness itself, the trail to the undead."

The Children of Lilith

"Where?"

"The Path into Darkness."

"But why?"

"To find the children of course."

"We're going into the...the...the Well of Souls? I don't think I'm ready for that just yet. How do you even see where we need to go? I can't see a thing."

"That's because there is nothing to see. There is no earthly substance, no things to touch, no light to banish the darkness—endless emptiness."

"How can that be? Infinite nothingness?"

"Your earthly consciousness cannot wrap its head around infinity, but trust me, it exists here, and it will take us if we do not guard ourselves. Remember your memories. Hold them up against the force of this empty place."

"There is something that will attack us here?"

"No, there is nothing. Just nothing. It will sap your energy, steal your thoughts, seek to imprison you in an abyss of nothingness."

"Well, I'm glad you didn't try and scare me or anything."

"I'm just warning you. Be prepared. Guard yourself against the despair and sorrow; it exists here where no other thing can. This is no place to not take seriously. Now let's get going; I don't like this place any more than you do."

"How do you find your way when there is nothing here?"

"With this, it will show us the way." Colm held up the amulet of containment that he had snatched from the chest of the child.

"So? Can we walk in..um..nothingness."

"Nope. There is nothing to stand on, no trail to follow. We follow the spirit imprisoned in this triquetrum; they are separate but one. We must only focus on it and the life force that cannot escape it. If we can find them, we must help them past the despair and hopelessness of this place."

"Can we do that? Like bring them back?"

"No, I suspect not. We will free them if we can, but what happens after that we cannot know."

"Again, this just keeps getting sadder and sadder."

"Heartbreaking. Stay close to me in your thoughts. We will walk in the sunshine again soon Annie, I promise."

Annie had experienced the silence of deep night far in the wildernesses of the world. In her travels with her father, she had listened to the sand whisper across the dunes of the desert, and the faint scratch of pines moving in a breath of air, but she had never experienced the absolute silence of an infinity that contained no vibration or life. The only sound was the pounding of her heart in her own ears. She sensed that they were moving, but did not know how. She reached out with her thoughts looking for Colm. His thoughts answered immediately, voiceless he spoke in her head.

"That's very good, Annie! Very good. Now we can proceed more quickly. Stay with me now."

"It feels like we're moving, but moving where?"

"What do you feel? Give it a moment, clear your heart. What do you see?"

Annie felt the fear in her chest and the pounding in her heart.

"Take a deep breath, slow your heartbeat."

Annie took a deep breath and let it out. *'Mom, what should I do?'*

'Follow the amulet, lead the way, the druid will not be strong enough, lead the way.' The voice was not her mother's.

"Hand me the amulet Colm." Annie's voice had changed to one of strength.

"Are you certain?"

"Step behind me and give me the token."

As soon as she touched the amulet, the image of a young boy flashed into her mind. She spoke to him in her thoughts.

"Hello child."

The boy looked up into her eyes, surprise in his expression.

"I am here to take you home."

"This is my home; I am home."

"No young one, we must away. You can sleep in your bed once again with your brothers and sisters."

"They are all gone; they left me here. I am home; I will stay. Leave me alone."

"No, you need to come with us, with me."

"I said no! I'm here. I'm here where I am needed."

"You will come with us young one, come along."

Instead of the small boy in her vision, a hideous demon appeared. Rising up, he dwarfed the two seekers, bulging eyes brightest red, open jaws snapped over deadly fangs.

"I will stay and serve the demon of night. I stay to renew her life force when she returns for me. Now you will join me in this endless night."

"Not a chance, step back foul beast." Colm moved forward.

"Begone weakling." The hulking monster swept his arm at the druid. Without another sound the druid's eyes rolled back in his head and he collapsed. "I will feast on this life force, I hunger."

"Touch him and die, you...you...you hellhound. I'm here to take you away, and I'm gonna do just that. Don't touch him again."

"Look at you! A child? I'm supposed to listen to a child? I will accept the gift of your puny heart as well."

Annie held up her open right hand, thumb touching her little finger. A bright light of scarlet blasted the darkness striking the creature in the chest knocking him backward.

With a look of surprise, he looked down at his chest and then roared a battle cry and attacked. Again the light blasted forward and the beast was forced backward again. Annie advanced, her hand outstretched.

"You will come with me young one. Leave him to me, foul creature. Return to the abyss."

Again, the horrible vision roared and attacked. Annie struck again, but the beast was only slowed in his assault. Closing fast, he threw his great arms around her, crushing her to his smoldering chest. Annie's breath was squeezed from her. She struggled uselessly, no match for the fearsome strength of the monster. She could not raise her hand to summon another flash of light. She began to weaken, her thoughts clouded.

'You have the amulet, be the light of justice. FIGHT ON!'

With an incredible blast, white light exploded in every direction. The beast was thrown backward. Annie stood above him, still aglow. Holding the amulet over him she spoke,

"Return to the abyss, release your prisoners. I banish you into the void never to return."

A wavering shadow, formless, a deeper darkness in an already dark place. For a moment it coalesced and then as if blown on a breeze, drifted away out of sight. An anguished and distant scream sounded in the unending night.

Where the form of the beast had been, there was now a small boy. His face streaked with dirt and tears.

"Are you my mother?"

"No, but it is time for us to leave this place now."

"I have to stay here, I have to wait until she returns for me."

"Who? Who is coming for you?"

"Us, all of us."

"Who?"

"We are the children of Lilith; she holds us here."

"She will never return for you, child, and I am here to release you. You and your kind, to be free at last."

Behind the boy, another child appeared and then another and another, until there were dozens. And then hundreds, reaching back through the ages of time, their numbers vanishing into the darkness.

"It is time to go home, children, to the memories of your hearts. Finally, to rest, no longer to despair." Colm McQuinn stepped forward, recovering from his own trauma.

A collective sigh rose from the throng as each one 'winked' out, vanishing to their rest and reward at long last, until they all were gone and there was only the emptiness of nothing again. As Annie watched, the amulet in her hand dissolved into dust and ran through her fingers.

"What now?"

"Now?" The druid turned to her, "Now we deal with Lilith."

The Grave of Lilith

"I thought we just did?" Annie was surprised, "You mean there's more?"

"Always more."

"How do we get out of this place?"

"We don't; we cannot."

"What! We're trapped here?"

"Yes," Colm stepped closer, his eyes glowing bright iridescent green in the darkness, "and no. For the next part, we have to be one."

Annie stepped back, suddenly uncomfortable with his closeness. "I'm not sure I know what you mean. But now you've found a new way to scare me."

"No, Annie. It's not like that. We need to join together, as one."

"I can't do that. What about Allegra? I'm not ready for any of that. What's wrong with you?"

Colm stepped back and chuckled, "No Annie, that's not what I meant. I'm sorry, I seem to forget how little you know of our ways. No, I'm sure Allegra would be fine with it."

"Well, she's a bigger person than I am then."

"Let me explain, I think we got on the wrong track."

"I mean, you're really handsome and all, and you seem pretty nice…but I'm not interested in a relationship with you. Especially not here! And besides, I'm only thirteen for God's sake!"

This time Colm laughed out loud. "Yes, we definitely are on the wrong track. Please, hear me out Anne of Present."

"Don't try to hypnotize me or anything…" Annie moved further away.

"Listen, or we will be here forever, and never."

"Forever? And never? What's that supposed to mean?"

"Okay, listening…that's good. Let's see…okay Annie try and imagine this place. You can't, right? Because you can't imagine a place where there is absolutely nothing. No stars in the sky, no earth beneath you; just nothing. Isn't that right? No matter how hard you try, your mind will always add something, because it must."

"Okay. I had that part already."

"The reason that there is nothing here is because this place does not exist."

"What are you talking about? We're both present right here, so it has to be something."

"Alright, but no it doesn't. This place is the place, the space if you will, between two moments. It exists in between the two ticks of the clock. The infinite nothingness, of the anticipation of the next breath of life, the next awareness of life."

"That makes no sense."

"We can make it as complicated as you like, but think about this. In school, didn't they teach you that everything is made of atoms?"

"Yes, of course."

"And didn't they say that there is infinite space between them no matter what the object is that they are a part of?"

"Yeah, sort of…They said that even though things feel solid, there is more space between the atoms than the space that the atoms occupy."

"Yes that's right! Okay, for the purpose of this explanation imagine that time is like that too. That is, the infinite space in the nano-second between moments, that not one second has ticked off the clock since we stood next to the bed with the children. We are still there, and we are also here but here and there are the same place. That is why the children never aged. How's that for blowing your mind."

"So?" Annie was understanding what he said, but understanding the concept of what he said was going to take a little more time. "So, what's this oneness we're supposed to become? I'm still not so sure about that part."

"I apologize, I should have explained first and asked later. We can't return, we can't get out of here unless we leave together because we arrived together. Our thoughts, our very substance has to want to move forward, and it has to be identical in every way. We have to become 'one' in purpose."

"When you say it like that, I understand. How do we do that?"

Again, Colm's eyes began to glow. "Come close, I am going to hug you, but in a friendly way okay? Whatever I say, you must repeat. You must repeat it perfectly Anne of Present, or we are doomed to eternity."

"So, kinda important."

"Very important."

Colm put his arms around her, she could smell his freshness of soap and lavender and feel the muscles of his chest and arms. It wasn't all that unpleasant.

Nóiméad go nóiméad; spásanna in am. Clog síoraí, arís beidh chime. Chuimhneacháin neamhaí, cas as an nua. Arís eile déanaimid chuimhneacháin an tsaoil, arís mairimid, chun grá nó achrann. Hearts mar aon, ár gcuid oibre déanta anseo, táimid ag iarraidh an nóiméad, athnuachan ár saol. Chun rúndiamhair an tsaoil níos faide ná an nóiméad."

As he repeated the chant, Annie repeated it with him, even matching the accent;

"*Nóiméad go nóiméad; spásanna in am. Clog síoraí, arís beidh chime. Chuimhneacháin neamhaí, cas as an nua. Arís eile déanaimid chuimhneacháin an tsaoil, arís mairimid, chun grá nó achrann. Hearts mar aon, ár gcuid oibre déanta anseo, táimid ag iarraidh an nóiméad, athnuachan ár saol. Chun rúndiamhair an tsaoil níos faide ná an nóiméad.*"

(Moment to moment; spaces in time. Eternal clock, again will chime. Celestial moments, turn anew. Again we join the moments of life, again we live, to love or strife. Hearts as one, our work here done, we seek the moment, our lives renew. To the mystery of life beyond the moment now.)

"No Annie! Don't touch him!" Elspeth and Allegra both leaped forward reaching for her to snatch her away from Colm.

"What? What do you mean?" Annie was standing next to the dusty bunk bed. Beside her Colm was just turning away from the rags and blankets, his hand still on the chest of the nearest skeleton of the five time-whitened bones of the children. The jolt of the return to the present second was too much and the room swam before her eyes. Colm slumped against the wall and put his hands on his knees panting.

"NO, YOU DIDN'T! You didn't really? Did you?" Allegra stood inches away from Colm's dirty shoes looking down at him.

Elspeth stepped forward and hugged Annie, "Here sit, boys grab that chair." She sat Annie down and knelt between her knees. "Deep breaths Annie, take some really deep breaths. Look—look at me! That's good; it's okay, we've got you. It's alright." Turning, she looked at Colm and Allegra. "Is he alright?"

"He gonna be, but only after he and I have a little talk!"

"He's got a few things to answer for, and there's no time like the present."

"I agree, how about it Mister. You took Annie with you, didn't you?"

"I couldn't help it. She touched me with the amulet."

"No she didn't; we stopped her."

"It's true, I touched him. Oh god Elspeth, I think I'm losing my mind."

"What troubles the One, why is she suddenly weakened." Micah stepped forward; Bracken also approached.

"She and the Druid have walked the path of the Dead, they are back from the Well of Souls."

All of the five elves stepped back, "Only one of the Ancients or the son of Dagda may walk the path. How is this possible?"

"It seems this is a time for explanations. You will know sooner or later. Sooner is available. Annie, can I borrow you for a moment. And let's step outside. This may take a little room." Allegra spoke gently to Annie.

Two elves assisted Annie over the wall and supported her out to the clearing. Colm had recovered enough to walk on his own. As soon as she reached the grassy area beyond the trees, Allegra turned and faced the troop.

"Druid, if you please." Colm stepped up and took a place next to her. "Annie stand in front of us. Bracken, please." The dire wolf stood forward and turned. Annie put her hand on the great shoulder. "Elspeth, the summoning please?"

> *"Scéal sean, eagna a dúradh. feiceáil*
> *mar atá tú, is sine le fada"*
> *("Story of old, wisdom foretold. appear*

as you are, oldest by far.)

The elves quietly looked in wonder as Elspeth addressed them, "Maybe not quite so close boys." As they stepped back several steps, she began again, "Behold! The wisdom of the ages. The dead rise again, the Eldest of the Eldest!"

Allegra burst in flaming light, armed as a warrior, great staff in her left hand, A bright shield on her left arm and the flaming crown of the Queen of Aeaea on her head.

"And eldest of his kind, son of Dagda and the Queen of Fairies and Fey, descendent of Boru the Valiant, Highest Druid of his kind."

A great hooded figure clothed in darkness and a staff of smoke stood to the right.

"And the Queen of Fairies, both high priestess of the Fair folk and the Black Queen of the Underworld, The 'Taker of Souls'!"

In a flash of bright red fire, Annie burst into flame. As the flames died, a tall woman, with flaming red hair and glowing eyes of bright blue stood. It was Annie, unchanged in appearance, a small smile on her face. As the elves gazed in wonder, she spoke: "Annie, always Annie, except when I'm not."

Bracken, his hackles raised and head lowered as if ready to attack approached Annie and then he turned and took his place on her left. Annie put one hand on his great shoulders and smiled again. There was another flash of red flame, and she stood in a long, hooded robe of deepest midnight blue, two Elvin Stars, one red, one sky blue flashed bright in the winter sunlight.

Bracken did not change in appearance, still

incredibly fearsome, his face drawn into a horrific snarl, his hackles raised.

"I serve the One, I serve Anne of Present," he rumbled

As one the elves and Ellspeth dropped to one knee.

Walking away from the buildings, Elspeth stepped beside Annie, "Well done. Really well-done Annie, Circe would have been so proud of you. Your powers are growing so fast that I can watch the changes as they occur. How do you feel?"

"I'm fine, but things are happening so fast…too fast really. It doesn't seem like there is any rest between them. I would like to spend about a week just floating in a hot tub and thinking about nothing. I used to be pretty good at that sort of thing."

Micah hurried and began to walk beside Ellspeth, filled with awe and questions.

"And the Three have gathered as well."

"And a good thing too. We've still got Lilith to deal with."

"She is bound to the grave; she cannot escape."

"Oh, she'll find a way. She always does." Elspeth smiled a sardonic smile. "We can't guard a gravesite for eternity; it's not possible."

"But for now, she is still bound, yes?"

"For now yes," Colm answered, "but the amulet has been destroyed. Its power was a part of her. It's something that can hardly go unnoticed. Time could be short. We will stand against her if we can, but she is subtle and she has immense evil within her. If she battles us, our combined strength should be enough, but if she chooses another way—we might have some difficulty."

"What do you mean…some other way?"

As they approached the grave of Lilith, others had already gathered.

"I took the liberty of bringing them, we stand against her, there is evil here, we can sense it." Patch confessed.

"It's alright Patch, we would have gone for them if you hadn't."

The three men stood apart. Michael at the foot of the grave, Gabriel on one side, Raphael on the other. All of their eyes on the barren ground in front of them.

"How did we not know of this Olivia? How did no one know of the defeat of Lilith?"

"I'm afraid it might be temporary Michael. Your daughter and the druid have destroyed the key. The triquetrum may no longer be effective, the circle is broken."

The three immediately dropped into a fighting stance, moving together ready to touch.

"Not immediately, but I'm afraid very soon. We can summon her, but we must be prepared for whatever comes out of that hole. Otherwise, she may escape. It is a rare occasion when this much power is gathered in one place. It is unlikely she will wish to face us if she can find another way."

"Bring her forth; we stand ready." All five of the elves stepped in front of the three, weapons drawn. "We fight for Anne of Present. We honor our pledge. We fight to the death!"

"Allegra?"

"I am ready."

"Druid?"

"Do your worst—witch."

Elspeth smiled in spite of herself, "You say that like it's a bad thing. Annie, Bracken?"

"I guess."

"Yes, bring her if you can. Let us deal with the evil. It is an honor to stand with the strength of the races once again." Bracken still stood close to Annie's left.

"So mote it be."

Elspeth stepped to the headstone and spoke;

"Níl aon fhocal ann, níl aon litriú ann. Tá an t-olc a chodlaíonn thíos níos faide ná teanga na sean, a neart san olc a dhéanann sí féin. An chéad bhean le hAdhamh, concubine Lucifer, gadaí na n-óg, gan ocras go deo ar níos mó de rud ar bith, éist le mo ghlór, glaoim tú as an tuama coimeádta seo. "

(There are no words, there is no spell. The evil that sleeps below is beyond the language of old, her strength in the evil of her own making. First wife of Adam, concubine of Lucifer, thief of the young, forever hungering for more of nothing, hear my voice, I summon you from this tomb of containment.)

Everyone present braced themselves. Those with weapons held them drawn and ready, but nothing happened. No witch of evil appeared. No disturbance of the ground. There was only the silence of winter in the snow-covered forest.

Elspeth standing next to the stone marker sighed

and her eyes rolled up in her head. She collapsed to the ground. Before they could react, Allegra did the same thing, falling to the ground as if suddenly asleep.

"It's Lilith! I don't know how she's doing this, but it's the only thing it could be." Michael was not fooled. The group contracted, their eyes in every direction. They surrounded Annie, providing a ring of protection against something they couldn't see.

"Hello Michael! Long time, a very long time since last we met."

Standing on the barren ground of the grave stood a tall thin woman, dressed in rags. Her face was haggard, and her deeply sunken eyes were black as night.

"Lilith, it is time. We have come to banish you, beyond the veil, and beyond the other world of that side."

"You? Really? I doubt that very much," and with that she was gone. Only to reappear next to Rafer, her hand inches away from his forehead. With a touch, he collapsed to the ground and Lilith was gone. Again, she appeared standing on the grave.

"I can do this for as long as you like Michael."

"We will defeat you in the end Lilith."

"No you will not old friend, your strength and fury has no power against me."

Micah leaped forward, his sword raised and slashed at Lilith in a wide arc. The sword seemed to pass through her from one side to the other with no effect.

Lilith smiled, "Would you care to try again elf?"

Micah repeated the sword stroke and again the sword passed through the body of the succubus without hurting her.

"You see how insignificant you all are; you cannot hurt me. No one that walks the earth has power over me. Only those that have walked the Path of the Dead, have that power. I see only one here in this group of misfits, the necromancer and he is no warrior."

"I can still smite you Lilith if you will not submit," Colm stepped forward.

Lilith did not seem to move, but Colm McQuinn suddenly collapsed to the ground twitching.

"You see? I walk between the moments, the infinite time that exists within time itself. I am here as you see me," she disappeared and in an instant stood next to Gabriel touching his forehead. As he fell heavily to the snowy ground, "and now I am here. No time has passed, but I could have lived a lifetime in the moment between the moments. There is no foe that can fight my strength."

"I have walked the Path of the Dead, and I know the moments between moments." Annie stepped forward and through the rank of elves.

"You, a child? Now I'm forced to face a child! A child, honestly? I believe you have finally reached rock bottom if this is your final resort." She winked out and appeared in front of Annie, her hand poised for the deadly touch. "Forgive me, you are a little too old for you to serve my interests, but beggars cannot be choosers sometimes." She smiled and reached forward. "Oh well, shall we?"

Annie reached out and snatched a handful of the rags of her sleeve and they both were gone. In a wink, Annie reappeared in the middle of the barren grave. She was on her hands and knees, breathing hard, sobbing as those that had been rendered senseless by Lilith began to recover. Annie, sobbing deep shuddering breaths crawled slowly to the edge. Reaching out with one hand she touched the grass and snow beyond the ruined ground and collapsed.

"Annie, Annie…are you alright?"

Elspeth and Allegra were the first to recover. They rushed to the graveside, careful not to touch the unholy ground.

"Come back to us, Annie. Come on, you can do it."

Annie at the edge of the barren ground, made one more effort but again collapsed in a faint. The women rapidly pulled her free. Rolling her over, they called to her. "Annie, come back. Annie come back to the land of the living. Come back child."

Without speaking or opening her eyes, Annie raised her right hand. There in her right hand, on an exquisite chain of brilliant silver hung a jewel encrusted pendant. The daisy wheel triquetrum of the witch.

"Oh great goodness! Her power and protection is stolen! She is banished beyond the underworld." Honest tears sprang to Elspeth's eyes. "Oh, dear child, you have done it!"

ISABELLE AND MICHAEL NELSON

The Quest of Five Stones

Annie lay on the bed, surrounded by fairies. Some were holding food or drinks for her that she could not eat, others hovered overhead, worried expressions on their faces. The five elves stood outside the bower, allowing entrance to only those absolutely necessary. For two days she had slept, waxing in and out of delirious dreams and nightmares. Elspeth and Allegra had attended to her day and night, but she had not improved. As the time passed, she slipped further and further away, her movements less and less frantic. Finally, they called for the druid.

Colm McQuinn stood at her bedside for a very long time, listening to her breathing, his fingers on the pulse in her wrist. One hour passed and still he stood in silence, then two hours passed and still he did not move. At last, he stepped out of the bower, his face and brows drawn down, as everyone gathered around him.

"She has fought a fight that none can imagine. Alas, for one so young to face a foe of such evil and strength, she has shown bravery that I doubt many could match, and it has taken the very last of her strength. The call of the Path to Darkness is loud in her ears, and she cannot resist it for long. Although she is trying, she has already started down it and the voice of her heart is growing ever more faint. I fear that something may be luring her back. I must go and find her. If I do not, and soon, her spirit may break and she will be lost."

"Take me with you Druid." Michael Abbott stepped forward.

"I am sorry Michael, I know how you feel, but the Guardian cannot walk the path, nor can one of the thirteen. Only the son of Dagda, or the soul of the Eldest can pass through the doorway and hope to return."

"Then I must go." Allegra stepped forward.

"I am afraid that you must, my love. We must combine our strength to find this wonderful child. It may not be easy."

"Then we should begin immediately." Allegra looked resolute, but her voice trembled revealing the fear beneath the surface. "First we must have a talisman, a guide so that we might return." She looked about.

"I have the perfect suggestion," Olivia stepped forward. "Here is one that knows both this path and the other. From the fires of hell itself, to the icy shores of Lake Superior to the jeans pocket of this wonderful girl, these may help you to find this little one, or perhaps help her to find herself." There in the palm of her hand were Annie's five small agate stones. "'The light shines in the darkness, and yet the darkness did not overcome it'. These are close to her heart, she may hear their call.

Godspeed to you, we must await your return."

"We shall return before your heart beats one more time—or never." Colm's face was set, his brows furrowed, his lips in a tight line. Reaching out he placed one stone on Annie's forehead and one over each closed eyelid. As he placed each stone he chanted quietly, repeating the chant with each stone.

> *"Anns na beàrnan eadar, chun an dorchadas thall, beàrn an dorchadais, an t-slighe neo-aithnichte. Lorg an leanabh seo, till i dhachaigh"*
> *(In the spaces between, to the darkness beyond, the void of darkness, the path unknown. Find this child, return her home.)*

Finally he placed one over her lips and the last one over her heart.

"Take my hand Allegra, and under no circumstances let go. We must not become separated."

Allegra stepped forward and took the druid's hand, gazing into his eyes, "I will not be separated from you in this life, or in whatever lies beyond the void. My heart will always know where to find you."

"So be it." He placed his hand on the stone over Annie's heart.

> ***"Lorg an leanabh seo, till i dhachaigh!"***
> *(Find this child, return her home!).*

All five stones began to glow and then flashed bright.

§§§§

"Well, this is rather unnerving isn't it?" Allegra's spoke into the darkness.

"Yep, every time. Here take this." He handed her a glowing blue orb. "It doesn't really help, because there really is nothing to see, but it's comforting in a way. By the way, you don't have to whisper here. Even if you think something will hear you."

"What's next? Should I be prepared for something?"

"Next? Next we look for the stones and see where they lead." He opened his palm and the fifth stone glowed fitfully in his open hand. "They will want to be together, so we follow them to wherever they lead us."

"Or shouldn't you say, whenever they lead us?"

"Clever. Yes, there is no wherever, but there isn't a whenever either. But okay, we are actually looking for whenever, aren't we? You continue to amaze me."

"This is no place, or time, for any of your sweet talk young man. Lead on." Colm could sense her smile in the darkness.

Holding out his hand with his open palm, slowly he turned in place. In one direction more than any of the others, the stone in his hand glowed brighter. "We have a direction to go, shall we?"

"How?"

"The stone will take us, but do not try to resist. It's easier if you try not to think about anything at all actually."

"Easy for you to say. You've been here before; this is a completely new nightmare for me."

"Every time is like a first time. Just keep me in your thoughts and we'll get where we're going together."

A bright spot in their vision began to grow, seeming to grow closer and closer. The stone in the druid's hand grew brighter and brighter. The vision in front of them became clear, gathering light as it came into focus.

"What is that?"

"That is where we're going—apparently."

"Who goes there?" The vision rose up, a warrior standing before them. A bright light shining from her forehead, eyes and mouth, with sword drawn and face haggard. "Speak or die!"

"It is I, friend not foe. Companion of the One, Druid High Priest of the Order of Thirteen."

"Mother? Have you seen my mother? Roison of West March. I must join her; I hear her voice. She beckons."

"No!" Allegra moved forward, "Annie, listen to me. It's me, Allegra. The voice is not Roison of West March. It not the voice of your mother!"

"You LIE! She beckons, and I must find her." The vision turned to go. "I feel her loneliness."

"Anne of Present, Morganna of old, you must awaken from the longing of your heart!" The druid held up the remaining stone, holding it out in front of himself. "Do not hear the call of the deep, your story is yet unfinished."

"No! She beckons. I can save her."

Allegra moved forward, radiant in the darkness. Reaching, she at first touched the sleeve of the warrior, then did the same with the other hand.

"We are here Anne; we are here because we love you. Ever we will need you in our lives."

The tall warrior did not struggle against her.

"I am here as well Annie," Colm placed a hand on her arm. "Without you, our lives would not be whole. Feel our need, our love for you. Come away with us, and meet the sunshine."

"I feel the loneliness here. I must stay even if I wish to leave."

"No Annie, we have the talisman. We can take you home. The voices that beckon sow misery and sorrow, come away to happiness with me." With a sudden move Allegra wrapped her arms tightly around the tall woman, holding her tight. "Colm, whatever you do, **DO IT NOW!**"

Next to the bed, beneath the bower of ivy and rose, Annie Abbott opened her eyes for the first time in three days. At the bedside, Colm McQueen and Allegra collapsed, their foreheads on the bed, both breathing heavily.

Annie looked around at all the worried faces. Reaching out she touched the druid on the forehead gently raising his face to meet her gaze.

Smiling down at him she said, "I think we could all use a nice cup of tea."

Walk into Night

As nightfall began, they gathered at the gate of the little stone cottage. Two of the elves, Ash and Raisa were to stay behind. Raisa would travel back to the Smoke Mountains to carry word of what had already happened to the Red Queen. Ash would stay with the witches to assist in preparation for any further attempts from the mortals or Cian and his underworld army.

The Three shouldered heavy packs prepared especially for a long walk that would be hundreds of miles. The three remaining elves, Micah, Mink and Link danced about light on their feet and anxious to be on their way, their green eyes aglow in the growing darkness. Bracken stood patiently at the left hand of Annie, ready when she was. Annie, with a small backpack, looked at the three women.

"Well…I guess we're ready. It sounded like a good idea when I was talking about it in the daylight. Now I'm a little scared."

"The light shone in the darkness, and the darkness did not overcome it." Colm McQuinn stepped up. From his pocket he produced the five agate stones and returned them to her. "Let this be of some comfort to you, even when hope might seem lost." He smiled at her.

As he spoke, the stones began to glow brighter and brighter. She closed her hand and dropped the stones into her jeans pocket. "That's what I mean...no respect. They wouldn't do that for me." His smile went all the way into his eyes. "Take care friend, I will meet you there."

"You're going to be there too?"

"You bet, I'm taking Elspeth's car; I'll be there in time for corn flakes tomorrow."

"Wait a minute! I didn't say you could take the Maserati!" Elspeth pretended to be upset.

"Elspeth, I promise I'll get it detailed for you in Nashville. Michael really messed up the upholstery; remember?"

"Humph, you better be careful Priest."

"Oh I will...Witch!"

Olivia approached the gate and handed Annie a bundle. "Food for travel and a nice pot of hot tea. It will stay hot for a few days so make sure you drink it before it cools dear. Godspeed to you all." Turning the dire wolf, "Protect her at all costs Bracken, you will be the last line of defense should all else fail."

"As you speak, so shall it be."

"Okie dokie, let's go. I guess."

The elves sprang off into the inky blackness of the night. Raphael and Gabriel went next. Bracken turned to Annie, "Fear not my Queen, I see as well in darkness as in sunshine. I will guard your steps."

ISABELLE AND MICHAEL NELSON

At the back of the group Michael walked with Patch hovering over his shoulder as they guarded the rear of the group.

"I kind of envy the druid to be honest. It's a long walk of more than a few days. It would be great to be able to drive there instead." Annie mused.

As she finished her sentence, a cold rain began to fall.

"We'd need a pretty good-sized vehicle to move all these people in Annie. We would have to find one, rent it or buy it and we don't really trust anyone right now. There isn't a single one of us that is unknown now. There has been a watch set for us. Our appearance and our skills have been broadcast far and wide."

"Great!" So even as we speak, they're watching for us to make a mistake?"

"Yes, but they also think we are at the glen and staying at the glen. If we move out from under their watchful eyes without them knowing it, we have an advantage. While they watch the wood and glen of the Dell of the Hedge Witch, we will not be there."

"How long before they realize that the chickens have flown the coop?"

"I'm confident that the women can create plenty of diversions that will entertain the evil ones for quite some time. You've seen what Elspeth alone can do. The other two are no less talented. It would have been fun to see what they come up with."

"Well, no matter what I bet it would be more fun than walking a couple hundred miles in the dark." Annie huffed a little.

"An inconvenience but no more than that. The air is

324

clear, the stars are bright and the company is good. I would rather be a little inconvenienced than caught in an ambush at some out of the way gas station or convenience store." He looked down at her with a meaningful expression.

"I understand Dad, I'm just making small talk. Honestly? I was getting a little bored back there. This is fine, at least for tonight. I don't know how I'll feel by the time the moon is full."

"It will be past full before we get to Vaughn House. As I remember, this is beautiful country; it would be great for you to see it in the light of day."

"What about towns, and people? Won't they see us and report us or something? I'm the only one of us that looks even slightly normal. I mean, elves really look like elves; people would notice that. And Bracken, geez don't even get me started on him, he's like the nightmare you can't wait to have."

"My Queen?"

"No offense, Bracken. You just look so fierce, it would really scare people, that's all."

"Then that is a good thing." There was distinct pleasure in his voice.

"We could walk right down main street in the next town, and no one would notice us Annie."

"What, how does that work?"

"We are all cloaked. The magic of the elves will go ahead of us. It is a real boon to have them in the vanguard. You remember how that works, cloaking is how we usually interact with the real world. At best, there are those that are sensitive enough to feel us as we pass by. For others, they will feel the breeze on their faces, the leaves that suddenly rustle and then stop, or the wind chimes that suddenly gently clatter and then stop. To them, we are only a passing zephyr, unnoticed and unremarkable."

"Then why don't we just go during the day?"

"In the daylight, we would still create shadows, as the sunlight reflected our substance if not our forms. We would not only be detected, we would be frighteningly apparent, and the alarm would sound, both for our pursuers and the local emergency responders. We would freak them all out."

"So, this is better. I get it. Another adventure, but this one is only a *minor* inconvenience."

"Yep, walk by night, sleep by day."

"I'll let you know how I feel about it at the other end."

"Fair enough."

They walked in silence while Annie considered what her father had told her. As usual, she had lots of questions but very few answers. It took her a while to sort out which ones were the most important to her, and then she dropped back to where Michael was walking again.

"So no one can see us—ever?"

"Well some of us are more transparent than others. The elves for instance, are creatures of fantasy and lore, as are the fairies. You, however, are a girl just like any other girl that lives on the earth until you assume a different identity. I'm not sure what happens then."

"But don't people know about us?"

"They talk about us, they make great stories about us as you already know, but it is a rare occurrence when any of them interact with us. And when that happens, a whole new set of legends springs up around the experience."

"I don't understand; we are walking around among them. They can sense our presence, but they don't know what they sense?"

"Exactly."

"But we are fighting a war to protect them from the rise of evil, and they don't even know we exist?"

"Exactly. But, just like us, their world feels the evil, the negativity. Look at the world today. Not just in the United States but everywhere in the world. People have lost their trust in each other; their greed and avarice have overpowered their sense of integrity. They want what they want, and they see everyone else as opponents. People who are trying to take their share of whatever it is that they covet. They don't honor their fellow man; they have learned to hate."

"But that's not our fault, is it?"

"No, absolutely not! The evil that is rising is not just from our world. It is from theirs as well, but the two are just reflections of each other. However, the influence of evil, the evil that is rising in our world exists the same way we do. Many can sense it; some embrace it even if they cannot explain it. Slowly, they cross over into minions of those that would change the course of both mankind and our kind. We resist the evil not just for us, but because we are the first defense for their world; we do it for them too."

"So, we are fighting for our own survival? And theirs too?"

"Our world would be the first to fall, because it

takes longer in their world for evil to find a host. When it happens in their world, the evil becomes a pandemic and sweeps the face of the earth and brother fights brother, father fights son. The great world wars were testament to the strength that the forces of evil can muster. Those that fought for right and compassion defeated those of pain and suffering but barely, even when the armies of the world stood against it."

"But we would go first Dad?"

"Yes, because we stand, almost literally, at the gates of hell. We do what we can to prevent it from escaping. We are the avenging angels of old, and we fight for every living thing on this earth and beyond."

"Wait! I never thought of it that way before! Michael—Michael the Archangel! From the bible? You are the avenging angel that they wrote about in the Old Testament."

"Well, yes and no. I'm the latest edition, but they had no other way to explain us back in antiquity, so it became its' own legend."

"And Gabriel and Raphael, my gosh Dad! You are all angels from forever ago!"

"And Lilith, first wife of Adam and concubine of Lucifer. The list goes on and on, but all of those ancient lessons have been diminished by the 'enlightenment' that is rife in our world today. Those lessons of the need for vigilance against the creep of evil and lost the sense of importance."

"But religions, all of them, preach peace and love. Why don't people just do that?"

Michael laughed a sad laugh in the darkness. "Because it interferes with their quest for the house in the suburbs, the hundred-thousand-dollar car in the garage, and the corner office with a floor to ceiling window. As a result, we must stand against the force that is rising almost at their behest."

"I don't want any of that, but I'm starting to understand that I am part of the answer."

"Every creature that draws breath is part of the answer my lovely girl. You just happen to be able to do more about it than some others."

"I am so far behind Dad. How do I catch up?"

"What was it that the old willow said about reading the roots? All the trees that have gone before, their forms above the ground have long since passed, but the network of the roots still communicates with those that still live, and the tree roots talk with each other. We are your roots, we who would stand the line."

"But it's too little too late Dad. My brain is already full, and I can't learn fast enough."

"You also have a secret weapon Sweetheart. Look inward. Roison, your mother, is waiting for you to ask; she can be your guide to the secret pathways. Beyond that there is her mother, Felicity, Queen of the Highland Shire, Avenger of the death of the great one, Brian Boru. They stand ready to guide you and offer wisdom, but you must ask."

"What about Morganna?"

"She is there as well, as is Kehlen, the Taker of Souls. I would wager that there are very few of us that have so much information available as you do."

Annie walked again in silence, considering what she had just heard. A ghostly figure rushed up from the darkness, its eyes gleaming.

"There is a force ahead of us. They guard the road beyond; they look for us." Mink whispered.

"I will handle this myself," Bracken growled.

"No don't Bracken!" Annie placed a hand on the great shoulder. "If you do that, they will know we are on the move; it will get worse."

"Very good Annie! That's thinking!" You could hear the pride in Michael's voice. Turning to Mink, he asked, "What do you think?"

"There is a less traveled way, but we do not know it. We could avoid those who wait."

"Is it longer than the way we're going?"

"Yes, more difficult, but safer—we think."

"Lead on. We will follow."

As the rain increased, the company turned to the south, moving downhill until they reached a small stream that chuckled through a rocky rapid. The three elves moved off into the darkness, and Bracken guided Annie to the right side of the running water and once again turned east. As they picked their way along the creek's edge, the elves rushed back. Micah, his green eyes ablaze appeared in front of Annie.

"It is a trap, an ambush is ahead. They are advancing. We must flee!"

"No! We must move forward. They mustn't be allowed to push us into a box where they can fight us at their leisure." Michael peered into the darkness ahead. "We must make a stand. Find us an open space where we can maneuver Micah." He was already shrugging out of his heavy backpack, turning he yelled, "Bracken get her out of here!"

"What is your wish my Queen?" Bracken did not want to leave a fight if he could help it.

'The One will lead in battle, the One must lead now.' The ancient voice spoke in her memory.

"I will stand and fight." Annie's voice was strong and powerful. "And I will lead!"

"Annie no! You've got to get out of here!"

"No Dad. Step back, I have this. All of you, step away."

Annie shed her backpack and stepped into the creek, the icy water a shock as it splashed against her calves. The group could now hear the advance of the evil ones. Through the thick underbrush, occasional glimpses of their red eyes shown in the night.

'Sisters, I face a foe of greater numbers. I stand alone. Show me my strength!"

In the rain and gloom, the already faint image of Annie clouded deeper until where she stood was now a black hole of darkness. She raised her arms across the small stream, palms down over the fast-running stream.

"Gabe, step into the stream. Face forward. Now stand still. Rafer, stand to my left, and I need more rain and a breeze if you will."

Turning, she held her hands out over the water she spoke;

> *Bràiste na fìrinn, uisge na beatha.*
> *Eirich an aghaidh bhreugan,*
> *cuir crìoch air ar strì.*
> *Cluinn mo ghuth, tha mi ag àithneadh,*
> ***SLEEP NO TUILLEADH!***
> *(Bringer of truth, water of life.*
> *Rise against lies,*

end our strife.
Hear my voice, I so command,
SLEEP NO MORE!)

Ahead of the darkness of Annie, Gabriel began to glow. The water of the creek, rapidly receding, disappeared upstream behind them, leaving the creek bed dry beneath their feet. Gabriel cried out as if in pain.

"Stand fast Mariner!"

The image of Annie rose higher into the air, a pillar of smoke in the darkest of night.

"Wind Warrior! Now!"

A moaning wind roared, carrying a gale of rain that raged down the valley, sweeping past as the wind moaned through the forest. Reaching out in each direction she grasped overhanging branches of the great trees that grew at the water's edge.

"Luchd-dìon beul-aithris,
freumhaichean gliocais
Tha an ùine air tighinn.
As sine de ancients,
bidh ceuman olc a 'brathadh ar
talmhainn.
Rise agus Vanquish!
SLEEP NO TUILLEADH!

(Guardians of lore, roots of wisdom
The time has come.
Oldest of ancients,
footsteps of evil tread our earth.
Rise and Vanquish!
SLEEP NO MORE!)

Gabriel's form stretched in a spasm. His back

arching, his head thrown back. All around him the wrenching sound of destruction grew in a crescendo of violence as the ancient trees that lined the creek bank uprooted and began marching downstream. Behind him a wave of water rose, taller than his head and then taller still.

"Cleanse the earth!" Annie's arms dropped and her palms thrust forward.

The great wall of water swept past them, a cataract of immense strength that stretched from creek bank to creek bank. The sound of the roar of water only matched by arrival of the ancients upon the advance of the evil ones ahead of them. The sounds of chaos, and pain filled the night as the wind howled down the valley.

"Now! Back to the road! Quickly!" Annie, again appeared as Annie as she picked up her backpack and began to climb the steep hillside. "They're going to be busy for a while. Let's get past them."

"That was brilliant Annie! A flash flood in a tight canyon, in the middle of an intense storm. They may suspect that we tampered with it, but they might not. Really brilliant!" Michael beamed in the night, as Rafe and he supported the immense figure of Gabriel who was staggered by the forces that had passed through his body.

As soon as their feet touched the road after the long climb, Annie turned to Michael.

"Lead them away Guardian."

"What are you talking about Annie. I can't do that. I won't do that. Don't let this change your thinking Sweetheart. We're going to be fine."

"No Dad, we're not. This is a setback for them, but it won't take too terribly long before they put two-and-two together and come up with five. This wasn't just a freak storm, C'mon! It's almost Christmas Dad; nobody has storms like that in December. They'll be on us in a jiffy. You've got to lead them away, or we're doomed."

"I have to stay; I have to keep you safe." Michael's face contorted in indecision, "I should never have agreed to this. This trip was a mistake."

Gabe and Rafe both approached from behind. Gabe still breathing heavily, and Rafe supporting him.

"Any doubts that I might have had, or ever had? Those doubts are gone after what you just put me through Annie," Gabe panted.

"I agree, I have the power, but you commanded it," added Rafer.

"So, it's settled."

"What is settled?"

"The Three must lead them away. They don't know how many are with you, but they will definitely figure out who attacked them down in the creek bed. So they know the Three are trying to go somewhere to do something. So they will follow you—if you make it obvious where you are. While you do that we will continue on."

"We? Who is we?" Michael was getting angry. "Who can do better than we can?"

"I will ask Bracken to accompany me."

"I would ask no more of my Queen." Bracken rumbled and leaned against her left shoulder.

"We defend the One, as long as we draw breath."

Micah spoke but the three tall elves stepped in front of Annie, facing Michael, their hands on their weapons.

"I have fought many battles. I have earned my place among the defenders of the Queen. I go as well." Patch swooped across to Annie and hovered above her shoulder.

"Dad, I love you but we cannot walk halfway across the United States and fight every single opponent along the way and hope that all of us will survive. Look what I did to poor Gabriel just a few minutes ago."

"Duly noted," Gabriel spoke from where he stood with his hands on his knees and still breathing hard.

"Dad, I know I'm thirteen-years-old, but I'm a lot older every day, and I'm a whole lot older than I was seven months ago when we opened that box from the attic. It's important, and I'm starting to think that it's time. Lead them away for me please?"

"But Annie, I promised to protect you. Don't make me do this."

"Then protect me. Lead them away."

Rafer put his hand on Michael's shoulder, "She's right Michael. Just one or two of us wouldn't be enough to draw them off. They would know that the one left behind hid the real treasure. It's all of us or none of the Three."

"Go Dad. Here watch, just to reassure you."

Annie stepped back several paces. "Micah? Bracken?"

In the darkness of the falling rain, Annie began to glow and then in a burnished bright flash she stood before them, hooded and cloaked in the darkest of robes. Beside her stood the dire wolf, head lowered, hackles raised, teeth bared. In front of her stood three tall warrior elves, each brandished deadly weapons, and over her right shoulder, Patch threatened with her sword drawn.

"We are stronger than anything that can stand against us as long as we are not separated. Go! Lead them away."

Gabe straightened up, "She's right Mike. Our task is to protect her. There is nothing that says it has to be a fight every time. A little deception, with a little misdirection would protect her more than drawing every enemy to one spot and erasing all doubt that she is with us. We need to go and spread bread crumbs behind us so that they follow."

"I know it's the right thing to do; I just don't want to do it." Michael was shifting from one foot to the other.

"We will meet you at Vaughn House Dad," Annie stepped forward and wrapped her arms around the big man, "I love you Dad. I'll race you there."

"What? You think you can beat us in a race?" Rafe's smile could be heard in his voice. "Game on!"

"I have a secret weapon."

"Oh yeah? What is that?"

"Bracken? Let's get going." The huge dire wolf stepped forward and in one leap Annie was astride the beast. Annie grasped two handfuls of thick fur on his shoulders and turned to the elves, "Let's go boys!"

The great beast howled into the rainy night and leaped away into the darkness. From out of the darkness Annie's shouted voice drifted back; "See you at Vaughn House! Don't be late!"

Character List

Michael Abbott - Annie's father, Professor of History, The Guardian, Leader of the Three

Annie Abbott - Redheaded twelve-year-old, with an abundance of curiosity

Rafer Tate (Raphael) - Native Sioux, Wind Warrior and protector, One of the Three

Gabe McDonald (Gabriel) - The Mariner, Protector of the Guardian, husband of Elspeth, father to Allegra, One of the Three

Elspeth - White Witch of Rose Hall, wife of Gabriel, mother to Allegra

Allegra - Guardian of the light, Annie's best two-legged friend

Circe - Eldest of the thirteen, Queen of Aeaea, bewitcher of men

Patch - 800-year-old fairy warrior of the forest realm

Bracken - Ancient dire wolf, Lord and leader of his kind, companion to the Druid Queen, protector, friend

ISABELLE AND MICHAEL NELSON

Olivia - Red Witch of the Dell, holder of secrets, wife of Michael Abbott

Thomasina - Fairy protector of the Dell, Leader of the Forest realm

Old One (Willow) - Keeper of the history, and lessons of lore

Colm McQuinn - Druid Priest, eldest of his order, scientist, necromancer

Micah - Leader of the Elven Warriors

Ash, Mink, Raisa and Link - Elven Warriors of the Smoke Mountains

Dagda - King of the Tuatha De'Dannan, (the good guys)

Cian - Son of Balor, Evil leader of the Underworld, King of the Fomorians (the bad guys)

Kehlen - Queen of the Underworld, Taker of Souls, mother of Cian

Tuatha De'Dannan - The magical realm of witches, druids, fairies and elves

Fomorians - Denizens of the underworld, demons, sprites, evildoers and mischief makers

About the Authors

Isabelle Nelson is a current Junior at Saint Ambrose University double majoring in English and Secondary Education with a minor in ESL (English as a Second Language). Her plans are to become a high school English teacher and later teach English abroad. She hopes to pursue her master's degree following a few years of teaching. She has always loved to read and recently discovered her passion for writing. She credits her love of it to her parents and many educators who have supported her endeavors with the craft.

Michael Nelson is a retired physician who also writes under the pen name Michael Deeze. After thirty-eight years in a rural house-call practice, he retired to pursue hobbies, and be near his adult children and grandchildren. In his spare time, he decided to write down some of the deeply personal memories of his life before practice, and the wonderful experiences of a house-to-house practice with he and his team in the Amish communities of northern Wisconsin.

This is the fourth novel for him, and in his opinion the most fun because he shared the work with his young daughter. "Imagine the treasure of working with your treasure to produce treasure. What a gift."

Coming soon, as the story continues

The Ghost of Vaughn House

A blanketing heavy fog hung just below the level of the streetlights softening the surrounding light and creating bright glowing halos of white around each one. At the foot of the hill a grove of ancient magnolia trees dripped moisture in the cool still air. In the small hours beyond midnight no sounds disturbed the peace.

From beneath the shadows of the spreading magnolia trees three shadows were in motion. The three figures were moving quickly, separating and spreading out into the open space ahead of them, moving forward in a crouching run their demeanor one of caution and haste as they hunted.

Moving soundlessly, the hunters searched and listened in the fog ahead, alert for any danger. They moved separately but in the same direction, slowly working their way up the vast expanse of lawn. Objects beyond the fog could not be seen but were felt. The stealthy hunters disappeared into the cold mist.

As they faded from sight another dark shape, only a shadow, flowed forward from the deeper darkness. The shadow, darkness against the darker space of the surrounding tree trunks appeared huge moving slowly, flowing forward. At the edge of the shadows, it stopped —waiting. The figure was almost imagined more than seen, its presence malevolent, the subject of a children's nightmare. It waited for the three to return.

A wailing police car, its flashing lights reflecting off of the overhead vapor howled by on a nearby street. As it did, the dark shadow dropped to the ground, just another shadow beneath the massive trees.

Within moments, all was silence again.

Annie rose from behind the massive dark form of the dire wolf. "It's okay. This happens a lot around here."

"I have not walked among the mortals for an age. They have multiplied." Bracken's rumbled voice echoed in her brain.

"Yes, and with each generation, they grow more detached from others and increasingly ignorant." Annie knew that the words were true, even if they were not hers. The voice went on, "But their doom is our doom."

"The elves have moved far forward. Should we follow?" Bracken was wary.

"One last sprint Bracken. We're so close, I can feel it. Should we fight or should we flee? Tonight, if we must, we fight! Let's sprint my friend, catch up to the elves." Annie pulled her hood over her head and loosened the sword at her belt. Leaping astride the great wolf she leaned forward and whispered in his ear, "let's sprint!"